NO MAN'S

GHOST

NO MAN'S GHOST

JASON POWELL

The following is a work of fiction. Names, characters, places, events and incidents are either the product of the author's imagination or used in an entirely fictitious manner. Any resemblance to actual persons, living or dead, is entirely coincidental.

First hardcover edition June 2023 by Agora Books
An imprint of Polis Books, LLC
62 Ottowa Road South
Marlboro, NJ 07746
www.PolisBooks.com

For the men and women of the Harlem Hilton Family, past and present. Thank you for taking me in.

-1-

WHEN A WINDOW ON the sixth floor exploded, the crowd across the street gasped and backed away. A firetruck in front of the building had a ladder extended to the roof and the man climbing it paused at the sound of the blast, before continuing up quickly. On the ground, residents of the building rushed out of the entrance in pajamas and robes or shorts and t-shirts, some wrapped in bed sheets. They ran, bent low, hands over their heads, ash and glass and small debris falling around them. Police tape stretched from a lamppost on the corner to a green sanitation garbage pail dragged to the middle of the street, and cops waved the residents behind it to join a crowd of passersby who'd stopped to watch.

Those from the building huddled together at the front of the crowd and looked on in awe, wringing their hands or rubbing the backs of their arms. From where they stood, every visible window on the top floor was in flames. The building was only six stories high, and the heat from the fire could be felt at street level.

More firetrucks arrived. Firefighters poured from them, looked up quickly, then hurried to the building. A long hose made up of smaller ones connected together snaked its way from the side of a firetruck to the street, onto the sidewalk, then disappeared inside. More residents ran out, dodging the firefighters and hopping the hose, to join their neighbors across the street. On the top floor, black smoke began to seep from behind the fire in one of the windows; a thin, shifting cloud silhouetted against the night sky. The flames from that window flickered stubbornly, pulsed, then finally disappeared altogether. Water splashed out in spurts, raining down on the street below, and the crowd cheered.

The smoke from a second window turned black and the fire in that window went out too. A firefighter appeared in the first window, using a tool to knock shards of glass and charred wood away. The people on the street applauded at the sight of him, and the cheers grew louder. The firetruck in front of the building had another man climbing the ladder now, obscured occasionally by the new smoke coming from the windows. Those in the crowd with children crouched to the kids' height and pointed him out.

Then two paramedics pulling a stretcher ran past the crowd to the building. From the entrance, two firefighters, one walking backward, came out carrying someone underneath the arms and knees. Either by chance or discretion, it was difficult to see the person being carried; but the firefighters weren't struggling, which gave some in the crowd the impression that whoever it was didn't weigh much. Someone small.

The two paramedics paired up with the two firefighters and got whoever it was onto the stretcher. One of the medics started pushing on the person's chest while the other held an oxygen mask over their face, and together they rolled the stretcher to the back of an open ambulance. The two firefighters went back inside.

At the front of the crowd, furtive looks were exchanged and for a long moment, no one spoke. Then some obvious questions were asked, and an unofficial and unorganized census began. Next door neighbors looked for each other and made sure kids and elderly family members were out of the building and accounted for. Friends looked for friends who didn't live on the same floor but lived in the building. Nearly everyone looked for the young girl with autism who lived on the fifth floor. She lived with her single mom, and everyone was relieved to find them both near the back of the crowd, on a bench.

Then the search narrowed. Each floor above the first had four apartments and everyone seemed generally confident that those who lived below the top floor had made it out safely. But what about the four families on six?

Two were accounted for right away. One family was away at Jersey Shore for the long

Fourth of July weekend. The man who lived next door knew that because he'd been asked to receive a package for them. He and his girlfriend were in the crowd with everyone else, and though they were obviously upset about the fire, they were physically okay. Firefighters had practically knocked his door off the hinges, he said, and rushed them out of the apartment. He didn't know the status of his neighbors in the other two apartments—a couple in one, a widowed old lady in the other—but from what he was looking at from the street, he feared that if they weren't out by now, then they weren't okay. He said so, and those who heard him agreed.

The crowd looked back to the sixth floor. Flames still flickered in a few of the windows. Men could be seen in others, on their knees, or duckwalking with flashlights on their helmets or coats, one behind the other, aiming a thick hose at a corner unseen from the street. Then a rumbling sound like thunder, a crash, and they were gone.

A cloud of dust and smoke, flecked with glowing embers, rolled ferociously from the top floor like a tide. It spread out above the street and again the crowd gasped and retreated.

Across from them, firefighters outside the building shouted

to each other and into their radios. One of the men from the roof was back on the ladder, holding on to the rungs, unmoving. Two more men climbed to the top of the truck and called out to him, but if he heard them, he didn't show it.

At the entrance to the building, firefighters streamed out, apparently uninjured, looking up once they cleared the threshold. They peeled oxygen masks off their faces and joined their coworkers, worry and sweat on their faces.

The man on the ladder started down then, moving slowly, but doing it on his own. The two at the foot of the ladder waited for him, but stared at the windows on the top floor, where muffled shouts could be heard behind the cloud.

More firefighters exited the building, some with soot on their coats and helmets. Paramedics and emergency medical technicians ran to the entrance to meet them, but the firefighters waved them away and joined the others in the street, looking up.

Then a distant alarm started from the top floor. No one in the crowd across the street had ever heard the sound before, but it was eerily high-pitched, and the look of unease on the faces of the firefighters made those who saw them worry. When the alarm started, a fireman in the street said something on a radio clipped to his chest, and five other firefighters near the entrance grabbed a sled full of tools and ran inside the building. The dust cloud was dissipating, and as it did, the sound of the alarm grew clearer.

Then another one started up there. Out of sync with the first, but same eerie high-pitched tone, same anxiety from the firefighters on the street. Then a third.

The cloud had cleared enough that the windows were again visible. Everyone in the street, both in front of and behind the police tape, looked up at them. Fire burned somewhere inside, behind a few of the windows. In the others, darkness. No movement. Just a creepy chorus of alarms.

The fireman in front of the building who'd spoken before spoke again into his radio, and others started waiving to another group of paramedics, who pushed a stretcher covered in bags through the crowds. At some point a second hose line had been stretched into the building, and the medics lifted the wheels of the stretcher over both lines on their way to the entrance.

Though the sun had long ago set, the temperature was still high. New York City was on its fourth day of a heatwave. Some of the fire from the building had been washed away, but much remained and could still be felt below. Despite those things, many in the crowd looked at the worry on the faces of the firefighters or up at the windows, listened to the alarms in the darkness, and shivered.

A woman from the fifth floor, the autistic girl's mother, chewed her bottom lip and stroked her daughter's hair. She turned to the man from the sixth floor and asked, "How did this start? Do you know?"

The man shrugged. "Only God knows," he said. But he was wrong.

TWO STREETS AWAY, OUT of the glow of the lights from the emergency vehicles, the man who started the fire leaned on a gate and watched the growing crowd. He was wearing a bright shirt and was afraid that if he got any closer, he'd be spotted.

An ambulance sped away from the building and passed him, lights flashing, sirens wailing. There was only one person in the front, which meant there was someone in the back with a patient. The man turned his head and watched the ambulance until it turned a corner and was lost to sight.

And he laughed.

-2-

CHARLES DAVIDS LOOKED THROUGH the steering wheel at the speedometer and did his best to fight the anxiety. Barely five miles an hour. This was insane. How was traffic so bad and why was he apparently the only one affected by it? All around him, drivers in other cars sat comfortably behind their wheels, unbothered. A woman to his right, steered coolly with her left hand while smiling broadly at a video on her phone in her right. Charles looked away from her and shook his head. Squeezing the wheel, he closed his eyes for only a second and sighed.   What was this like, he wondered. In some ways it was like being in one of those hidden cameras shows where you know something isn't right but everyone around you is acting as if it is. But in a more accurate way it was like nothing at all. Nothing abnormal about heavy traffic early evening on a Friday. This wasn't a social experiment testing his patience. It was just New York City.

Almost an hour earlier, Charles had left the NYC Fire Academy and was now headed to his new firehouse, Engine 99. Located in Harlem, Google Navigator had estimated that it should take about a thirty-six-minute drive to get there. Charles glanced at the time on the dash and squeezed the wheel again, clenching his jaw.

"C'mon," he muttered, leaning forward. "Move! Please!"

At twenty-four years old, Charles had lived in the city all his life, but never really had to deal with traffic before. He'd only gotten his license ten months ago because the Fire Department application process required it. He knew about the city's traffic, of course. Everyone did. But this… How could he have left an hour early yet still be twenty minutes late?

The time on his dash showed six minutes after four p.m. He knew that night shifts in the fire department started at six p.m., and that the unwritten rule was to report for duty an hour early. But he'd also heard that while he was on probation, he was expected to report an hour earlier than everyone else, which, at this point, was impossible.

The other side of that coin, however, was that he wasn't actually working the night shift. His graduation from the academy wasn't until tomorrow. Charles was only going to Engine 99 now to introduce himself and bring the cake every new member was expected to bring to their firehouse once they were assigned to it. He'd stay longer if invited, but he wouldn't be on the clock.

So? Were they expecting him at four or at five? Or at all? Maybe Engine 99 wouldn't know they were getting someone until he arrived at their door. Charles didn't know how it worked but figured it was better to be safe than late, so he aimed to be there early.

So much for that.

He looked now at the screen of his phone. Google Navigator said he'd arrive in eleven minutes. Okay. It was silly to worry, he knew that. He had no control over what time the fire academy instructors let the class out. Neither could he control the afternoon traffic in New York

City. It was unreasonable to worry about things he couldn't do anything about. Still…   Up ahead, a narrow spot opened to his left, and Charles made an aggressive lane switch that was rewarded with blaring horns he barely noticed. He passed two cars on his right and was happy with the decision. He looked again at his phone nestled in the dock on the dashboard to see if his ETA had shortened at all, and it hadn't. Disappointed, he took a deep breath and blew it out slowly.

Then twice more. In deep, out slow. He relaxed his grip on the wheel, and the muscles in his back began to loosen. Then, he made the mistake of looking over at the cake box nestled in the foot well of the passenger seat, and his heart started to race again.

EARLIER, BEFORE CHARLES AND his classmates had been dismissed, the head instructor had cautioned them all about starting off on the wrong foot. Today, he reminded them, was their one chance to make a good first impression.

"The first thing they're gonna notice is your greeting," the instructor said, referring to the other members of the firehouse. "No one cares how you look. You all look the same: shaved heads, fairly good shape, frightened. Who gives a shit? They're gonna notice how you greet them."

The instructor was a tall thin man, all muscle and bone. He smiled as he walked slowly up the center aisle, fingers laced casually in front of him. "In your first month here," he continued, "you all walked around with your heads bowed and your shoulders up. Now you baldheaded freaks are walking around with swag, patting each other on the ass because you think you're big shit for getting through the academy. And that's fine, that's good. You *should* be proud of yourselves," he added, sincerely. "But when you go to your firehouse, you're back at the bottom again. Probation will be over after a year or so, but you'll still be on the bottom of the totem pole until your house gets another probie assigned; *if* they get another probie assigned. So first things first, lose the swag. Everyone you meet tomorrow is sir or ma'am until they tell you differently. That clear?"

"Yes, sir!"

Charles hadn't been in the military and his first couple of weeks in the academy were spent awkwardly learning to stand straight and quickly salute everyone who was superior to him before loudly greeting them with a sir or ma'am. But the head instructor was correct—by the end of the fourteen-week academy, the salutes had become a bit slower and the greetings somewhat quieter.

"The second thing they'll notice is the cake," the instructor continued from in front of the stage. "For your sakes, I hope you guys took my advice and went to an actual bakery and not some corner store café or something."

Charles had. Tuesday, when they'd been reminded of the tradition of bringing a cake, he'd gone to a bakery that same day, rather than waiting for yesterday.

"Remember, you only get to make one first impression," the instructor continued. "If you bring a crappy cake and they throw it on the floor, that's all anyone at your house is gonna talk about for the next few days. And, if they throw it on the floor..." he shrugged, "...it'll be your job to clean it up."

CHARLES PULLED OFF THE FDR Drive at exit 21, sped up on a yellow light, and blasted through the intersection. He glanced at the map on his screen and the arrival time turned from eight minutes to seven. He looked over at the bakery bag in the passenger side footwell and felt a knot form in his throat. What if he'd overdone the cake?

The place he'd gone to was the closest five-star bakery he could find at a location he could drive to without having to worry about parking. A small place in a hippie neighborhood called Sweet Art by Felicia. Inside the small shop, the name began to make sense. On the dull pink walls were framed photos of famous paintings recreated as cakes. Charles saw what he thought was Mona-Lisa with a slice cut from her right shoulder revealing a chocolate cake. In another photo, fondant was used to sculpt The Last Supper, and instead of bread, Jesus and the disciples had plates of cupcakes.

Toward the back of the shop, a green and pink checkered tablecloth draped a large waist high round table. On it were rollers and spatulas, plastic bowls, cookie cutters, and cupcake trays. Three kids stood around it, listening intently to a woman. She had a bowl of icing in one hand, a spoon in the other, and was wearing a green apron.

In front of the wall, to the left of the entrance, was a traditional glass counter with different elegant pastries on display, and beside that were refrigerators with ready-made cakes inside. Behind the counter, a young woman wearing an apron and consulting a clipboard, stood in front of a cabinet with jars filled with sweets. Charles went that way and when he was close, she looked up and smiled.

"Hi. How are you?"

"I'm good, ma'am, thank you. I was wondering if you could—"

"How old are you?" she asked, cutting him off.

Charles frowned, thrown off by the question. "I'm twenty-four."

"I'm twenty-five," she said, smiling. She pointed a finger at him. "Don't call me ma'am."

When Charles laughed, she said, "Sorry. What were you gonna say?"

"Um," he looked away, taking a second to remember. "Uh, I need to get a fancy cake for next week," he said. "But not like a wedding cake or anything. I have to bring it to a firehouse full of guys."

"Hmm. Okay."

"I don't know if it really even needs to be a cake," he continued. "It has to be some kind of pastry, but it has to be fancy, and it has to feed a bunch of people. Do you have, I don't know, fancy cupcakes or something?"

"Yes, of course," she answered brightly. "Come with me." She placed her clipboard on the counter, then led him to a section filled with cupcakes in different sizes with different colored icing in elegant designs.

"Those are nice," Charles said, pointing to a row of large cupcakes with icing designed to look like leaves. "But do you have them in different colors? You know, something masculine?"

"Masculine?" She smiled, lifting a brow. "Cupcakes?"

Charles smiled too, but worried. The cakes and cupcakes behind the counter were nice, but they looked regular. They might taste amazing, who knew, but that wouldn't do him any good if they ended up smashed on the floor.

"What about a pull-apart?" the woman asked enthusiastically.

"I'm sorry?"

"A pull-apart. It's like a cake made up of cupcakes held together by icing or marshmallow. And we can shape the cake to something firefightery. You know? Like, I can give you red velvet cupcakes and vanilla cupcakes and put them together in the shape of a firetruck.

Oh!" She turned and hurried back to the jars. After a moment, she was back with one filled with what looked like action figures. She opened the jar, put on a plastic glove, and took out a small candy firefighter in full uniform. "We can draw a window on the cake and put him inside!"

Charles noticed her smile and it made him smile too. She was beautiful and sincere, but it was her excitement that sold him.

11

This was perfect: a custom cake made specifically for the occasion. What could go wrong?

"That would be perfect," he told her.

"Not today, right? For Tomorrow?"

"Or Thursday if that's possible. I'm bringing it Friday but can't pick it up that day." "Thursday it is. Anytime," she said pleasantly.

Charles smiled again. "Thank you, ma'am."

She scowled dramatically. "Libby. Not Ma'am"

Charles raised his hands. "Sorry."

"Ma'am is my mom," she said, nodding toward the woman at the table with the kids.

"But she wouldn't let you call her that either. Not in her own shop. Libby and Felicia will do just fine."

Charles smiled at her, glanced at her mom, then back at Libby. He was suddenly glad for a reason to come back for the cake when it was done.

He'd done that, yesterday but hadn't seen either Libby or her mother. He asked the woman who was there to thank Libby for him, and she promised she would. He'd been slightly disappointed, but the cake looked great, and he felt better when he saw it.

But now, as Charles stopped for another red light and watched the time to arrival drop to two minutes, he was less confident. A *cupcake* cake? With candy action figures? For a firehouse full of grown men?

The woman's voice on Google Navigator told him to make a right and his destination would be on the left. He squeezed the wheel, once more, sighing deeply.

"Here we go!" he muttered.

ENGINE 99 SHARED A firehouse with Ladder 88 and the chief of Battalion 5. As Charles was stuck in traffic on the

FDR, Lieutenant Josh Calahan was sitting behind the desk in the office of Ladder 88. He was leaning back in an office chair, feet crossed at the corner of his desk, staring at the ceiling, listening to Sade, when Matt Quincy walked in.

Matt was a lieutenant assigned to Engine 99. He was younger than Josh by fifteen years or so, but Josh admired him. At only thirty years old, Matt was one of the youngest lieutenants in the department and was on track to become one of the youngest captains. In September, Josh would be celebrating his eighteenth year on the job, and in his nearly two decades, he'd met thousands of members of the department. He liked most he had met and loved many. He disliked a few and hated only one. Matt was his favorite.

"Joshy Jobs," Matt said, dropping his shoulder and letting a gym bag slide off it, to the floor. "What's up, man?"

Josh pulled his feet from his desk, smiled, and stood. "What's up, Matty? You working tonight?"

"I am, sir. You too?"

"You and me, brother. I'm ten-eight and ready for fire duty."

"Nice!" Matt answered. "Just coming in?"

"Nah. I worked today." Josh looked at the time in the corner of his computer screen.

"Why're you here so early?"

Matt checked his watch. "I wanted to get a workout in before I relieve the captain," he answered. "I may not get a chance later. The Engine has a new probie from the academy stopping by tonight."

Josh's face brightened. "Fresh meat?"

"You know it."

"Who is it?" Josh asked. "Anyone we know?"

"Don't think so. A kid named Davids. I don't think he has any connections on the job."

"Oh, okay," Josh said. "Can we do good cop, bad cop?"

Matt laughed, shook his head and shrugged. He said, "I'm just gonna be myself. But I'll try to keep a straight face."

Josh beamed. "Fair enough. Let's wait downstairs. You go work out after."

CHARLES HAD FOLLOWED GOOGLE'S instructions and made the right onto the street the firehouse was located on. On his left he passed a tall apartment building attached to a community center. The address 2 West 143rd Street was boldly stated in rusted bronze letters above its doors. Further down the street on the right was a playground. There were several people sitting on benches near a basketball court watching ten guys play a full court game. Many of the men playing were half naked, and from the looks of their physiques, Charles figured the decision to go shirtless was probably more for comfort than from vanity. Across from the playground, immediately following the community center, separated by a wrought iron fence, was a parking lot full of cars. Attached to the lot was the firehouse.

Charles pulled over in front of the lot, careful not to block the entrance, and put the car in park. He took another deep breath and released it slowly, then stepped out. He walked around the hood to the passenger side, opened the door and grabbed the cake. In the park behind him, the people sitting on the bench closest to the gate watched him. Charles was tall, a few inches over six feet, and was in his dress uniform, minus the blazer. a tie at the neck of a sky-blue button-down with a fire department patch on the shoulder and navy-blue slacks with a near perfect crease. He did his best to smooth out the wrinkles on the shirt, but being tall and stuffed into a car for an hour made them resilient. He set the box down and checked his armpits for stains. They were clear and he was glad about it because what could he have done if they weren't?

He grabbed the box, stepped out of the street onto the sidewalk and looked up. The firehouse was a plain, unassuming three-story building. Large white brick with two red garage doors, ten feet high and six feet wide on either side of a standard door. Above that door was a large sketching of two firefighters: one holding a hose line, the number 99 on his helmet, the other holding an axe with the number 88 on his helmet. Above the garage door on the left, in metal framed letters, "Engine 99." Beneath that was the date it was established. Above the garage door on the right, "Ladder 88" and the date it was formed. Below the sketching and above the center door, medal letters read, "Battalion 5," but with no date.

Charles took one more deep breath before making his way to the center door. As he passed it, the garage door on his left started to rise. Bells jingled as the door rolled up on clanky tracks. He swallowed, breathed out through his nose. Behind the rising door, he could see the expanding legs of a man standing next to a large garbage pail on wheels. Charles balanced the box in one splayed hand like a tray and stood straight. The door rose higher, finally revealing a tall, dark-haired guy with a hand on the pail, looking down at his phone. Charles twisted his chin left and right to loosen his collar. The man with the pail looked up, spotted him, and grinned.

Charles took in a breath, raised a rigid hand to his brow, and said loudly, "Probationary
Firefighter Charles Davids reporting for duty, sir!"

The guy inside smiled broadly now. He dropped his phone in a pocket and shook his head. "Put your hand down, bro, I'm just a firefighter. You don't gotta salute me." He held out his hand. "Joe Bahms. Nice to meet you."

"Good to meet you, sir," Charles said, taking his hand.

"Call me Joe. Or Bahms, 'cause there's a bunch of Joes

here. But not sir."

"Yes, sir."

Bahms laughed and shook his head. "Come on in, buddy. Let me just put this in the dumpster, then I'll take you to the captain and show you around."

"I'll do it," Charles said, trying to balance the cake while reaching for the pail.

Bahms waved the offer away, saying "No, no. I got it," but Charles grabbed the pail and tried to pull it from him. Bahms grabbed his hand. "Charles, right? Charles?"

"Yes, sir."

"You're doing the right thing, bro. You are. As a probie, you should be trying to do as much as you can," he said, still smiling. "But you don't even officially start until Monday, right?

You're more like a guest right now. You're not gonna get in trouble for not taking this from me." Charles felt hot beneath his collar, uncertain what to do.

Bahms smiled again. "Trust me: you're gonna have plenty of opportunity to throw out garbage over the next twenty years. I'll get this one."

Bahms walked the pail to the curb and used two hands to pull the bag, drop it in a red dumpster to the right of the doors, then roll the pail back to where Charles was. Charles hadn't moved. He was uncomfortable. At the academy it'd been drilled into his head that if he wasn't doing anything and someone senior to him was, then he was doing something wrong. Today was his first day at the firehouse. *Everyone* was senior to him. Bahms watched him, chuckled and shook his head. He shoved the pail and it rolled inside and coasted to a stop just to the left of the open garage door. He reached for the box and said, "Thank you for the cake. Welcome to the house, bro."

Charles handed him the cake and they walked in together.

Inside was just as plain and functional as the outside. Four feet from the entrance, and directly between the two garage doors, was a small, enclosed office. The housewatch, he figured. A room in the front of most firehouses where a member could monitor who came and went, as well as announce over the loudspeakers whenever there was an emergency to respond to.

In front of him, fifteen feet away from the open garage door, was Engine 99's firetruck, red, white and yellow, facing the doors, ready to roll out at a moment's notice. To the right of that was a pickup truck with a cap on the back. The pickup was painted the same red and yellow as the Engine with a number 5 painted on the sides. The chief's car. Next to that was Ladder 88's truck, slightly longer and taller than the Engine and facing the garage door on the right. On the wall to the left was an open door with an exit sign above it. Beyond that, were metal racks about six feet tall with helmets on top and firefighters' uniforms inside.

Charles looked around and for a happy moment his anxiety was gone. This was what he'd been looking forward to. He hadn't always wanted to be a firefighter, but once he did, the idea consumed him. In the academy, all the other students seemed to have family already on the job. Or close friends or neighbors. They all seemed to have come in knowing more than him, and even up until yesterday, Charles wasn't yet sure he was exactly ready to do the job.

But in this moment, as he stared at the trucks and the bunker gear, the uncertainty was forgotten. He looked around and was happy. And he tried not to smile.

Bahms was saying, "We'll go put this in the kitchen and then I'll introduce you to the boss. I think the captain is still here. He's not working tonight but…" He trailed off and turned toward 88's truck. On the other side of it, a stairwell leading up to the second floor, rose out of sight. Two men in conversation, walking slowly, were halfway down the stairs.

"Salute *these* guys," Bahms whispered, and Charles looked at him. "They're both lieutenants and they'll say you don't need to salute them going forward, but it's a nice touch if you do it the first time. Okay?"

"Yes, sir."

"But wait 'til they're in handshake range."

"Yes, sir."

"Boss!" Bahms called over to the stairwell.

The two men stopped talking and looked over. They paused on the stairs, looked at each other, and smiled. The one closest to the foot of the stairs continued down, then rounded the banister and headed in Charles's direction. The one still on the stairwell was short and stocky. His body was in a space between muscular and chubby and looked as if he was recently the former but was heading toward the latter. He had a full head of hair, but it was thin and transparent. His face was red and worn, but like a tired man, not an old one. He walked down the stairs somewhat dramatically, planting his feet and pausing slightly on each step before moving on to the next. His eyes were on Charles and he seemed to sneer.

The other man was the opposite. He was young and thin and wiry. He bounced on the balls of his feet as he walked, and his full head of hair bounced to. He smiled immediately and started his outstretched hand toward Charles long before he was in reach.

Charles saluted. "Probationary Firefighter Charles Davids, reporting for duty, sir."

The smiling man waved away the salute. "Matt Quincy," he said. "I'm a lieutenant in 99.

I'm one of your officers. Charles, did you say?"

"Yes, sir."

Jason Powell

"Welcome, man! It's good to have you," he said, and Charles believed he meant it.

A moment later, the other man arrived by his side. Up close he didn't look mean, so much as angry. As if Charles had knowingly offended him and refused to apologize for it.

He folded his arms and ran his tongue across his teeth with his mouth closed. He lifted one eyebrow, looked Charles over and nodded slowly. "Who are you?"

"Probationary Firefighter Davids, sir."

"You got a first name, probie?"

"Yes, sir. Charles, sir."

"Charles. That your cake?"

Charles looked over at Bahms, who was holding the pull-apart box in both hands.

"Um, yes, sir."

"Then why the fuck is this man, with, what, nine years on the job, holding it? Something wrong with your arms?"

Charles flushed. His heart rose to his throat and the heat beneath his collar spread behind his ears. Why *had* he given the cake to Bahms? The garbage had already been thrown out, the pail already pushed inside. What did Charles need his hands free for? He really was an idiot.

"Something wrong with your arms, probie?" The lieutenant asked again.

"N-no, sir. Sorry." Charles turned to Bahms to take the cake back and found him chuckling. He looked over to the Engine boss, Matt, and he was laughing too. So was the other man.

"I'm fucking with you," the third man said. "Josh Calahan. Call me Josh." He held out his hand. "Welcome, brother."

Charles let out a sigh and a small groan escaped with it. He took Josh's hand and laughed. A mixture of emotions made his legs weak, and he squeezed Josh's hands harder than he intended. "Nice to meet you, sir."

The three men stood in a semi-circle around Charles and smiled at him. He let go of

Josh's hand and took the cake back from Bahms, who said, "Let's go put that in the kitchen. The men like nosh around this time anyway."

"Good to meet you. We'll talk later," Matt said, slapping his shoulder, then headed back toward the stairs. Josh turned left toward the housewatch. Bahms led Charles in the opposite direction toward a door on the back wall behind the trucks.

"Do *not* call him Josh." Bahms said once they were out of ear shot. "Keep calling him sir or call him Lieutenant. Or Lieu, you know, like short for lieutenant. I don't know why some officers do that. They forget how things work when you're new. If you called him Josh, the men would rip you a new one."

"Okay."

"Try to remember everyone's name as quick as you can. But I don't care what the bosses tell you, call them by their rank or call them sir."

"I will. Thank you."

They walked past an open space behind the trucks with a few couches facing a small table, to the door on the back wall, and pushed through into a kitchen. Charles was hit by a blast of cool air and it felt great. Bahms walked straight to a counter in the back, took the box from Charles, and opened it. Libby really had done a great job. The pull-apart was about a foot and a half long, in the shape of a fire engine. The layer of icing on top of the cupcakes was smooth and continuous. More icing had been added to form the details of the truck: doors, tires, windows. And in the driver's seat, a small candy action figure. Bahms looked down at the cake and smiled broadly.

"Nice touch."

Charles smiled back and felt his shoulders start to relax. Bahms stepped away left into a dining area. A long wooden table with twelve chairs around it dominated the area. In the corner was a metal stand with a tray of silverware. Bahms grabbed a butter knife and came back to the counter. "I'm gonna try this now," he said.

Then two tones, one high, one low sounded throughout the building. Bahms stopped and turned an ear toward the ceiling where the speakers were. An automated voice spoke slow and loud through them.

"Engine! Ladder! Battalion!"

"Gonna have to wait 'til later," Bahms said. "The house has a call." He tapped his ear and pointed at the speaker. "Pete is in the housewatch. He'll say what the call is for."

Charles looked at the speaker, a dusty cone-shaped object with chipped red paint on the outside. Four fast bells sounded and then a man spoke, clear but urgent. "Everyone goes! First-due for smoke!"

Bahms dropped the butter knife on the counter and hurried toward the door. "Just hang out," he called over his shoulder as he pushed through the door. "Make yourself at home." The door closed behind him and the man on the loudspeaker—Pete?—spoke again.

"8989 Douglass Boulevard, between 148th and 149th. Smoke, apartment 4B. Three and two with the chief, Engine and Truck both first-due. Giddyup!" Then four fast bells again.

Charles stared at the kitchen door, feeling awkward. Should he be doing something right now? Should he wait in the kitchen? Outside the door he could hear the trucks starting up and people moving around. He decided to wait. Out there he might be in someone's way. In here, he was fine. He couldn't get in trouble for standing in one spot, could he?

Turning to the counter, he closed the box, then took the cake over to an industrial-sized refrigerator with two glass doors and opened the one on the left. The door was heavy and manufactured so that it closed automatically to stop the cold air from escaping. Charles stood in the arch of its swing and used his back to keep it open. The shelves were mostly full. He put the cake half on a shelf to balance it with one hand and used his free hand to maneuver bowls and dishes around it to create space.

From behind him, the kitchen door burst open, and Joe Bahms was there in full uniform, smiling.

"Wanna go to a fire?"

"Yes, sir," Charles answered, and hustled through the door after him, heart racing.

The cake box had only been half on a shelf. When Charles let the box go, it fell forward toward the glass door, which closed automatically, and caught it as it dropped. The door pinned the box against the shelves and kept pushing.

TEN MINUTES LATER, CHARLES was between Bahms and Pete on one side, and Matt on the other. They were standing on the curb outside of 8989 Douglas Boulevard, looking up at the building. There hadn't been a fire. Someone had done a poor job cooking potatoes and their neighbor had smelled the smoke and panicked.

As the other firefighters were coming out of the building and back to the trucks, Bahms and Pete took the opportunity to explain to Charles what everyone had done and why. Charles stood beside them, hands folded behind his back, and listened intently. This wasn't a real fire, but he could still learn from it. Whether he felt ready or not, he might be doing this for real someday soon.

So he listened. And again, he tried not to smile.

-3-

EARLIER, WHILE CHARLES WAS walking into the firehouse beside Bahms, Alan Johnson walked into the lobby of 8989 Douglas Boulevard, humming. He was in a great mood. His day had been mostly uneventful, but last night had been awesome, and even the memory made him smile. He walked to the stairwell, looked up, and sighed, then started the hike up the stairs to the sixth floor.

Alan considered himself an average man, and he was. Average height, average weight, neither fat nor thin. He kept himself in okay shape, he thought. Good enough. Not a muscle head, but not a couch potato either. A woman at the foot of an out-of-service escalator might see him and ask him for help bringing up her bags, but he probably wouldn't be the first choice of a weightlifter at a gym looking for a spotter. And that was okay with him. He had energy for what he needed energy. Coming home was the worst part of his days because he lived on the top floor of a walk-up and going up six flights sucked. Nevertheless, he could do it fine. And even as he climbed the stairs his good mood was unchanged.

Alan was coming from work. His friend Kimberly had a shoe store and after taking days to decide a name, had called it Kim's Shoes. She wasn't very inventive, but she was a good friend, and a fair boss and she paid Alan a decent wage to manage the stockroom and replenish the sales floor. She'd even given him a set of keys so that he could lock up after cleaning whenever he worked the later shift.

Kim's Shoes was a small spot in Harlem, sandwiched between a florist on the left and a hair salon on the right. Kim's had a storefront entrance on Amsterdam Avenue and a back exit that led to an alleyway where they dumped their trash. The hair salon had the same setup.

Lately, Alan would hangout near the back exit after closing, in hopes that Vanessa, who worked in the salon and usually locked up at night, would take the garbage out. Very often she did, and the two would talk. The talk eventually evolved and last week she finally showed him her tits. Then last night he brought her into the stockroom of Kim's, and she showed him everything else.

Alan smiled at the thought. When he reached the top floor, panting a little, he was still smiling. Then he opened the door to his apartment, looked inside and stopped. To his left, the bedroom door was open when it shouldn't have been. Fridays were his wife's late day. What was she doing there?

He'd been holding a bottle in a brown paper bag. Now, he stuffed the bag in his back pocket, pulled his shirt down over it. He took a step inside, and a crunching sound cause him to look down. Glass from a shattered candle was at the foot of the wall to the left of the door. He frowned at it. What the hell was this? What was going on?

Alan stepped in cautiously, avoiding the glass, and closed the door behind him. He dropped his keys on a table beside the door where Candace kept their mail.

"Hello?" he called softly. He didn't ger a response, but from the bedroom, he thought he could hear breathing.

Heavy breathing.

No. No, not that. He was imagining it. She wouldn't.

He stood where he was a moment longer then took several deep breaths and marched over to the bedroom entrance.

Candace stood inside near the window, her back to the door, trembling. She was alone. Her arms were folded, and her head down. The ceiling fan was on, rustling loose hairs on her head. A pair of her shoes and her purse were on the floor between the bed and the door. The bed hadn't been slept in, but the top sheet was rumpled and wrinkled as if someone had laid on top of it.

At the foot of the bed, Alan saw his tablet, the screen blank. It hadn't been on the bed when he'd left for work. He stared at the blank screen and thought about what it might show if it were on, and he groaned.

Candace turned and faced him, her eyes red like the first part of a Visine commercial.

"What?" Alan asked, doing his best to sound concerned. "What happened?" He'd already figured it out, but he asked anyway.

CANDACE JOHNSON TAUGHT SECOND grade at Public School 329 in Harlem. Earlier in the day, she'd had to excuse herself while teaching a summer school class. She had gradually felt a sharp pain in her abdomen, and heat on her forehead head and cheeks. She was sure she had a low-grade fever and was afraid she might pass out. When in the restroom she'd found blood in her panties, she told her principal, Lucy, and they pulled a paraprofessional from another classroom to watch her students. Lucy had offered Candace a ride, but she called a cab instead and left for an Urgent Care, conscious of the pounding in her chest.

Hours later, when she had gotten home, she was weak, and not just physically. She'd walked into her bedroom, stepped out of her sneakers, and dropped her bag on the floor. She sat on her bed, elbows on her thighs, head in her hands and tried hard to ignore the knot in her throat. Candace thought about the last few hours and about Alan and about the past. Even before the diagnosis, she'd already known what happened. She knew the pain. She knew the signs.

They had been fighting a lot more than usual. Alan's drinking had become too big a problem to ignore, but it wasn't just that. It was everything. Alan hung out with his friend Rob all the time and he nearly always came back high as a kite. He was impossible to talk to like that and he seemed uninterested in talking to her when he wasn't. Now and then there'd be good days and Candace would see the person she'd fallen in love with. But those days were few and far between.

Still, after the Urgent Care, she'd been conflicted. On one hand the experience reminded her how they once were, years ago. The first time she found unexpected blood. A moment that could've been the worst of her life but wasn't because of him. Because of how he cared for her. How he seemed to understand the trauma of losing a baby was more than just physical. She felt an indescribable void in the days following that first time, and Alan filled it.

But on the other hand, Candace had been so stressed by the state of their relationship lately, that she didn't even notice she was late. She didn't know there was a baby to lose.

Candace stood and pulled the cord on the ceiling fan, then curled up at the foot of the bed and closed her eyes. She was startled when the desk by the window began to vibrate. She lifted her head and saw Alan's tablet, then lowered her head again, ignoring it. When it vibrated a second time, it occurred to her that she'd never seen it left unattended before. Candace pushed herself up, got her feet on the floor, and went over to the table. The screen was lit, showing a preview of a new text message. Someone named Vanessa had sent a heart emoji.

Candace's pulse raced as she punched in the four-digit code and a thread of messages between Alan and Vanessa filled the screen. Text and pictures. As she read through, an ellipsis appeared at the bottom of the thread. One of them was typing something.

It was Alan. He wrote: ***Thinking about last night got me excited. Wanna take your break at three o'clock and help me with this?***

A minute passed without a response and Candace realized she wasn't breathing. She gasped for air and swallowed it and tears fell. A moment later, a message from Vanessa popped up in a blue dialogue bubble.

Middle of the day! And a second later. ***Would love to but can't. Sorry, babe.***

And that was it. Over the next couple of hours, Alan received one text message from Rob and one from his bank alerting him that he had just made a forty-seven-dollar purchase at Best Wine and Spirits on Amsterdam Avenue. Aside from those, the screen remained blank.

Candace tossed the tablet on the bed and stared at it, her jaw trembling. The heel of her left foot drummed a beat against the rug and her vision blurred behind her tears. She walked a broken circle crossing her arms then grabbing her waist then grabbing the back of her neck, no movement lasting longer than a couple of seconds.

She was madder at herself than she was with him. How stupid she was to think, to hope, that what happened today might be made better by a man who would sooner chose a bottle over her.

Candace left the bedroom dazed, her cheeks and head feeling hot again. Tears continued streaming down her face and she wiped them away with the bottom of her shirt. She walked around the living room, then grabbed a candle off the table near the sofa and threw it at the front door as hard as she could, screaming with the effort. It shattered against the wall and pieces skittered across the floor.

She was sweating now. She grabbed her waist and walked back to the bedroom, stood beneath the fan and tried to steady herself. She hated to cry.

When she heard Alan's keys she stepped closer to the window, took a deep breath. She wouldn't cry in front of him.

He called out and she ignored him. The day outside the window was ironic. Beautiful, clear and calm. When she heard Alan come into the room, she steeled herself and waited a beat before turning to face him. They held each other's eyes.

He said, "What? What happened?"

Candace said, "Vanessa. Who is she?"

ALAN HADN'T ANSWERED HER. It took two people to fight. One of the first lessons his dad taught him. One of the only lessons as it happened, because by the time Alan was ten years old, his mother had successfully run his dad off.

She would start stupid fights too, his mother. A stay-at-home mom who must've spent her time alone just thinking about new things to bitch about. His dad would come home from work and she'd complain about him being gone for so long. But if he stayed home from work, she would complain about him not doing anything with himself. Once, when Alan was eight, his dad had come home from an office birthday party and brought Alan a piece of chocolate cake with vanilla icing. The moment he got home, his mother started in on him, yelling about one thing or another. At some point early in that fight, the cake was thrown at his dad and the icing wound up splattered against the wall. His dad didn't react. He just dragged Alan into Alan's bedroom and locked the door. They played Nintendo with the volume high while his mother banged on the door and continued her ranting. His dad said, "Just ignore her, Al. Just ignore her.

It takes two people to fight. She can't fight with herself, so just ignore her."

Alan remembered that as Candace stood in front of him, face in tears. An overreaction if you asked his opinion. He was certain she had gone through his tablet, but so what? So some woman was sending him nudes and dirty messages. That's not proof anything happened. What was she crying about? An assumption was what. And that wasn't fair. It was even, he believed, in the constitution or something that if you couldn't prove it, then it didn't happen. Innocent until proven guilty, right? She didn't know if he'd actually done anything wrong, which meant he didn't. It took two people to fight, and he wasn't in the mood for it, so he didn't answer.

They stared at each other for forever until she stood up straight and wiped her face.

"Get out."

And there it was: his way out. Alan nodded. The bottle was starting to burn a hole in his pocket anyway. Rob was probably off work, and he could help Alan kill a couple of hours to let Candace cool off. Alan was very thirsty now that he thought of it.

"Good idea," he said. He turned around, left the room, and headed to the front door.

"Let's cool down," he said over his shoulder. "I'll be back before too late."

"Don't."

Alan turned back and Candace was at the door to the bedroom, arms crossed over her chest. Tears rolled down her face like rain on glass.

"What?"

"Do *not* come back. Get a bag, pack your things, and don't

come back."

Her body trembled every time she took a breath and Alan watched her, disgusted. All this because, what? A few messages? She didn't even know anything! He patted his pocket to locate the bottle, then grabbed his keys off the table and turned to the door. There were blotches of candle wax against it and the wall beside it. It was wax, but what he saw was vanilla icing.

He shook his head. Women. Fucking ridiculous.

OUTSIDE THE APARTMENT, IN the hallway, there had been a commotion. A smell like burnt toast filled the air and a low rumble of chatter came up from the floors below. Alan's neighbor next door, Mrs. Tabacco, an old lady who'd become a widow last year, stood in front of her open doorway, near the stairs, with her arms folded and a frown on her face. The door that led to the roof was open at the top of the stairwell and a fireman in full gear made his way down. Mrs. Tabacco stepped backward into her apartment but left her door open. When the fireman reached the foot of the stairs, she began coughing, and he turned to her.

"What's going on?" she demanded. "Is there a fire?"

"No, no," the fireman answered. "Someone just burned some food on their stove. Caused a small smoke condition, but you guys are okay." He looked from her to Alan and nodded. "You don't need to leave your apartments. There's no fire."

Mrs. Tabacco stuck her head out and looked over at Alan. She frowned again, then disappeared inside her apartment, muttering about idiotic people unable to use a damned stove, for crying out loud. The two men looked at each other, smiled and shrugged. The fireman told Alan to take it easy, then went down the next flight. Alan, still pissed about Candace, followed him down.

"I *will* take it easy. 'Bout to go have a drink. Gonna be a nice night."

"Nice," the fireman said. "There's a nice breeze out there. Good night to hang out."

On the fourth floor, the door to apartment 4B stood open. Alan peered inside on his way down and saw a man fanning a hand-towel toward an open window. He didn't see any smoke, but the air looked dim, like looking through a dirty glass. In the lobby, the firefighter held the door to the building for him. Alan nodded a thank you and stepped outside. At the curb were two firetrucks, lights flashing, with a bunch of firefighters putting things away in compartments and climbing inside. Alan looked around and saw three other firetrucks at the traffic lights or rolling away down the street with no lights on. The fireman from the roof walked past him and held up a hand.

"Alright, brother," the fireman said. "Have a drink for me too. Be safe."

"You, too. You guys roll pretty deep for a burnt pot or whatever," Alan joked. "What do you send if there's a real fire?"

The fireman stopped and smiled. "This. At least this. More if it's bad or if we need it. Whoever called about this said there was a fire. Or smoke. Or, you know, something that means there might be a fire. We didn't know it was only burnt food 'til we got here. We send five rigs—five, you know, firetrucks—and a chief, to start with. If we need more, we send more. If we need less, we send some guys back."

"Damn," Alan said. "That must suck, rushing all over the place for bullshit. Especially at night."

The fireman smiled again. "Sucks more for you all. Especially at night. This is our job; we get paid to rush every-

31

where. You guys being disturbed or woken up for bullshit is worse."

"Yeah," Alan agreed. He looked away from the fireman toward the trucks. At the curb, a young guy in a button-down, tie, and slacks stood with the firefighters, looking out of place like an unlucky fan posing with the wrong team. With his hands behind his back, he nodded at everything the others said to him. Obviously new.

"Better safe than sorry," the fireman from the roof said. "It could always be something worse than burnt food. Anyway, take care, bro."

"Yeah," Alan said again, his anger at Candace forgotten. He watched the fireman go join the others at the trucks. Something he'd said lingered in the back of Alan's mind, but he couldn't figure out what. Something, good he thought. Something that made him want to smile.

-4-

THE NEXT DAY WAS Charles's graduation from the
academy. The probies were each given five tickets for guests,
and because there were three hundred of them, the department
used the auditorium of a super church in Brooklyn for the
ceremony.

Charles didn't have a need for five tickets. He didn't have
a need for one. His only family in New York was his mom and
one of his brothers, and he didn't invite either one of them.
He'd always been very close with his mother, but even more
so after his dad passed. His father had been relatively young
and healthy, and his death was a surprise. A month after his
funeral, when Charles received the acceptance letter to the fire
academy, his mother wasn't very happy. When she thought
of her youngest child as a firefighter in New York City, she
thought of terror attack documentaries and Hollywood mov-
ies. If Charles would've invited her to the graduation, she
would've gone, but she wouldn't have liked it. So he didn't
invite her. He didn't invite his brother because his brother was
antisocial. Instead, he gave his tickets to other graduates who
had more than five people in their lives who would be happy
to be there.

After the ceremony, Charles posed for pictures with
friends he'd made, holding up their completion certificates.
Some arranged to meet up later for a celebratory drink.

Charles agreed to join them but wasn't really sure he wanted to. He thought of the other graduates going off with their families to restaurants or home-cooked meals or parties in celebration, while he was on his way home to his empty apartment, and a spirit of celebration just wasn't in him.

In the parking lot of the church, Charles tossed the framed certificate and his uniform cap on the back seat of his car, then climbed in behind the wheel with no idea where to go. He didn't want to go home. If he went to visit his mom, she'd see the uniform and feel bad for not knowing today was the graduation and for knowing why he didn't tell her. So that was out. He didn't want to go to a restaurant by himself in uniform because he'd feel weird being alone, so that was out too. He sat back and looked through the windshield at a graduate posing with a woman who was either his girlfriend or his wife or someone hoping to be one of the two. His arm was around her shoulder, and both her arms were around his waist. She wore a hot pink dress, and a small crowd milled around watching, not so discretely.

Charles smiled to himself, reached forward, and started the car.

SWEET ART BY FELICIA was open and empty of any customers. The smells of vanilla and cinnamon hung in the air like perfume. Music from a piano played low through speakers near the door. Some famous pianist, Charles figured, to keep with the artistic theme. He didn't know anything about classical music or classic art, but he felt that the theme fit nicely in a bakery. In his experience, which wasn't extensive, small businesses did well if they had an old timey, through-the-ages feel.

When he entered, Libby and her mother Felicia were at the round table where Felicia had been the other day. More bowls were on the table this time, filled with different ingredients you might expect to find in a cake. They worked in separate bowls, wearing aprons dusted in flour. Both looked over when Charles walked in, and he was excited to see a smile spread across

Libby's face. Her mom smiled too, a look of amused surprise. Libby rushed off to a sink beside the counter and rinsed her hands. She dried them on her apron and crooked a finger at Charles.

Heart racing, he smiled and walked over.

"We saw you on the news," Libby beamed. "You graduated today!" She untied the apron from her waist, pulled it over her head, tossed it behind the counter, and hugged him.

Charles inhaled sharply, and time stopped. He'd heard the phrase before but never experienced the phenomenon. Libby stood there on her toes, arms around his shoulders, and he could feel his heart beat against her chest. He hadn't been sure she'd even remember him, and suddenly, somehow, they were holding each other in a tight embrace.

Except, not really. Libby was holding him, but he hadn't returned the hug. When time stopped, he'd become super aware of everything. He was aware that his reflex was to wrap his arms around her waist, but that doing so may seem too personal. He was aware that her hair smelled like apples, which seemed very appropriate. He was aware that New York City was in the middle of a heat wave, and he'd been in his full uniform for nearly six hours and, under those circumstances, he wasn't completely confident in his deodorant. He was also aware that as happy as he was to have Libby embracing him, it was a little awkward in front of her mother. And he was aware that time didn't stay stopped; if he didn't react soon, it would be awkward for a whole other reason. He let himself breathe and wrapped one arm around her back.

After a second, Libby pulled back and met his eyes, her smile as broad as when he'd come in. "It's so crazy," she said. "We were literally just talking about you and the pull-apart." She brightened and grabbed his shoulders. "How'd it go with the pull-apart? Did they love it?" Charles looked at the excitement in her eyes and couldn't bring himself to tell her the truth. Not after all the work she'd put into the cake.

He said, "They loved it. It was gone in ten minutes."

"Yay!" She laughed. She grabbed her face. "I don't know why I'm so happy. I feel like I helped you win a bake sale or something."

Charles laughed too. "You were amazing. Yesterday was my first day meeting everyone.

It was a great first impression thanks to you."

She blushed. "My cheeks hurt, I'm smiling so much. I'm really happy for you."

"I appreciate it, Libby. Thank you."

"You remember my name!"

"How could I forget? You made my night."

Blush. "Well, you never told me yours."

He told her and they shook hands and she laughed. Then she brought Charles over to the round table where her mom had been watching.

"This is my mom," she said, rubbing her back. "This is the firefighter I did the cake for the other day. Charles."

Charles said, "Nice to meet you, ma'am."

"Felicia," Libby's mom said with a smirk. "Not ma'am. I know how they make you all do in the fire academy, calling everyone sir and ma'am and all that, but if you want a free graduation cake, you better knock it off in here."

Charles laughed. "Yes, ma'—yes, I will."

"Congratulations on graduating."

"Thank you very much."

"Did your parents go to the ceremony?" Libby's mom asked.

"No, ma'am. Sorry. No, Miss…Felicia, they couldn't make it."

"Just Felicia. And I'm sorry," Libby's mom said, scraping cream off the sides of the bowl with a spatula. The sweet smell reminded Charles that he was still hungry.

Libby frowned. "Did anyone go to your graduation?" "No, but don't feel bad. Most of my family is out of town." "No wife or girlfriend?" her mom asked.

Charles laughed. "No. No wife or girlfriend." The two women stole a glance at each other, but Charles saw it and it made him smile.

"Well," Felicia said, standing straight and setting the spatula down. "Libeth was incredibly happy when she spotted you on the news earlier. It's a tremendous accomplishment, graduating. You two go over to the fridge and you pick out a cake for yourself. Free of charge."

Charles's heart began to race again. She, Libby, had spotted him on TV in a crowd of three hundred people all wearing the same uniform. She'd been discussing him with her mom.

She hugged him. Those were signals, right? He wasn't misreading this. And even if he was, what was there to lose?

"Actually, I stopped here right after the graduation," he said, shifting his weight slightly.

"I haven't eaten anything yet. My mom would kill me if I had dessert before my meal." The two women smiled at that.

"I don't know what time you close or what time you guys get off, but I was wondering if you'd want to join me for dinner tonight. Nemo's down the street is nice, you guys ever been there?"

"Yeah, a couple of times." Libby smiled. "But we have plans tonight."

Charles nodded, wondering if his cheeks were visibly red. "I get it. Thought I'd ask." No one spoke for a moment. then Charles said to Libby, "Do you mind if I leave you my number?

Maybe we could rain check? I get hungry a lot."

Felicia grinned again and glanced at Libby. Libby hesitated, then said, "Let's go now. I can take a break for lunch. It's just across the street." Charles smiled and Libby smiled back. "I get hungry a lot too," she said.

Charles stepped toward the door and Libby went behind the counter to grab something.

Felicia looked at Charles and said, "Be safe out there. Probation is a hard fourteen months." Charles was surprised by that. "I know all about firefighters," she said, and although she was smiling, it sounded like a warning.

CHARLES AND LIBBY LEFT. Libby may have been underdressed, and Charles overdressed, but Nemo's didn't have a dress code, and this wasn't an official date and they were both hungry, so they didn't care.

They ordered fish and chips (Libby) and fried chicken with rice (Charles) and were good with the pitcher of ice water their waitress brought them when she introduced herself—"Jenn with two Ns." They ate and talked about themselves and asked about each other. Charles spoke about being the youngest in his family and spoiled by his siblings and how that made the academy a wakeup call. Libby spoke about her mom teaching her to bake and about having a dog "but not a dog," and how she met her parent's for the first time at the bakery.

"How does that work?" Charles asked.

"Adoption," she answered after finishing her water. The straw made an empty tunnel sound when it sucked up air, and

Charles grabbed the pitcher and refilled her glass as she set it down.

"Thank you." She smiled, and Charles was hit again by how beautiful she was.

"You're welcome. I'm shocked you're adopted. Your mom and you look like twins."

"We don't," she said plainly. "You just think so because we're the same complexion and we wear our hair the same. And, I don't know, maybe we have the same expressions? That happens with people who spend a lot of time together. It was the same with my mom and dad. *They* look related. But not really. It's just 'cause they spent their whole lives together. They became so much alike."

Libby looked into her glass, her smile fading slightly. She rubbed the tabletop with the side of her thumb on one hand and played with the straw with the other hand. She held her finger over the mouthpiece of the straw and lifted it from the water. Then, once the straw cleared the rim, she'd lift her finger and watch the water in the straw splash back into the glass. When she looked up after only a moment, she seemed tired. Like the train of thought she was on had taken her on a long ride.

"Tell me about your family," she said, sitting up straight. "Where are they? You said most of them aren't in New York?"

Charles watched her a moment before he answered."Yeah," he said, "We're all scattered. One of my sisters is a Marine. She's at Camp Lejeune in North Carolina."

"Oh, nice! A family of service."

Charles shrugged. "Her, yes. I haven't really done anything yet."

"Stop! You joined the fire department. That's a selfless thing."

He smiled but shrugged again. "Another sister is a professor in Africa. Cape Town, I think. A third sister works for a publishing company based in Norway. And…I have three brothers who are missionaries. They're funded by the church my family goes to. They're in Haiti right now. Haiti or the Philippines, I don't remember which."

"Wow. You guys are…your parents must be proud. And easily bored. How many was that? Six kids including you?"

Charles smiled. "That was seven including me. Seven of nine. I have another brother who lives in New York, not too far from my mom, but he's part shy, part antisocial, part recluse. He doesn't even have a cell phone."

"And number nine?"

"Another sister," Charles said, pushing his shirt sleeves back above his elbow. "She passed away a couple of years ago. Heart complications."

"Oh, I'm sorry." She reached over and touched his hand. "I didn't mean to bring it up."

"It's fine." He smiled. "We're okay now."

Libby held on to his hand and Jenn came back over. "Can I get you guys some dessert?

Coffee?"

Charles lifted an eyebrow to Libby, and she pressed her lips together, squinted, then shook her head.

"Just the check, please," Charles said, and Jenn smiled and laid it face down in a leather holder on the table between them, then walked away. Charles and Libby both grabbed it.

"I got it." Charles smiled.

"No. This is for your graduation. I'll get it."

"No, no. The free cake is for my graduation. This lunch was a thank you for your help with the pull-apart." He used a little more force on his end of the holder.

"Nice try," she said, frowning, using both hands now. "You paid for the pull-apart. Your business was thanks enough."

"Libby."

"Charles!"

"Okay. Okay, how about I pay for this one and you have dinner with me next weekend?" he said. "I can tell you all about my first week in the firehouse and you can tell me about how you have a dog but not a dog."

She squinted and thought about that. "Can I pay next weekend?"

"For yourself? Sure. Probably."

Libby smiled and released the holder. "Fine."

Charles threw some bills in and gave it to Jenn when she passed.

"I'll bring you your change."

"It's yours," he said.

"Well, thank you." To Libby she said, "Next weekend, make it Saturday. I'm off Sundays." Then she turned to Charles and flashed a smile. "Not that I was eavesdropping."

OUTSIDE THE BAKERY, LIBBY fanned herself and looked up at Charles. A few customers walked around inside, but not many.

"Can I ask you a question before we go get your cake?" Libby asked.

"Yeah, of course."

"Where are your parents? Why didn't they make it today? You made it seem like you all are so close."

"We are. Well, we were. I mean, my dad died. Last year," he said and Libby's face softened. "I didn't invite my mom today because she's not happy about this. About me being a firefighter. She's worried, you know? My sister passed, my dad passed, six of us are overseas or in potentially dangerous places. Well," he shrugged. "Maybe not Norway, but you know. My mom's scared she's gonna lose someone else."

"I get it. I'm sorry." Libby said and touched his arm.

Charles said. "Did your dad pass, too?"

Libby took her hand back, surprised. "My dad's not dead." She looked between his eyes like she was going to say something else but didn't. Instead, she grabbed the handle on the door.

"Come," she said. "Let's go pick out your cake."

-5-

SATURDAY SUCKED FOR ALAN. It sucked because Friday sucked, and the two days were really just one long crappy continuation. The sun may have gone down and come back up but there'd been no night's sleep to separate those two events. Not a good night's sleep, anyway.

After he had spoken with the fireman in his building, he met up with Rob and they'd gone to Mikey G's pub near West 125th Street. He'd told Rob about Vanessa, and the fight with Candace and how she overreacted.

Rob said, "They take that shit seriously, man." He was looking down the bar at a redhead bartender who he often fantasized about but never spoke to other than to order drinks.

"What shit?"

"Cheating, man. They don't like that. Women will stay with a dude who smacks the crap out of them every other day, but once he cheats…" Rob shook his head. "That's it."

WHEN ALAN RETURNED HOME, he hadn't been completely drunk, but he'd needed to hold
the handrails to make it upstairs, and it took a lot longer than it should've. It was nearly midnight when he got in and he was conscious of the noise he made in the hallway. He didn't feel like sitting through another argument, so he com-

posed himself outside, determined not to wake Candace. That turned out not to be a problem.

When Alan walked in, Candace and her friend Hanna were on the couch, looking at their phones, a magazine between them. They had moved a fan that was normally kept behind the couch beside the coffee table in front of it. The TV was on, but muted. There were open boxes beside him at the door and at the couch and at the entrance to the bedroom. Alan looked into one near his leg and saw a bunch of his things. When he looked up again, the women were standing.

"What is this?" he asked, feeling his cheeks flush. The windows were open and the fan was on, but the apartment felt like a bathroom after a shower.

"Your stuff," Candace said. Her face and eyes looked as if she had been crying, but her voice was calm and strong. "You can move them out next week or get them into storage or whatever. But you can't sleep here." She combed her hair behind her ear. "I would appreciate it if you gave me the keys, so I don't have to change the locks."

"What are you talking about?" Alan asked, genuinely confused. "Why?"

Hanna said, "Are you for real? Did you just ask why?"

Alan ignored her. He stood up straight, giving his best impression of a sober man.

"Candy, I know you're mad—"

"Do you even know what happened today?" Hanna continued. Her fists were balled, and she leaned toward him. Hanna was thin and muscular. She wrote books for a living, but she spent just as much time at the gym as she did at a desk. Alan glanced at her fists, then met her eyes.

"What're you talking about? It was just a fight. You weren't even there."

"To her, asshole," Hanna said, stepping forward. "Do you

know what happened *to her* today?"

"Hanna." Candace placed a hand on her friend's shoulder and Hanna turned. Candace shook her head and Hanna looked back at Alan, revulsion on her face. She bit her bottom lip, breathed out, and stepped back, putting her arm around Candace's shoulders.

"You're pathetic," Hanna said to Alan. "You have, like, a disease or something. You need help, you know that? Like serious help. You don't deserve her."

He didn't answer.

Hanna shook her head again. "Get out of here," she said. "When you come back for your things, I'll be here. She says to give you a week, but I wouldn't test my patience if I were you."

Alan looked from Hanna's eyes to Candace, and she looked away. She studied the ground taking long, deep breaths. Although they were probably the same height, she looked small in Hanna's arms. She looked fragile and soft, and he wanted to hug her. He was reminded of the beginning when they were dating. Years ago, she had gotten pregnant and miscarried, and when she returned from the hospital, she looked defeated and small. Just like now. He wanted to take care of her then. He wanted to take away the pain. Obviously, the miscarriage wasn't his fault, but he wanted to make up for it. He wanted to make sure she never felt sadness again. He proposed later that month, and it made her so happy. Things were good. He didn't know when that had changed, when or how things had gone bad. But if he'd been able to make her happy before, why not now?

He wiped his mouth with the palm of his hand and stepped closer. "Look. I'm really sorry."

The fan by the coffee table oscillated, and at one end of its rotation it would ruffle the pages of the magazine on the couch. Apart from that, the apartment was silent.

"I'm sorry," he said again. "Candy, I know I messed up. But it was only this one time, I swear."

Silence.

Alan stepped closer and Hanna's body tensed, but he ignored it. "I know I messed up,

alright? But I'll never do it again. I swear. Okay? I shouldn't have fu—slept with her. I didn't enjoy it and I'm sorry and I will never do it again."

Candace looked up and Hanna dropped her arm. Candace's eyes welled up before tears rolled down her cheeks, but her face stayed exactly the same. She blinked away more tears and when she was done, he saw the same look in her eyes that he saw in Hanna's.

Rob was right. That was it.

WHEN ALAN LEFT, HE called Rob to see if he could sleep at his place, but that hadn't worked out.

"You know Jackie hates you," Rob had said. "She won't let you stay here."

"Screw her."

"Not if you stay here, I won't. Sorry, man. G'luck."

Frustrated, Alan sat on a bench across the street from his building and considered his options. No way in hell was he going to a shelter. Those places were filthy. And he wouldn't go to a motel in the area for the same reason. He didn't want to go to midtown and spend two or three hundred dollars on a hotel, and he couldn't go to Kim's shoe store to sleep in the office because the keys to the store were on the same ring as his house keys, which Hanna made him drop on the table near the door before he left. Pissed and hot and hungry, he went to a bodega on West 145th Street and bought a beef patty and a bottle of water. He ate it outside, standing on a corner. Across the street in a Ritechek, a twenty-four-hour check cashing place, he spotted a milk crate under a long counter against the window. He finished eating, then crossed the street, went inside the Ritechek, flipped the crate on its side, and sat down to figure out his next move.

Alan sat for hours, drifting in and out of an uncomfortable sleep. When he saw a *Daily News* truck pull up to the grocery store across the street and drop off a bundle of papers, he realized the night was over. It was Saturday and he had to work.

ON HIS WAY INTO Kim's, he'd stopped at a Dunkin Donuts. He was hungry again, tired, and nearly hungover. He ate a bagel with butter, a toasted coconut donut, and drank Gatorade as he walked. And afterwards, although he still had an unbelievable headache, he felt ready to work.
Inside, Kimberly was ringing up a customer. She smiled and said good morning, and Alan walked past her to the stockroom. He sat on a metal foot stool and massaged his temple with one hand while balancing the open Gatorade on his knee with the other. Kimberly came in a moment later, walked over to him, leaned forward so her face was near his, and took a deep breath.

"You're drunk," she said, standing straight, pinching the bridge of her nose.

"Huh? No. I'm good."

"Alan, you're drunk. You smell terrible and you look like crap." She sighed. "What is wrong with you? Why do you do this?"

He didn't answer. He wasn't in the mood.

"Go home, Alan," she said. He looked up and she was in front of him, arms crossed over her chest. Kim was a tall woman with powerful shoulders. With her hair tied back the way it was, she looked like Mr. Clean standing over him. "Go home," she said again. "Sober up. This is the last time, Al, I swear. If you do this again, I gotta let you go. Don't put me in that position.

You understand?"

Alan looked at her, incredulous. It was almost unbelievable. Her too? She was supposed to be his fucking friend.

He pushed off the stool, stood on shaky legs, and felt his head spin. He grabbed it with both hands and dropped the Gatorade bottle, which bounced once before landing on its side, blue liquid spilling out onto the carpeted floor.

"Shit," he said, and stooped to pick it up.

"Leave it." Kimberly reached out to steady him. "Alan. You need to stop this. Seriously. Candace isn't gonna put up with this forever. You're gonna lose more than your job if you don't cut this out."

Alan shrugged her hand off his shoulder. He stood up straight, waited until he felt balanced, then walked out. Kimberly said something behind him, but he hadn't heard it clearly and didn't care.

The heat outside didn't help his mood. He stood beneath the stupid awning and glared out at the street, again unsure of what to do. He couldn't go home, not like this. He didn't know if Jackie was at Rob's, but Rob was probably at work, and he doubted Rob would let him stay at his place alone. Jackie wouldn't like that, and Rob acted like a punk when it came to her.

A dark-haired woman with a yellow sundress walked past him on the sidewalk and he turned to watch her in case the wind blew. Once she passed him, she turned and went into the beauty salon next door to Kim's.

Alan smiled to himself, feeling instantly better.

Following the sundress, it occurred to him that he had never been inside before. A couple of women were in chairs

Jason Powell

under big dome dryers. The sundress was at a counter talking to an employee she seemed to know. Another woman sat in a chair with her back to a sink and her head inside getting her hair washed by Vanessa. Alan smiled again and went that way.

Vanessa didn't notice him until he put his hand on her waist. She stopped what she was saying, looked up and gasped, and her expression surprised him.

"Hey," he said, because he didn't know what else to say. "I—"

"Excuse me one minute, sweetie," Vanessa said to the customer, panic in her voice. She looked around the salon and dried her hands on a hand towel beside the sink. "Come with me," she whispered to Alan, avoiding his eyes. She started to go toward the back but changed direction and headed instead for the front door. He followed and they walked out the way Alan had come.

Outside, Alan was nervous but wasn't sure why. He stepped close to kiss her, but she flinched and ducked away. She walked hurriedly out of sight of the front window where the women inside the salon had all stopped to watch, and when he followed her to the corner, her face was red.

"What the hell are you doing?!" she demanded, her voice a loud whisper. "Are you crazy? You know I'm married, right?"

"What are you...? What do you mean?"

"What do you mean, what do I mean! They all know him." She held out her hand to the salon. "What the hell are you thinking?"

Alan didn't answer.

Glaring now, Vanessa said, "Don't come back in. We're done. You ruined a good thing. Okay? You just—we're done." She folded her arms and leaned away from him, her eyes flicking back and for the between him and the salon behind him.

49

Alan's head throbbed. He closed his eyes and massaged his temples again. It was probably his own fault, what he was feeling. There was no reason he should've been surprised or disappointed by what was happening. None at all. Hadn't this been his whole weekend? Hadn't this been his whole *life*? He opened his eyes again, looked down at Vanessa, and hated her. He stared at her a moment, considering, then turned and headed for the door to the salon.

"Hey," she shouted behind him, but he ignored her. He pushed open the door and leaned in.

"I fucked her!" he yelled. "Two nights ago, after work. In the back, there." The women inside gaped at him, mouths open.

He backed out to the street, and when he turned and saw the look on Vanessa's face, he felt a little better.

THE REST OF SATURDAY was just as crappy. He fell asleep on a shady stoop some streets down from his apartment and someone called the police. He wasn't arrested but he was told he couldn't sleep there. Later he went to McDonald's and fell asleep at a table and the fire department came and woke him up. They said people had been trying to wake him for a while and thought he was unconscious.

"An ambulance is on the way," one of the firemen said. "We just came to make sure you were okay. If you want to get checked out, the ambulance will take a look at you, but if you just wanna sleep, it'd probably be best if you go home."

So, he did that. He waited outside his building for someone to come out or go in, and when some goth teen finally did, he slipped inside, went upstairs, and knocked on his apartment door. Candace should've been off from work. He knocked and waited. And waited. He rang the bell and knocked again and waited some more. His neighbor, Mrs. Tabacco, opened her door and scowled at him. She stepped out into the hallway, looked at his closed door and scowled again, then went back inside and slammed her door.

He'd spent twenty minutes in the hall before giving up and stamping down the stairs, frustrated. Frustrated and maybe a little embarrassed. As he exited the building, an Uber pulled out of traffic and stopped at the curb. Nothing happened for a moment, but then the door opened and first Hanna then Candace stepped out. Candace looked amazing and for some reason that made his heart sink. The women were smiling as they approached the building entrance but stopped when they spotted him.

Hanna asked, "What are you doing here?"

"I need to get some of my things. And, and a shower."

"Wow," Hanna scoffed. "Is that a joke?"

"It's my place too!" He hadn't intended to yell.

"Not anymore," Hanna said. She answered calmly, but Alan saw her body tense again.

"Go shower at Victoria's house."

"Your clothes are in a box," Candace said, drawing his attention. She took out her keys from a purse she carried, and walked past him, eyes to the ground. "Grab them and get out."

Alan tried again. "Candy…"

Candace opened the door to the building and paused with her key still in the lock, the knuckles of her fist holding the purse flat against the glass pane of the window. She looked down at her shoes, then up at his eyes.

And he began to cry.

It wasn't an act, and he was shocked. It must've been ten years since the last time he cried. He hadn't felt it coming, but now he couldn't stop. Alan cried and felt the stress of the weekend cascade out of him. He'd messed up. He knew that. Hanna was right, he didn't deserve Candace. He knew that too. But that could change. He loved her, and she loved him. What else mattered?

"I'm sorry," he choked out. "Just gimme a chance. I…I'll do better this time."   Candace didn't respond. She was silent for an uncomfortable moment, then looked back down and turned away. She took her key from the door, then met his eyes again.

She said, "Get your box, then get out." She pushed the door open, and Hanna came from behind Alan following her inside. When Hanna looked back at him, she was smiling.

He stopped crying.

AROUND MIDNIGHT HE WAS back on the crate in Ritechek holding a Poland Spring bottle filled with vodka. Outside, three fire trucks rolled down Douglass Boulevard, lights and sirens.

Alan took a sip from the bottle and shook his head, mad at himself for having cried. He thought of Hanna's face when she passed him. Thought of the smile. He rolled his eyes and took another sip.

After only a couple of minutes he saw the fire trucks again. Going back the way they'd come, no lights, no sirens. Must've been a false alarm.

He brought the bottle up again but stopped before it reached his lips. That was it!

His heart began to race, and he closed his eyes, trying to organize his thoughts.

Okay. What could happen if he called? He'd be in trouble, but only if he was caught. That meant he couldn't use his cellphone. Phone companies listened to calls and tracked locations all the time. Everyone knew that. Fine. He looked through the window at the payphone on the corner. That should work, right?

Alan stood and looked over to the cashier's window across the customer area to his right. Two people, one guy and one girl were working, but neither paid him any attention. He turned away from them and went outside. A lot of people were out. Not really a surprise for a Saturday night in the summer. People walked past him and either crossed Douglass or waited on the curb for the light to change so they could cross 145th. No one looked at him. Why should they? He was just a regular guy making a phone call.

His heart hammered his chest. He wiped his palms on his pants and picked up the receiver, then hung it up again. It had to be planned out, he wasn't good enough to freestyle. Eyes closed, Alan mouthed a couple of drafts, started to laugh, and was surprised by it. He opened his eyes again, serious now, nodded, then picked up the receiver and dialed.

One ring, then, "9-1-1, what's your emergency?"

"H-hi. I'm on…there's a fire in my hou— my apartment is on fire."

"Sir, are you inside your apartment?"

"Yes, no! No, I'm outside, but I think my wife is inside."

"What's your address, sir?"

"It's 8989 Douglas Boulevard, apartment 6B."

"Sir, are—"

Alan hung up. He practically ran back inside Ritechek and dropped onto his crate. The two cashiers looked up and looked him over, then went back to what they were doing. He sat with his hands on his knees and rocked. Felt like he was having a heart attack.

Sirens. Not two minutes since he called, three trucks sped by his window, blaring their horns. Alan ran outside again and looked up the street as the trucks pulled over in front of his building. Somewhere in the distance he could hear more trucks approaching, and he ran back inside. This time the cashiers frowned at him. He didn't care. He was thinking about his apartment, wondering what was happening inside. Would they knock on the door, or would they just break it down? Was Candace already asleep? He didn't love the idea of the firemen seeing her in bed because she barely wore anything in this heat, but he did like the image of her and Hanna being woken up from a peaceful sleep while he sat in this damn check cashing place.

Would the firemen be mad at her? Would she be pissed at them? Either way, this was going to ruin her night, he thought.

And he laughed.

-6-

MONDAY MORNING CAME TOO fast for Charles.
The start of his first official day at the firehouse and by the
time he'd left his apartment and was in his car, he felt as if
he'd forgotten everything he learned during his four months in
the academy. He drove, distracted, to a supermarket near the
firehouse and tried not to panic. His memory loss was probably normal, he thought. Just nerves. But why? His last visit
there ended fine.

Friday evening, when they had gotten back and spotted
the mess in the kitchen, there was an eternal moment when
no one spoke, and Charles stopped breathing. But then they
all laughed or applauded and shook their heads. Joe Bahms
helped Charles clean it up, and as they were crouched down
picking up the cupcakes, Pete Dufresne, the Pete from the
housewatch, walked in. He looked down at them, shook his
head, and said, "And you wanna be my latex salesman."

No one seemed mad and everyone seemed friendly, and
Charles had gone home feeling good about being assigned
there. But on this day, Monday, as he walked around the
supermarket trying to figure out how many eggs and packs of
bacon he should bring for breakfast, he felt the same way he
had in his car on his first trip there.

Charles took a calming breath and headed for the row of
registers. He'd settled on two pounds of bacon and an eigh-

teen pack of eggs. On his way to checkout, he grabbed four newspapers. The line at the register moved smoothly, but when an older woman two customers ahead of him thoroughly searched her bag for exact change, Charles felt his anxiety build.

Six thirty. The day shift at the firehouse started at nine, so he needed to be there at seven. The supermarket was only three blocks from the firehouse, but the woman at the register was in no rush and the guy in line behind her, licked his fingers and paged slowly through a circular full of coupons. Nevertheless, when Charles got to his car, he had more than twenty minutes to go just three blocks, so things were fine.

Then they weren't.

Charles tossed the groceries on the passenger seat, then jogged around the hood to the driver's side and saw it immediately. The driver's side front tire, completely flat. He'd been in the grocery store for what, five minutes maybe? Seven? How could it have gone completely flat so fast?

Calming breaths wouldn't work for this. Twenty minutes was more than enough time to go three blocks, but was it enough time to change a tire, *then* drive three blocks? He didn't think so. He ducked inside the car, opened the glove compartment, and took out a fire department parking placard he'd received at the academy. He stuck it in the windshield so he wouldn't get a ticket, grabbed the groceries, locked up, and started walking.

A block from the firehouse, a car horn beeped behind him, and he turned.

"Charlie! What's up, bud?"

A 2006 Camry pulled up level with him, Joe Bahms behind the wheel, arm hanging out the window, smiling and nodding to the music coming from his stereo. Charles smiled back.

"How's it going, sir?"

"You're pretty early," Bahms said, glancing at his watch. "Nice touch." A car behind his tapped their horn and he looked in the rearview. "See you in a bit," he said, and sped up.

Halfway up the street, he turned into the parking lot. When Charles got there a minute later,

Bahms was out of his car, holding a bag of groceries near the side door. Charles went that way.

They shook hands. "You walk to work?" Bahms asked, surprised. He punched in a combination on a lock above the knob, then turned it.

"No, sir. I got a flat in front of Foodtown. I didn't have time to change it. I'll take care of it after work."

"That sucks. Is it secure?"

"The car?"

"Yeah."

"Yes, sir. It's locked."

"Joe. Joey. Bahms. Even Joseph. Not sir. And good, we'll take care of it later."

The lights were dim inside and they walked quietly to the back. A workbench along the back wall was covered with wood shavings and a half full box of wooden door chocks. The radio above it was on and low, tuned in to a classic rock station. Bahms pushed through the kitchen door and held it for Charles.

"Thank you, sir."

"Not sir."

"Bahms. Sorry.'"

"No worries, buddy." Bahms smiled. "I know they drilled that into your head. We'll get it out of there." He went into the dining area and dropped his bag on the long table. There were no chairs around it this time. They were stacked instead, on the far wall.

"Alright, Charlie," Bahms said. "Listen. You and I have similar schedules, so we'll be working a lot together. I'll probably by overseeing a lot of your training." He took out a newspaper from his bag and laid it face up on the table. "Obviously, there are a bunch of guys with more time than me who are gonna train you and drill with you too. But I'll teach you more of, like, you know, what you should be doing as a junior man in the house and as a probie.

Okay?"

"Okay." Charles pulled out the newspapers from his bag and placed them beside the other. Bahms took out a paper bag of bagels from his bag and placed it on the table near the center. Charles grabbed the eggs and bacon and started to place them in the center of the table as well, but Bahms stopped him.

"First lesson," he said. "You're a probie. You get paid crap, we all know that. Don't spend so much on breakfast. Bring one thing to eat and one paper."

"Okay."

"Everyone who comes in for a day tour brings in one thing and a paper. It's not your job to bring in a paper for everyone who may want to read one. If you're the only one coming in for the day, then there'll only be one paper. Not a big deal."

"Okay," Charles said again.

"Good move getting something you gotta cook, though. As a probie, you should be making breakfast, not just bringing bagels or donuts or things like that. You always wanna be busy, so something easy to make but that requires actual cooking is a nice touch. Good job."

Charles smiled, his anxiety fading.

They dropped the food by the stove then went back out to the main floor.

"You don't have friends or family on the job, right?"

"No, sir."

"Okay. I know you spent nearly five months in the academy, but I'm just gonna talk to you as if this is all new to you. Okay?"

"Yes, of course. It *is* new to me."

Bahms pointed a finger at him. "That's the right answer. Everyone here will constantly tell you things and teach you things, and because there are forty or fifty of us, you're definitely gonna hear the same things a bunch of times from a bunch of people. But each time you hear it, just nod and listen and keep your mouth shut. Act as if it's the first time you've ever heard it. Get it?"

"Got it."

Bahms led Charles over to the gear racks where off-duty members hung their uniform pants, coats, and helmets.

"First thing you do when you come in is get ready for the shift. Pull your bunker gear off the racks and place them next to the rig. Make sure they're good to go. Pants and boots are good, gloves are good, hood is good, helmet and jacket are good. If you have any tools in your coat, which you should, make sure they're where they should be. Then place everything near the rig so that the minute someone going home comes downstairs, you're ready to relieve them."

Charles nodded and grabbed his gear from the space they gave him Friday. The boots they wore with their uniform pants came up to the calf and were wide at the opening. To save time, the pants were scrunched down around the ankles of the boots, so when a firefighter stepped into the boots, they stepped into the pants as well. Charles checked everything Bahms had said to check, which didn't take very long because none of those things had been used yet.

Seeing his last name on the back of his coat temporarily

removed his anxiety and he was proud.

"Speaking of rigs," Bahms said. "Don't ever say firetruck. Say rig."

"Rig. Okay."

"That's important." Bahms smiled. "Especially because you were assigned to an Engine company. You're gonna see, if you haven't already, that there's a battle between Engine companies and Ladder companies. It's a joke, but still. Both groups think they're harder workers than the other. Either groups' rig can be called a rig, but Ladder companies are usually referred to as Trucks. So you *never* call an Engine's rig a truck. Get it? It's like…it's like calling a grown woman a girl."

Charles gave a small laugh.

"Seriously, bro." Bahms chuckled. "Engines are Engines. Ladders are Ladders or Trucks.

Engines are never trucks. If you remember only one thing from today, remember that."

"Will do," Charles said.

"That and the coffee."

"The coffee?"

Bahms nodded slowly and smirked. "The coffee."

UPSTAIRS ON THE SECOND floor of the firehouse, Josh Callahan was in bed, staring at the ceiling in the Truck office. The morning light gave it a blue glow. Over the last few hours of the night shift, the ceiling had gone from a black blur to a cloudy shadow to this blue haze. Josh had tossed and turned all night and wished for sleep, but never received it. Now it was too late, he could hear movement downstairs. He checked the time: five minutes to seven. It had to be the probie down there. No one else would be here this early.

Josh pulled the sheet off his legs and sat up in the bed

against the wall across from his desk. It wasn't often that a night shift would be slow enough for anyone to get proper use out of the beds, but Sunday night had been pretty quiet. The whole house had gotten a call for fire at 8989 Douglas Boulevard that had turned out to be a prank call, and the Engine had gone on a couple of calls for emergency medical service alone, but aside from those three runs, no one had left the firehouse after midnight. That type of night was exactly what Josh needed after the day he had Sunday, and he was disappointed that he hadn't been able to take advantage of it.

SUNDAY STARTED LIKE MOST days had recently, with Josh awake before the alarm clock.

At home. In bed alone. His wife Mildred was home, but she hadn't slept in their bed that night. She hadn't slept in their bed any night since their daughter Athena went off to a summer college program in Italy a little over a month ago.

Josh had been awake for hours. He'd managed to fall asleep but was awoken sometime in the night by Mildred coming up the stairs and going to Athena's room. He wasn't sure what time she had gotten home. Wasn't even sure where she'd been. He thought about getting up and going to her to try and talk this thing out, but after an internal debate, he decided against it. The middle of the night wasn't the time. Instead, he turned over to the empty side of the bed and tried to go back to sleep but never did.

Later that morning, Josh made breakfast and considered having the conversation again while they ate, but Mildred never came down. When he'd finished eating, he wrapped her food and left it on the counter near the stove, then went down to the basement. Their daughter was an art history major and an amateur photographer. Josh was building a wall unit with shadow boxes that would display her work. A useful distraction for him.

He worked on it a few hours, then wrapped up around three in the afternoon and went upstairs to shower. Mildred was in the living room with the television on, her feet tucked beneath her, arms folded on top of a couch pillow on her lap. She heard him walk in, turned that way, and pressed her lips together in a smile.

"How's it going down there?" she asked.

Josh shrugged. "It's coming out good. I think she'll like it."

"She's gonna love it," Mildred said. "If she were here, she'd be down there every day, photographing you doing it."

Josh smiled. "Yeah, but it's hard to surprise her nowadays, ya know? I wanna see her face when the pictures are already in the shadow box, know what I'm saying?" Mildred smiled again, then turned back to the television.

Josh: "Did you eat?"

"Breakfast?"

"Yeah. Or anything."

"I did. I ate what you fixed, thank you."

"Yeah, of course, you kiddin'? No problem."

The TV controller lay on the coffee table, out of reach from her but not far. *Family Feud* on the screen. The family guessing had three of the top five answers already revealed and no strikes. Josh looked at Mildred's profile. Her eyes were unfocused. She was looking at the screen, but she wasn't seeing it.

"Mildred," he said carefully. "Listen…"

"Josh." She turned to him again and he saw exhaustion in her face. She was worn out.

"Please?"

He swallowed and nodded. "I'm, uh…I'm gonna go shower. I'm working tonight."

She pursed her lips again. "Be safe."

"Okay."

WHEN JOSH HAD GOTTEN to the firehouse two hours later, he pulled into the lot and sat in the car. The readout on his dashboard showed fourteen minutes after five. He was breaking the one-hour rule. The guys wouldn't break his balls about it, but he hated that he was late. He felt bad that he hadn't yet gone in to relieve whatever Ladder boss was working. Still, he sat in his car.

Josh watched the time on his dashboard tick another minute away. The car hummed as it idled below the soft blow of the air conditioner. The motor caused his seat to vibrate. He rubbed his wedding ring with the pad of his thumb and stared out the window. He sucked on his bottom lip, and he could taste the mouthwash he used earlier. Another minute ticked away.

He unclipped his seatbelt and freed his arm. He needed to move, he couldn't sit there all night. He sat up straight and covered his face with both his hands, then took a deep breath and exhaled. When he moved his hands away, another minute had passed. Shaking his head, he sat back. Outside the lot, a young girl with a white husky were in front of the lot's gate. It took a crap on the ground, and she left it there. He reached up and grabbed a tuft of hair behind his ear and looked at the clock. Another minute gone. He really had to go to work. Still, he sat in the car.

When he finally walked inside, it was a quarter to six and everyone working the night shift was going over the rigs.

"Brothers!" he said to the group as a whole, and those who heard him turned and smiled. One firefighter on his way out to the lot held out his hand and said, "Joshy Jobs. What's up?"

"Brett, how ya makin' out? Good?"

"Yessir."

As Josh set his gear up by 88's rig, more guys spotted him and smiled. He smiled back and meant it, the last hour forgotten.

THE NIGHT TOUR HAD been fun and relatively routine, if not slow. Apparently, the prank caller from 8989 had called the night before as well. False alarms were generally annoying, but more so that night because if not for that call, Ladder 88 would have had no runs after midnight and the men could've enjoyed a rare shutout. Nevertheless, even if that call hadn't come in, Josh probably wouldn't have slept.

Now he sat on the edge of the bed listening to whomever it was moving around downstairs. There were at least two people. One of them was definitely the probie. The other was likely Bahms. He probably came in early to help the kid out. Bahms was good that way. If he weren't married, Josh would've fixed him up with Athena.

Standing and stretched, Josh made his way to the bathroom. There he peed and brushed his teeth, then looked in the mirror and shook his head. An old man looked back at him, shaking his head too. Josh had about two more hours before his shift ended, probably less because the captain always came in early. Those two hours would be fun because work was always fun. But after work, he'd be alone with that jackass staring back at him. That would be less fun. He shook his head again, then looked away from the mirror. He'd cross that bridge when he got to it. Right now, he wanted to enjoy himself. After splashing water on his face and drying it with a paper towel, he headed downstairs to give the probie a hard time.

-7-

COFFEE, BAHMS SAID, WAS an important tool in the
firehouse. Almost as important as a hose line or an axe or a
saw. Charles didn't drink it himself, but the way Bahms talked
about it, he'd probably be the only one."

"For day tours, you should wake up early or come in early
and start two pots of coffee.

Then grind beans for two more." They were back in the
kitchen and Bahms pointed to everything as he spoke. "It may
seem crazy," he said. "But if one of the senior guys or one of
the bosses woke up looking for coffee and didn't find any, and
you were here, there'd be hell to pay."

"That's no problem," Charles answered. "I'll remember."

"Good. Order of priority," Bahms said. "Set up your gear,
start the coffee, go up to the locker room to change. Come
down and start breakfast."

"Got it."

They headed upstairs, quietly and Charles thought the
place looked a lot bigger than he remembered from a couple
of days ago. When he got to his locker and saw his last name
printed on the door, he smiled again.

DOWNSTAIRS, HE FOUND TWO filters of coffee beans
already ground up and slid them into the coffee maker Bahms
had showed him. Then he pinched away two more filters from

a stack and started the grinder. The machine roared to life, churning like an ice maker and Charles flinched. He hadn't expected it to be so loud. He moved closer to it, nervously, hoping to muffle the noise, willing it to finish fast.

To his left, the kitchen door eased open and Josh, the Lieutenant from Friday, was there with his palm flat against it, a tired frown on his face. Charles watched him, feeling a heat spreading beneath his collar but trying to ignore it.

"Good morning, Lieutenant."

Josh didn't respond. He looked between Charles's eyes and continued to frown. He was shorter than Charles and for some reason Charles felt uncomfortable looking down at him.

"I'm sorry," Charles said, waving at the grinder. "I didn't know it was gonna be this loud."

Josh frowned a second longer, then snorted and shook his head. "Damn. You're a nice guy, aren't you?"

Charles exhaled and smiled. "No, I don't know. This thing is so loud in the silence. I thought everyone was gonna wake up and kill me."

Josh swatted the air. "Nah, you're okay, kid. Don't worry about shit like that. No one really sleeps here, anyway." He pushed the door wide and walked into the kitchen. "This your first day? Your first real day?"

"Yes, sir."

"Got your shit all squared away? Your gear and everything by the rig, ready to ride?"

"Yes, sir. Joe—Bahms helped me with that."

"Good, good," Josh said, nodding. "Joe's a good dude. Great firefighter. He's got some time under his belt, and he's always been a heads-up dude, know what I mean? You do what he did—what he *does,* and you'll be alright. Got that?"

"Yes, sir. I will."

Josh checked the time on his watch then looked around.

He stood with his back to the kitchen door and leaned closer to Charles. "Listen, kid. It's the men's job to show you the ropes here, but can I give you a tip?"

"Yes, sir, please," Charles said, leaning forward, too.

"Stay on top of the toilet paper."   Charles frowned. "I'm sorry?"

"In the bathrooms," Josh said. "There's one out there on the apparatus floor," he said, pointing behind him. "There's a few more upstairs. Toilet paper is an important thing in the firehouse, okay? I'm serious, kid. Probably more than it is in, you know, nine to five jobs or whatever. You know what time the lunch break is in the firehouse?"

Charles thought about that. "There aren't lunch breaks."

"Exactly right," Josh said, pointing a finger at him. "We don't have any scheduled breaks. We're ten-eight twenty-four seven, know what I'm sayin'?"

"Yes, sir."

"You know your codes, right? What's ten-eight?"

"Yes, sir. Ten-eight means unit is in service and ready for duty."

"Exactly right."

Charles grinned and neither man spoke for a moment.

Josh: "What was I saying? Oh, toilet paper. No, no, breaks. We don't have regular breaks. We're outta the house in sixty seconds from the moment those tones go off because that's what the public expects. Know what I mean? They're callin' for help and we're not dickin' around, we're going to help. So we eat when we can and shit when we can and rest if we get the chance. You're the probie; it's your job to always make sure there's toilet paper in every stall, get me? We don't got time to be hopping around from stall to stall, tryna wipe our asses. Know what I mean?"

"Yes, sir."

"A heads-up move," he said lifting his eyebrows and lowering his voice, as if to impart a confidence. "What I used to do when I was a firefighter in Brooklyn, I would set pre-wipes up on all the rolls, you know? Like just take a handful of tissue and fold it neatly and put it on top of the rolls. This way, if a guy is shitting and the tones go off, he doesn't have to pull it off himself. It's already there ready to go."

Charles nodded slowly. "Got it," he said. "That's a good idea."

"Just a suggestion," Josh said in a normal tone. He stood up straight and stretched.

"You're working with the captains today. Both Engine and Truck. You might've met Captain Emmett for a second on Friday."

"Yes, sir."

"Good. So, remember what I said. I know he's a fan of the pre-wipe."

ORDER OF PRIORITY, CHARLES thought as he stepped out of the kitchen. Lt. Calahan poured himself a cup of fresh coffee and Charles went to make a quick check of the bathroom on the main floor. There was a nearly new roll of toilet paper there and he spooled a few sheets and folded it four times, then laid it on top of the roll. After that, he went back to the kitchen to start breakfast.

In the academy, a couple of the instructors would sometimes go around and ask probies, what abilities they had. Were they good with tools? Did they play any sports? Could they cook?

Charles had been slightly embarrassed to answer no across the board. The instructor who'd asked, shook his head at that and said, "when you get to your firehouse, fake it 'til you make it." Charles thought about that, as he grabbed two pans, and was very grateful when Bahms walked in and offered to do the eggs while Charles did the bacon. They cooked side-by-side and Bahms told Charles what a morning tour would look like. As they spoke, guys from both the Engine and the Ladder trickled into the kitchen sporadically, looking well rested and happy about it. Everyone knew Charles's name, even some he hadn't met before, and everyone asked if this was his first tour. They all grabbed coffee and sat at the table and shared the papers and talked about how welcome a slow night was.

The eggs were finished before the bacon, but Bahms didn't put them on the table until Charles was done. Charles took the last of the cooked pieces and stacked them neatly on top of the rest, then put them in the center of the table near a bag of fruit. Kenny O'Reilly, a firefighter assigned to the Engine, had brought in the fruit, and thanked Charles when Charles went to slice the pineapple. That was an ability he *did* have.

The table was nearly filled with guys and three pots of coffee were gone. Bahms told Charles that probies didn't usually sit for breakfast because there might not be enough seats for everyone during the change of tours where more guys than will be working the next shift are in the firehouse. So they stood together by the stove and ate a quick breakfast.

When they were done, Charles went to the sink to clean the pans, and Kenny joined him.

Kenny said, "Listen, Charles. You're gonna learn a lot today. People are gonna be throwing information at you from all directions. If you only remember one thing today, remember what I'm about to tell you."

Charles turned the water off and looked at him. "Okay," he said, and wondered how many more "one thing's," he'd be told to remember today.

"It's about the bacon." Charles waited.

"Bacon is a serious thing in the firehouse," Kenny said confidentially. "Guys love bacon. They'd put it on every meal if they could. But Devin—have you met Devin?"

Charles cocked his head. "I don't think so."

"You will. He's here all the time. He used to be in the Engine, but he's a marshal now. Anyway, he became a health nut after his son got sick. The two of them eat only healthy crap now and he's always on everyone here about eating better. So we don't eat as much bacon as we used to. But everyone still loves it," Kenny said. He leaned closer. "Never stack the bacon like you did today. The grease pools at the bottom of the plate. Then the bacon is swimming in it and that makes it unhealthy. Guys'll feel guilty about that. When you're making bacon, put each slice side by side on the plate. You'll probably need three plates for all of it, but so what? We have a dishwasher. Or you could wash them after breakfast yourself when we're doing committee work."

Charles looked past him to the table.

"Alright, bud?"

"Yes, sir. I mean, Kenny."

"Cool. Don't forget. Very important." Charles nodded, uncertain.

BAHMS CAME OVER AND stood between them. He put his left hand on Charles' left shoulder and his right hand on Kenny's right.

He said, "I'm gonna go over the rig with Charlie if you don't need him for anything."

"Yeah, do your thing. I'll come with." Kenny said.

They were headed to the kitchen door when the tones went off. One high, one low, and the loud automated voice said: "Engine!"

Charles became aware of his heartbeat again and tried

70

taking a deep breath without really showing it. Bahms pushed through the door and ran towards the housewatch. Kenny and Charles followed him out to the garage area, with Kenny looking at Charles and smiling.

"Go time!" He said.

-8-

AT THE ENGINE, KENNY stepped out of his sneakers and into his bunker pants and Charles did the same. A moment later, two bells sounded, then Bahms's voice, loud through the speakers, said, "Engine goes, EMS. 2 West 143rd Street, apartment 16 George. Female caller states daughter giving birth, baby not breathing. Engine only, EMS." Then two bells again.

A pregnancy? Charles tried to remember what he'd learned about delivering babies, as he pulled his suspenders over his shoulders. Weekly medical service classes were part of the academy, but delivering a baby was talked about like winning the lotto. Or something less desirable. Firefighters had done it before, obviously, but none of the instructors thought it likely that these probies would have to worry about it anytime soon. Let alone possibly doing CPR on a newborn.

"That building's on the corner," Kenny was saying, pulling a handie-talkie strap over his neck and hurrying toward the back of the Engine. "Grab that radio!"

Charles went to where Kenny pointed and took a handie-talkie labeled "nozzle" hanging from a hook near the rig and threw it over his head and across his body. Bahms had come out of the housewatch and was pulling on his bunker pants while both Captain Emmett and Pete Dufresne jogged to the front of the rig.

Charles followed Kenny to the back of the Engine, where he was going through an opened compartment with a roll-up door labeled "EMS."

"We'll walk over," Kenny said, and handed Charles a small red duffle bag. Bahms appeared beside them and took a second bag as Kenny grabbed a third, then shut the compartment door. Captain Emmett was up front by the passenger door, stuffing his pants and boots in the footwell and saying something to Pete, who had climbed behind the wheel and started the rig.

Charles, Kenny, and Bahms followed the captain to the front of the firehouse. He carried a flashlight and pry-tool made for officers in one hand and turned on the handie-talkie draped across his body with the other. Bells jingled as the garage door on the Engine side rolled up. Behind them, Charles heard the air brakes on the rig release and the gears change. The four men ducked under the rising door, turned right, and sped down the street. Charles turned back and saw Pete pull the Engine half out of the firehouse, then stopped and reengage the brakes. The street was one way in the wrong direction, Charles realized, and understood why they were walking.

"You're holding the trauma bag," Bahms said to him. "It has all the first aid stuff. Four-by-fours, bandages, an OB kit, ice packs—all that stuff."

"Okay," Charles said. He was breathing heavy. He was still trying to remember what he'd learned about CPR and delivering babies and was wondering how he ever passed the exams. The other three looked intent but not worried. They were all moving too fast to call it walking, but not fast enough to call it a run. Power walking, maybe. Whatever it was, Charles was out of breath, and it wasn't from the effort. He took a deep breath to calm himself. He *did* pass the tests, he reminded himself. He'd scored well on the computer exams and practical's, and was officially a certified first responder, able to respond to medical emergencies and provide first aid care. And he wasn't alone. It'd be fine.

They arrived at 2 West 143rd less than a minute after they'd left and a police car with its lights on, but no sirens pulled over at the curb. The four men started up the stoop into the building, chocking the door open as they did, and two cops filed in behind them.

"16G?" one of the cops asked. He was tall, dark, and wide. His short sleeves struggled unsuccessfully to cover his biceps and his face was covered by a five o'clock shadow that looked painted on. He nodded when Charles looked back, and although his mannerism seemed friendly, Charles guessed most people were intimidated by him.

Captain Emmett looked over his shoulder at the officers and smiled. "How ya doin,

Grant?"

"What's up, Capt?" the cop said, and slapped the captain's back.

"Yeah, we're goin' to 16 George. What did you get it as?"

All six men were in the lobby of the building. Grant reached over and shook Kenny's hand, then Bahms's. "We got it as an aided female teen in labor," he said. He held out his hand to Charles. "Kenton Grant. How's it going?"

"Probationary Firefighter Charles Davids, sir," Charles responded, taking Grant's hand. Grant glanced at Kenny, amused.

Captain Emmett chuckled. "He's new, Grant. We'll get it out of him."

There were six elevators in the lobby. Half served floors one through twelve and half fourteen to twenty-one. The three they needed were all in use and going up. Bahms removed a key from a clip on his pants and put it in a slot labeled "fireman service" above the call button. He turned the key and all three elevators headed back down. The one in the middle was on floor seventeen when Bahms turned the key and it got to the lobby first. When the doors slid open, an elderly woman holding fistfuls of grocery bags stared at the digital display, confused. She caught sight of the group and brightened.

"Good morning, gentlemen. Is there a fire?"

"No, ma'am," Bahms said, stepping halfway into the elevator. "But there is an emergency. We do need to take this elevator from you, if that's okay."

"Oh, yes, by all means." The woman watched the ground as she chose her steps and exited. The group thanked her, and Captain Emmett told her that the other two elevators would be available for her any second. Bahms returned the elevators to regular service and Kenny leaned forward to hit a button. but stopped before choosing one. He looked at Charles and asked,

"Where are we going?"

"16G." Charles said, still trying to remember his training.

Kenny smiled and pushed the button for sixteen. The doors closed on the old woman standing in the lobby, the bags at her feet, waving.

CAPTAIN EMMETT USED THE butt of his flashlight to knock. "Fire Department!"

No answer.

He knocked again, harder. "Hello? Fire Department!" Nothing.

Charles heard a television somewhere behind the door in the apartment on the left. But that was it. Nothing from G. No baby crying, no woman crying, no heavy breathing. Nothing. Captain Emmett tried the knob and the door opened. He laid the flashlight flat against the door and pushed it along its arc.

The smell of blood and a taste like copper hit Charles, and

he unconsciously held his breath. The door opened to a short hallway that led to a spacious living room. As they stepped inside, Charles realized that the living room wasn't so much spacious as it was empty. If there was any kind of standard furniture inside, it would've seemed pretty small. Halfway down the hall, a doorway led to the kitchen. Across the kitchen, a second doorway led to the living room. The group looked inside the kitchen and found a young woman standing, back to the stove, facing them. She was wearing a men's large white t-shirt that fit her like a dress and nothing else. Her legs were splattered with dry or drying blood and her long black hair lay matted against her face and neck and shoulders.

Kenny squeezed in. "Hey. What's going on?" He sounded genuinely concerned, and he was.

She didn't respond. She lifted her left arm slowly and pointed through the other doorway toward the back of the living room, where Charles assumed the bedrooms were.

Kenny placed a gentle, gloved hand on her shoulder. "We're gonna go check on everyone else, sweetheart. We'll be right back for you, okay?"

KENNY O'REILLY, CHARLES HAD learned when they'd met on Friday, had been in nursing school when he took and passed the exam to become a firefighter. He continued in nursing afterward, taking night-school classes during the months of the fire academy. The fire department trained firefighters in basic emergency medical service, but Kenny was trained as a registered nurse, and every couple of years he would study and recertify. So, although as the probie Charles was expected to take point on EMS runs for training purposes, it was Kenny who led the way toward the bedrooms.

A fan in the living room intensified the odor when they crossed it. On the other side, a short hallway led into the corner of the apartment, where three doors branched off. The first door was the bathroom. Charles instinctively held his breath when they passed it but breathed again too soon and nearly gagged. The next door was closed and probably led to a bedroom, and from the third door the group could hear heavy breathing.

Pete's voice came over everyone's radios, startling Charles. "9-9 chauffeur to 9-9. EMS is on the scene and making their way into the building."

Kenny and Bahms covered the speaker on their radios with their palms and Charles mimicked them. Captain Emmett dropped his head to his and keyed the mic, "Ten-four, Pete." The group entered the third door. A pair of twin-sized mattresses lay on the floor, bare. A dresser stood beside them with a bunch of clothing spilling out. The window was closed, and another fan circulated hot, humid air. In the middle of the room, a woman with short brown hair, wearing a tank top and pajama pants, stood holding what looked like a bloody deflated football. An umbilical cord hung from it like a tail. The woman breathed heavy through her mouth. Her eyes were wide and her face, covered in sweat and tears, was an older, thinner version of the girl in the kitchen.

The group of men stopped a few steps into the room and stared at her, and she held her breath. A moment passed in silence, then she exhaled and said, "My daughter shit him in the toilet."

THINGS MOVED QUICKLY. KENNY crossed the room in two strides and took the baby from her. She handed it over without protest but didn't move. He turned from her toward the door, knelt, and laid the baby on its back. Charles dropped to his knees on the other side of the baby, and a second later Bahms was beside him. The two police officers pulled on gloves and started moving the mattresses out of the way.

Kenny placed two fingers on the inside of the baby's arm and closed his eyes.

"No pulse!" he said, and turned to the bag he carried in. Captain Emmett turned away, dropped his head to his mic again, and called Pete.

"9-9 to 9-9 chauffeur."

"Chauffeur."

"Pete, let Manhattan know we're ten-ninety-nine. CPR in progress."

"Ten-four."

While that was happening, Bahms took out an oxygen tank from his bag and connected a bag-valve-mask to it. Grant, the big cop, opened the baby's mouth and cleared it of fluids. Kenny set up a defibrillator and plugged in the pads that would detect the heartbeat, if there was a heartbeat, and Charles started chest compressions. With two fingers he pushed down deep at the center of the baby's chest and counted out loud. When he got to fifteen, Bahms had the BVM over the baby's mouth. Air from the oxygen tank inflated the bag attached to the mask. When Charles said fifteen, Bahms squeezed the bag and the baby's chest rose in response. Then Charles started counting his compressions again, starting from one.

Two EMTs came in after that, followed by the girl from the kitchen. The EMTs asked for an update and Captain Emmett told them quickly. They took out a couple of machines and a bunch of wires and took half a minute to hook them up, then attach them to the baby. Two minutes had passed, and the defibrillator told everyone to stand clear of the body. Those near the baby leaned away and held up their hands. The room went quiet. A robotic voice from the defibrillator broke the silence and said, "No shock advised. Resume CPR."

The other cop knelt beside Charles and took over giving

compressions. Charles tried to take over the bag mask from Bahms, but Bahms shook his head.

A commotion outside the room made everyone look that way. An EMS lieutenant walked in, followed by two paramedics. The lieutenant was a young woman, and Charles wondered briefly how she was already a boss. She greeted the captain, and he patted her shoulder and told them what had happened over the last three minutes. One of the paramedics spoke to one of the EMTs, a black woman with purple-tipped dreadlocks, and the other paramedic asked the baby's mother how long the baby had been unconscious.

The mother didn't answer, and before the paramedic could repeat the question, the defibrillator spoke again. Everyone stood clear, and those on the floor held up their hands.

Again, there was no shock advised, and Charles started to get back to his knees to take over CPR, but the EMT with the dreadlocks, whose shirt said her name was Towns, held a hand up to him to hold off. She asked for a pulse check and Bahms placed his fingers on the inside of the child's arm, then looked up, astonished. He shuffled closer and checked the other arm. Turning to Kenny, he said, "Check that. I think I feel a pulse."

Kenny did, and he too looked up, surprised. He said, "Nobody touch him," then took a pen light from one of the bags and put it on the baby's belly.

Charles glanced around. No one moved. No one breathed. No one took their eyes off the pen.

And it rose.

It was a small movement that Charles might've missed if he weren't looking for it, but the boy's stomach rose on its own and the pen rose with it. The cop, the other one, clapped his gloved hands together, said "Whoo!"

Charles's shoulders slumped with relief. He placed his hands on his thighs and tried to steady himself, but Towns said, "We're moving!" And time sped up again.

Everyone got to their feet, grabbing things. Bahms and Charles shed their gloves, then grabbed their red bags. Kenny bent over and picked the baby up, keeping the body flat. Grant picked up the oxygen tank, still attached to the BVM, which was still on the baby's face, and stood behind Kenny. The EMTs grabbed the bags they brought in, and the other officer gathered the two women from the apartment and told them to put some clothes on. The women were holding each other and crying, and what they were wearing was probably the furthest thing from their minds. But they grabbed a change of clothes anyway.

Captain Emmett led the way back to the elevator.

"9-9 to Chauffer."

"Go 'head, Capt."

"Pete, we're coming out. If you wanna go up to the corner and block the traffic on

Eighth Avenue; they're going to be headed to Harlem Hospital."

"Ten-four."

They took all three elevators this time, and when they got downstairs, Charles took the oxygen from grant and the officers ran to their car. The EMTs and Kenny got the baby situated on a stretcher in the back of their ambulance, then Kenny and Towns climbed out. Towns ran to the front and started the ignition and the police squad car pulled out in front of them. Pete had the Engine at the other end of 143rd, holding back a stream of slightly curious but mostly impatient drivers, coming south on Eighth avenue. The squad car's siren blared, and the ambulance wailed behind it, and they sped down the block, then merged one-by-one onto Eighth and sped off toward Harlem Hospital.

Pete reversed 99's rig onto 143rd and drove backward

to the firehouse. Charles and the rest walked in the street and made sure no cars coming the right way, blocked him. Charles's hands shook as he walked, and he gripped the strap of his bag to hide it.

When they reached the firehouse, Kenny and Bahms stayed in the street to stop vehicle traffic while the captain and Charles stood on either side of the garage door to stop any passersby. Pete nosed in toward a tree in front of the park opposite the firehouse, then reversed smoothly back inside. The rig hissed as he shifted to neutral and shut it down with the front facing the doors, ready to respond.

Outside, Kenny and Bahms stepped out of the street and met up with the captain and Charles.

Charles felt as if he was shaking but didn't think it was visible. No one said anything for a moment. Then the captain looked at Charles.

"So," he said. "Welcome to the fire service."

They all laughed, full of nerves. Pete joined them at the door and nodded to Charles. He was a middle-aged man with grey hairs scattered across his face even though he'd shaved. He always seemed amused with the world, like nothing ever really surprised or upset him.

"Everyone good?" he asked.

Kenny put a hand on Charles's shoulder and asked if he was alright. Charles said he was, but thought it sounded like a lie. Adrenaline coursed through his body, but he had nothing to use it for. His heart was racing, and if he looked as if he were breathing normally, it was only because he was doing his best to. He didn't understand the feeling and he hated it. The sight and smell of that baby were sad, and he was worried about his survival, but he could handle it. He wasn't freaking out. His heart had been racing from the anticipation of all this, but it was over now. There was no reason he should still feel this way.

"Do you guys need to take time?" Pete asked. "You need to washup?"

"Yeah, and we gotta restock," Bahms said. "But after we do committee work, can we run over to 145th and eighth? Charlie's got a flat that we gotta go take care of."

Charles looked up, surprised. "No, no it's okay, sir. Joe," he said. "Thank you, but I can take care of it when I get off."

Captain Emmett: "No. We'll do it now. Go restock the bags and wash up and we'll take the rig over and take care of it."

THAT'S WHAT THEY DID. Inside, the guys from 88 Truck were going over the equipment on their rig. Paul Oldman, a short, bald, muscular firefighter from 88, came over and asked if it was a legit baby delivery. He'd heard the report that Bahms had given out from the housewatch before they left.

"Yeah. Ten-ninety-nine for CPR on the child," Kenny said, pulling a new BVM from a supply closet near the front of garage. "The mother was just a kid. Probably didn't know she was in labor. Baby had no pulse when we got there."

"Geez. And now?"

"Yeah, we got one. It was faint, but the baby was breathing on its own. It's gotta be premature, though, it looked horrible. Don't know if it'll make it."

Paul nodded and turned to Charles. "Not what you expected, huh?"

"No, sir," Charles agreed. "But we handled it well, I think."

Paul smiled, kindly. "What's a ten-ninety-nine?"

Charles thought about it. "Uh, ten-ninety-nine is: unit involved in CPR." That wasn't right and he knew it.

"Close. Wanna try again?"

Charles thought some more. Pete and Bahms came closer.

Paul: "I'm not tryna put you on the spot, kid. It's okay if you don't know."

Charles waited. He was irritated with himself. He knew the codes down pat. During the academy, he'd made a cheat sheet with index cards to study from, and he knew them all cold.

But as he tried to picture it, all he saw was the baby in that woman's arms, small and deflated. He'd never seen a dead body before. And maybe he still hadn't. Maybe that one wouldn't count because of what they'd done to help. If so, he should've felt good. But he didn't.

He couldn't let it throw him, though. He said, "I'm sorry, I don't remember."

Bahms and Paul started to respond at the same time, then stopped. Paul was senior to

Bahms, but Bahms was in the Engine so Paul smiled and said, "Go ahead, Joe. My bad." Bahms said, "Paul is right, you were close. Ten-ninety-nine means that the unit is going to be operating for at least thirty minutes."

Charles nodded, annoyed with himself. He knew that.

"But you were close because that code is usually only given when the unit is doing CPR. Any other reason a unit would be operating that long should have its own code. Get it? Like if we were at a job—a job is what we call, like, a legit fire—if we're at a job, we're obviously gonna be there at least half an hour, but the code we would tell the dispatcher would be the code confirming a fire or emergency. Which would be...?"

"Ten-seventy-five," Charles answered confidently.

"Correct," Bahms and Paul said together. The other members of 88 Truck and both captains had wandered over and were listening. Charles was aware of their presence and tried to focus on getting the image of that cheat sheet clearer in his mind.

"What code do we give when we arrive on scene?" some-one asked.

"Ten-eighty-four."

Billy Pearson, from Ladder 88 said, "Women?"

Charles: "Sorry?"

"What's the code we give if we go into an apartment just packed with smokin' hot women?"

Charles laughed. "I don't know that one, sir."

Billy grinned. "Ten-sixty-nine, brother."

Emmett, chuckling, stepped up and led Charles out of the group with a hand on his shoulder, toward the rig. "Don't lis-ten to those degenerates. Go wash up, grab your car keys and we'll go over now."

Captain Gorm, the captain of Ladder 88, walked over. "You guys about to go do a drill?"

"Nah, Charles just has a flat up on 145th. We're gonna go change it out."

"Wanna *make* it a drill?" Gorm asked.

"Fagan and I were talking about going over airbags today anyway."

Emmett looked at Charles and raised an eyebrow.

"Yes, sir," Charles answered, shrugging slightly.

The captains nodded and Gorm went away. A moment later, Charles heard two slow bells, a pause, then three more. Paul Fagan, the senior man in Ladder 88, said over the loud-speaker, "Engine and Truck are going out. Multi-unit-drill."

Everyone was already on the apparatus floor. The Engine guys washed up quickly, then everyone grabbed their gear and started the rigs.

The battalion chief came out of the kitchen chewing a slice of bacon. Charles saluted him and the chief smiled and ignored it. He wiped his hand on his pant leg and held it out.

"Chris Leland."

"Probationary Firefighter Charles Davids, sir."

"Charles, good to meet you," the chief said. He walked away and asked Gorm what was going on. Gorm told him and the chief went into the housewatch. Four slow bells, then the chief's voice through the speakers. "Brian, shake it out, we're gonna go, too."

Charles was uncomfortable. He caught Bahms's arm as Bahms passed and said, "We can do a drill someplace else. I don't want everyone to stop what they're doing to change my tire. I

can—"

Bahms smiled, cut him off. "You're good, bro. This is what we do. We take care of each other, and we make everything an opportunity to train. Did you guys drill on airbags in the academy?"

"No."

"Exactly. As an Engine man, you won't get to use them often because it's a Truck—you know, a Ladder company tool. The only way you'll be proficient at it is if you drill with the Truck. This is what the firehouse is. No one is gonna blame you for having a flat. We were all gonna drill on something anyway, this is just two birds with one stone."

Charles didn't feel any better, but he didn't object again.

"Put all your gear on," Bahms said. "Every time we drill for as long as you're a probie, put on all the gear you would if you were really going on a call. It sucks in the summer, but it'll help you get faster at it and more comfortable. Practice like you play."

"Okay."

Kenny came over. "Did you tell him?" he asked Bahms.

"Just about to."

The two smiled at him, and Charles watched them, wondering what this could be.

Bahms said, "There are five positions in most Engine companies. You learned this in the academy, right?"

"Yes, sir."

Bahms nodded. "Go 'head. Rattle 'em off."

Charles pointed as he spoke. "Up front is the chauffeur and the officer." He pointed to the back seats, "Then in the back is the nozzle, backup, and control."

"Good," Kenny said. "Obviously, everyone in every Engine wants the nozzle position. That's the glory position. It's at the head of the hose line, so it's the person credited with putting the fire out. Because of that, most houses don't give that position to the probie for a few months. They have to earn it first." Charles nodded. It made sense.

Kenny and Bahms smiled. "We're not most houses," Kenny continued. "You're gonna have the nozzle today. And every day until you get a good nozzle job. A legit fire, not some car fire or brush fire or nonsense like that." Charles forced a smile.

"Nice, right?" Bahms asked, grinning.

"We're gonna go over the whole rig today," Kenny said. "We'll do a couple of drills with a dry hose line, and we'll go to a couple of buildings in the area and talk about stretching a line. And whatever else the captain or Pete wanna go over. I'm gonna back you up and Joe will take the control position. Sound good?"

"Yes, sir. Thank you."

The two smiled at him then got on the rig. Charles dressed, then climbed on after them.

He slipped his thumbs through the loops on the end of his sleeves and placed his hands, palms down on his knees.

Pete was the last to get on. He turned in his seat and looked back. "Kenny, what's the riding list back there?"

"Charlie's got the nozzle and Joey's got control."

"Okay. Good to go?"

"Good."

Pete faced forward and in a pretty good Ace Ventura impression he said, "We're going downtown."

The Engine left first, then the Truck and the chief last. The doors closed behind them and the chauffeurs each turned off their flashers once they were on the street. Charles looked out the window and a child holding the hand of his mother waved at the rigs. His mother waved too, and Charles waved back. He sat back and exhaled as quietly as he could.

He concentrated on ignoring the pace of his heartbeat, which in any case was returning to normal. He thought of what Captain Emmett had said earlier. *Welcome to the fire service.* And despite how he felt, he smiled.

-9-

AT 8989 DOUGLAS BOULEVARD, in the apartment
next door to the Johnson's, Sheryl
Tabacco was on her knees in her bathroom. She tried her
best to ignore the heat, but her gown clung to her as she bent
over her tub, and she kept having to peel it away so she could
move her arms freely.

It wasn't yet ten o'clock on Monday, but Sheryl had been
up for almost five hours. She gave up on sleep about halfway
through that time, got up, and started cleaning.

She started with the bathroom. A force of habit from when
Kevin was alive. Kevin worked nights for the Department of
Sanitation and his workdays ended in the early morning.

He'd come home, strip off his clothes, shower, then lay on
the couch so he wouldn't wake her. When she did wake up,
she'd wake him with a kiss or a nudge or a poke, drag him
to bed, and let him go back to sleep. Then she'd clean the
bathroom. She'd disinfect all the surfaces that he was likely to
have touched: doorknob, toilet, the faucet handles, the shower
handle, the towel rack.

That done, she'd thoroughly clean the shower walls and
the tub. She did this nearly every day for thirty-three years.
It was tedious and at times unnecessary since Kevin didn't
work every day. But Sheryl didn't work at all and didn't have

many friends or any pets or hobbies, so thorough cleaning was a task she had more than enough time for. She'd spend her mornings cleaning, her afternoons with Kevin, and her evenings with a book. Kevin once asked her why she spent so much time cleaning when the house was always spotless, and she'd answered, "So that the house is always spotless."

These days she did it for normalcy. There was a lot less movement in the house since Kevin passed almost ten months ago, and so a lot less need to clean so much and so often. Nevertheless, it was something to do. The hours were so long now, and the apartment so much bigger. The silence that surrounded her was heavy, and if she didn't keep herself busy, it might all be too much. Not to mention even when she tried to rest, there was always something screwing it up. Arguments and fights from next door; the fire department running all over the building like cockroaches. In the last few days, they had been in the building a thousand times and only once was there anything resembling a fire. They had banged on the Johnson's door in the middle of the night the last two nights, just to be gone three minutes later. No thought spared for the other people in the building, trying to sleep.

She thought about that, the fire department's late-night visit last night, and tried not to be angry. She scrubbed the spotless wall of the tub as sweat dripped from her chin, and she mumbled about how ridiculous things were.

AT THE SAME TIME, half an hour away in the borough of Queens, Lt. Matt Quincy was lying in bed beside his wife, Meghan. Neither of them had slept well the night before either, but they weren't angry. Sunday night, after seeing the Broadway show *Hamilton*, the two had wandered around Times Square, looking for a place to eat but not agreeing on anywhere. After a few minutes of that, they decided to return home, where Matt would cook something from the freezer.

Matt enjoyed cooking. He was excited to whip something up, but he never got the chance. After he put a pair of chicken breasts in the microwave to defrost, diced some onions and garlic and dropped them in a skillet, Meghan jumped off the stool at their kitchen island and ran to the bathroom. She'd been complaining of nausea all weekend and her unsettled stomach was a big reason they couldn't agree on a restaurant in the city. Matt wiped his hands on a towel hanging off the oven handle and followed her. He found her on the edge of the tub, leaning toward the open toilet, looking ill. Her face was damp and clammy, and she gasped for breath as she pressed her forearms into her belly.

"What is it?" Matt asked, concerned. "You think you got a bug?"

Meghan wiped her mouth with the back of her hand, spit into the toilet, sat up straight, and looked at her husband. "I think I got a baby."

"What!"

MATT POURED MEG A glass of water with lemon and told her to relax on the couch while he ran to the pharmacy.

"Don't worry about the chicken," he said. "I'll take care of it when I get back."

"Literally the last thing I'm worried about," Meghan answered. She crawled onto the sofa and hugged a throw pillow.

"Okay, I'll be right back. Wait, what do I get? Which, uh, what brand?"

"I don't know, babe. Whichever is the most expensive."

"Got it. You good?"

"Go!"

"Got it."

He went. Matt was a runner, so he ran there. The pharmacy was four blocks away and he got there in under a minute. Inside, he stopped at the entrance and looked up at the aisle signage hanging from the ceiling. He didn't see anything that said pregnancy tests or birth control or anything like that, and he didn't want to run up and down the aisles. Looking around, he spotted a young woman at the cash register unpacking Orbit chewing gum while watching him. He rushed over to her and she smiled and said, "Aisle three or aisle four."

He turned around and looked at the signage again. Aisle three said family planning and aisle four said feminine hygiene. He turned back to her and returned the smile. "You're awesome," he said. She laughed and he ran to aisle three. Scanning the shelves, he found three options. He grabbed the most expensive and ran back to the woman at the counter. She set aside the gum and took the package from him.

"Do you know," he asked, "is this a good one? Is it reliable?"

"I think so." She shrugged. "It's the most expensive." He laughed, a nervous chuckle, and she asked, "Are you guys hoping for a positive or negative?"

"Positive, definitely!"

She smiled. "I hope it is. This one is pretty easy. She just pees and then if she's pregnant, it actually says 'pregnant.' Like, on the screen."

"Sweet. Thank you."

She told him the price and he dipped his card. She bagged the test and waited for the receipt to print, then stuck that in the bag too. "Good luck."

"Thank you, you too!" he said, and ran out.

She laughed at that, then went back to the gum.

THE CASHIER WAS RIGHT, the test was easy. Meghan looked less nauseous when he returned, but a lot more nervous. She searched his eyes as he tore the plastic off the package, and when he had it open, she grabbed both his hands.

"What if I am?"

"That would be awesome!" he said, shocked by the question.

She smiled, leaned in and kissed him.

"Mmm," Matt moaned, "vomit breath."

Meg laughed and grabbed the test from him. She stood to go to the bathroom and he stood, too.

"Nope. You stay," she said, pointing at the couch.

"Are you serious?"

"I won't look without you. But I aim my urine alone."

So, Matt sat and waited. But not long. A minute after she'd closed the bathroom door, she was back in the living room and he was back on his feet. The test was in a paper towel. She smiled at him, shaking slightly. He wrapped his arms around her and kissed her forehead, then took her free hand.

Meg said, "Babe?"

"Yeah?"

"I didn't wash my hands."

He laughed and felt himself tense. He kissed her and felt her tense too. "You ready?" he asked.

"Let's do it."

They didn't sit down. She held up her palm and opened her fingers, and they lowered their eyes to the screen, both holding their breath.

"Yeah!" Matt yelled and punched the air. With his other hand, he squeezed hers too hard and she pulled it away, but she didn't really notice the pain. Her legs felt weird, like her body suddenly became too light and her legs didn't know what to do with the freedom. She'd only felt this way a few times before. Six years ago, when Matt proposed; two years ago, when her chart showed her as cancer free; last year, when her sister came home from deployment. It was an amazing feeling and a weird one. She'd never dabbled in drugs, but she imagined this feeling was the one people were chasing. And she loved it.

Matt turned to Meg and kissed her. She closed her eyes and wrapped her arms around his waist. He put his arms around her shoulders, and they stood there in the hallway between the kitchen and the living room. The microwave beeped four times to let them know the defrosting cycle was over. A dinner for two and a family of three.

THEY DIDN'T EAT. THEY held each other for another minute in the hallway then sat down on the couch and held each other some more. Matt held back tears, because he didn't want to cry alone. Meghan never cried, so he didn't let himself now. Instead, they talked about the future. They talked about what would definitely change and what might not need to. Definitely a new home, or at least an addition to this one. Guards on the windows, definitely. A dog. A vacation within the next six months, but probably not the first two. A bilingual babysitter. All those things were definite. Then Meghan brought up his job, and that wasn't so clear.

"You don't need to quit the department, but you said yourself there's a dozen different jobs that you could do outside the firehouse," she'd said. "Didn't they ask you to teach in the academy for a couple terms? You can do that, right? You won't get hurt teaching. The baby and I won't want you around forever, but at least a while. Who's gonna cook for us if you're gone?"

"That baby will be a gourmet chef before he can construct a proper sentence," Matt said.

"Or she."

"Or she! But, you know, a boy first would…."

Meghan put her fingers in her ear.

"Okay, okay."

She grinned and pulled her feet from beneath her and placed them on the floor. He pulled his up and laid his head on her lap, and she ran her fingers through his hair. "It sucks that I have to work tomorrow," she said. "I'm not gonna get any sleep."

"Me either."

But they did sleep. For a bit. The excitement and the talk made them hungry, and Matt finished the chicken. They fell asleep on the couch, after eating, for about an hour. When they eventually went to bed, they got comfortable and kissed good night, but neither of them went back to sleep. Meg stared at the ceiling and thought about being a mom. Matt stared at the wall and thought about all she had overcome. And they smiled in the dark.

When the sun rose Monday, they were both awake, staring at the ceiling. Meghan reached over and grabbed her cellphone from a side table near the bed to check the time. She sighed and whined and turned toward him, and he lifted his arm to make space for her.

"Can't I just quit and be a stay-at-home mom?"

"It's 2023, Meg," Matt said, seriously. "Women run the world. *I'm* gonna be the stay-at-home mom."

"Whatever. You go in tonight, right?"

This time it was Matt who sighed. "Yeah, I'm in for a twenty-four tonight, tomorrow day."

Meghan ran her hands across his stomach and hugged him. "Is Josh gonna be there?"

"Yeah, I think so. I think he's working consecutive nights Sunday night, Monday night.

Unless he got a twenty-four, then he's there for the day tour today. Either way, I should see him.

Either before he leaves or when we both come in."

"Okay. Make sure he's okay. Tell him I asked for him."

"I will."

"Good," she said. Meg looked up and kissed Matt quickly, then slapped his stomach and pushed herself up. "I gotta go bread-win. You know, it being 2022 and all."

"I hear ya."

She sat back on her calves, messed up her hair and looked down at him seductively.

"Unless you wanna try to give the baby a little brother or sister real quick."

Matt sighed and rolled his eyes. "Just like a man."

-10-

MONDAY MORNING WAS VERY different for Alan.
He woke up inside the Ritechek,
   surprised he'd actually slept. He had closed his eyes a few
minutes after three o'clock and didn't open them again until
the manager at Ritechek banged a broomstick against the wall
above his head at six to wake him. Alan woke up shocked and
confused and nearly hungover. When his mind cleared up his
surroundings, he was pissed and frustrated.
   Sunday night, he and Rob had closed out Mikey G's. The
redhead bartender was there, and Rob was too distracted by
her to be concerned with what Alan was saying. When their
night first started, Rob had been shocked that Alan had been
homeless for the whole weekend, but once the bartender came
over, his "wow's" and "that's crazies" were just fillers. He'd
stopped paying attention. Even when Alan told him about
Saturday night, calling in a fire at the apartment just to screw
Candace, all Rob did was stare at red's chest over the rim of
his glass and say, "Crazy. That's, wow."
   When they'd gone, Alan tried again to stay at Rob's place.

"AJ, Jackie is already jealous of you, and I only see you, like,
twice a week or something.
   She would kick both of us out if you stayed with me. Then
we'd both be homeless."

"Fuck you," Alan said defensively. "I'm not homeless."

"Good," Rob said, "then go home." He checked his pockets for his keys, and when he found them, he fished them out and stretched. "Later, man. Get home safe." He laughed as he walked away, and although Alan was pissed, he couldn't help but laugh too.

By the time Alan made it to Ritechek, though, the humor had gone. He pulled the door and felt the welcome but all too familiar blast of the AC. There were two dudes behind the glass this time, and they both looked up for only a moment before going back to whatever they were doing. Alan headed to his crate and sat down. Three nights in a row. This was ridiculous. And so unfair. He'd screwed up, fine; but it was one mistake. One! He didn't deserve this.

He couldn't believe it. This was so unlike Candace. They'd fought a million times and she had stopped talking to him on occasion. Once or twice she even slept on the couch or locked the bedroom door so that he had to, but they'd always gotten over it. Why couldn't she get over this? It was unlike her. There had to be something else. Something he was missing.

The thought made him feel like crap. What had happened? And why didn't he know?

Why hadn't he thought to find out earlier? Had someone died? No. Could she have been fired?

Maybe, but not likely. Her principal loved her. So, what? What happened?

Alan stretched a leg out and pulled his cellphone from his pocket. He looked at the battery icon and it was red. The number beside it said nine percent. He wiped the screen on his shirt, then pulled up the keypad and held down the number two. He watched the screen until it said connected, then he put the phone to his ear. There were five rings before Candace answered, and when she did, she sounded groggy and confused.

"Hello?"

"H-hey. Hey, babe."

"Alan? What's going on? What time is it?"

He pulled the phone away, checked the screen. "It's almost three p.m. A.M.! Three a.m.

Sorry. What's up?"

"Alan, what the hell?" Her voice was clearer now. He heard the bed creek and he pictured her sitting up on her elbows.

"Sorry, babe. Were you sleeping?"

"Are you drunk?"

Of course he was. "Of course I'm not!"

"Alan, I can't—" Candace cut off mid-sentence and Alan heard Hanna in the background. She was too far to make out, but whatever she was saying couldn't be good. "Alan, I have to go. I have to be up early for work. If you need to come get your stuff, Hanna will be here. You can come over whenever."

"Just hang up!" Hanna yelled from a distance, and Alan heard it clearly. Fucking Hanna.

She's the reason all this was happening.

"Listen, babe..." he started.

"Bye, Alan."

A quick beep sounded in his ear, then silence, and he looked at the screen. The call time flashed, then cleared to his home screen.

Not long after, when Alan's anger had reached its climax, he was back at the payphone.

"9-1-1, what's your emergency?"

AT SIX A.M. MONDAY, the manager of Ritechek called over to him to wake up. When that didn't work, he nudged Alan's foot, and when that failed, he banged the wall above Alan's head. Alan jumped up, tired and pissed, and was still feeling that way thirty minutes later when he was crossing 145th Street and almost got hit by a car. The dude driving the car didn't even slow down or tap his horn or anything. He just kept driving like nothing happened, and then stopped two streets up. Alan stood in the street and watched. A young guy got out and ran into the supermarket on the corner.

Alan, still angry, finished crossing the street and jogged to the supermarket. He peered in through the window but didn't see the driver. He turned to the car, looking it over. Break a window? He walked around it, considering. He'd have to break it then run, because it was bound to be loud, and although there weren't many people, the streets weren't empty. Alan checked the window of the supermarket again, quickly, then looked around for a brick or something to throw.

He didn't find one, but he did find a long, rusted nail and got another idea. A better idea.

Alan took the nail and went around to the driver's side where he was less likely to be seen from inside the supermarket. He bent and placed the point of the nail against the front tire and pressed hard. The back of the nail hurt as it pushed against his hand. He pulled the nail away and saw an indentation where it had been but no hole. He looked at his hand and found a small red circle in his palm and he grunted under his breath.

Alan pulled his t-shirt away from his neck and fanned his chest and thought about the problem. He stood quickly checking the store window again, then went back down to his knees and put the nail where he had before. Same spot. He held it there and straightened out his legs. Now he was bent over with his hands and the nail by his toes. He held the nail with his left hand and kicked the head of it with his right foot. The tire dented but wasn't punctured. He kicked it again and felt the nail slide through his fingers. Excited, he kicked it twice more, and when he was done, the nail was a quarter of the way through the side of the tire. Alan bent again, grabbed the nail, and twisted it up and down, left and right, then pulled it out and could both feel and hear the hiss of the air releasing. He sat back on his knees, satisfied.

He pictured the kid coming out and finding it and he began to laugh. Then he realized what he was doing, got up quickly, and headed to the subway.

-11-

HOW OR WHY CHARLES'S tire had gone from fine to flat in ten minutes was a mystery no one at the firehouse was particularly concerned about. It was an easy fix, and a chance to drill on a tool not often used. It was also an opportunity to help the newest member of the house.

Traffic had picked up when they got to his car, both on the sidewalks and in the streets.

Charles's car was parallel to the supermarket and right behind the crosswalk for 145th Street. It was an inconvenient spot to park three rigs and drill with thirteen men. So, Kenny, who wasn't wearing his bunker gear, got behind the wheel, while Charles and Bahms got behind the car and guided it around the corner, two streets down, and around another corner to a dead-end where the only street traffic was from people looking to do a U turn and the only foot traffic was from employees of a restaurant that hadn't yet opened for the day.

Pete maneuvered the Engine to the street corner, facing out of the dead-end. Fagan, from Ladder 88, backed the Truck up further down the street and stopped about ten feet behind the Engine, facing out. Brian O'Neil, the chauffeur for the chief, positioned the chief's rig at the entrance to the street so no cars would come down, then everyone got out and walked over to Charles's car. Chief Leland ducked back into the rig, grabbed a phone receiver on the console between the two front seats, and pressed the button on the handle to contact the Manhattan dispatcher.

"Battalion 5 to Manhattan."

The dispatcher: "Battalion 5."

"Battalion 5, Engine 99 and Ladder 88 will be away from the rigs for MUD. Please put our runs over the air."

"Ten-four, Battalion 5."

The chief grabbed an extra radio and handed it to Brian, who slung it across his body with his own. He turned the dial on the extra one to the Manhattan dispatcher so they'd be able to hear and talk to Manhattan without using the phones in the rigs.

Kenny parked Charles's car in the middle of the road, away from both curbs so that there would be enough room for everyone to operate around it. Before getting out, he popped the trunk and Bahms opened it. Charles reached in and grabbed the spare. He took it out and placed it on the ground, then reached in and grabbed his tools.

"You won't need those." Charles turned around and Fagan was there, fingers tucked into the waist of his bunker pants, grinning. His smile, Charles thought, could be either charming or intimidating. There was a thin line between the two and he certainly knew it. He was average height, with a full head of greying hair and a face that showed no wrinkles.

"Oh," Charles said. "Okay. Sorry, sir."

"Sorry for what?" Fagan asked, and he looked genuinely interested. The two captains, the chief, and Brian had come over near the head of the car. Kenny had gone to the Truck to help the members of 88 grab the airbags and the tools they would need for the operation. Pete walked up beside Fagan, pinched some tobacco from a tin he carried in his pocket, and placed it behind his bottom lip.

Beads of sweat rolled down Charles's forehead, into his

eyes, and he blinked them away. It wasn't as hot as it was going to be, but the sun was out and unhindered by any clouds or trees or buildings. His gear was heavy when fully donned like he had it, but he didn't think any of those were the main cause of his sweating.

"Why are you sorry?" Fagan asked again.

Charles tried a smile, shook his head. "I don't know. It's just a force of habit, sir."

"Saying sorry for no reason is a force of habit?"

Charles glanced at Emmett. The captain leaned against the hood of his car, a hint of a smile on his face. "No, sir," Charles answered, looking back to Fagan. "Saying sorry when I'm not sorry is a force of habit."

Fagan nodded, his smile fading away as if it had never been. "Yes, well, you've got fourteen months to learn to speak and act with purpose. Might sound like a long time, but it's not, so let's try saying and doing what we mean to say and do." He turned away from them and walked toward the Truck. "And my name's not sir."

"Yes, sir," Charles said automatically.

Fagan stopped and turned his head around to look at him.

Charles shook his head again. "Sorry. Fagan." He correct-ed.

"Are you really sorry? Or was that just a force of habit?"

Charles didn't answer and Fagan turned away. Pete stepped over to where Bahms and Charles were standing at the rear of the car. Bahms closed the trunk and laid a hand on his shoul-der.

"Listen. Fagan can be intimidating," Bahms said. "He's got over twenty years on the job—more time than most of the bosses. His patience can be short, but he's a good dude and a great firefighter. He's all-in on the job and he's tough, but if you show him that you're, you know, serious about learning, he can teach you a lot and you'll get along fine."

"Okay."

Pete: "You don't got a hair on your ass if you don't go up to him and say, 'Listen, buddy. I may be new, but you ain't gonna talk to me like a little bitch. You got that?'" He spit on the ground, lifted his eyebrows, and nodded. "Go! Go do that. I double dare you!"

Bahms laughed and guided Charles toward the tools laid out on the street. "Maybe only listen to Pete when he's talking about work."

THE GUYS FROM 88 finished gathering everything they'd need and placed them in a straight line. Fagan walked through everything talking so everyone could hear, but speaking mainly to Charles. The airbags he told them were neoprene rubber reinforced with steel and were extremely difficult to puncture but not impossible. They were flat when not inflated, and square shaped but came in different sizes, each rated to lift a different weight. When inflated, the center of the bag would rise about three inches, and at full inflation, the bag could only lift up to half its rated load capacity. The reason that was, he explained to Charles, was because when the bag was fully inflated, it domed like a pregnant belly and only the center of it would be in contact with the item being lifted. In this case, Charles's car.

Billy and Danny, two firefighters from Ladder 88, got to their knees with Charles and set up the equipment underneath the frame of Charles's car. They stacked two airbags of different sizes, the smaller on top, on top of wooden plates. When they were done, there was less than an inch of space between the undercarriage and the top bag.

Fagan got to his knees beside the assembly. "All of these bags have a load capacity high enough to lift the car by themselves," he said. "The airbag on the bottom is rated to lift four tons.

The one on the top, two tons." He looked at Charles. "How much will we be able to lift?"   "Six tons." Charles responded.

"Negative," Fagan answered. "Will the center of both bags have contact with the undercarriage of the car?"

Charles thought about that. "No."

"Then why would we take into account what the bottom one can lift?" Charles nodded but didn't answer.

Fagan said, "If I can bench two hundred pounds and you can bench three hundred, laying on top of each other isn't going to give either one of us the ability to bench five hundred."

Charles: "I understand."

"How much will we be able to lift?"

"One ton."

Fagan nodded and turned away, and Charles exhaled, irrationally embarrassed.

THE REST OF THE drill was just the operation, and Charles enjoyed it. They inflated the bottom bag first, then the top and the front of the car lifted off the ground on the driver's side. Paul Oldman cautioned Charles about putting any part of his body beneath the risen car, then

Charles and Bahms changed the tire. It was the first time he'd ever done it, and he felt a sense of pride.

When the tire was changed and the car had been lowered, Fagan asked, "Are we done?"

"Yes. Thank you, very much." Charles said. "For the tire and the drill."

Fagan flashed the smile. "We're done?" he asked again. "Is this how we leave the scene?

Tools out everywhere?"

"Oh. Sorry, no."

"No," Fagan agreed, smile fading again. "We're profes-
sionals. When we arrive to do a job, we bring the tools we
need and get to work. The job's not done until we accomplish
what we came to do and get out safely—with the tools we
brought in. They go back exactly where we found them, ready
to be used for the very next run, which could come at any
minute."

As he finished saying so, a ringing sounded in all three
rigs.

"Whoa!" Billy said, impressed. "What are you, psychic?"

Pete said, "Inconceivable!"

Brian turned the volume up on the second radio and held it
up to listen.

Bahms grabbed Charles's arm. "We all have a run. Let's
help them put this stuff away, quick," he said, and they joined
the others in packing up the tools.

The dispatcher's voice came through Brian's radio: "Manhattan, phone alarm box 1-1-2-
9. Multiple dwelling A. 535 West 150th Street, Broadway
to Amsterdam. Fire, first floor."

PETE HURIED TO THE Engine, Captain Emmett right
behind him. Captain Gorm climbed inside the Truck and
turned a touch-screen monitor on the center console toward
him. He pushed a button, half turned, and shouted over his
shoulder, "We're second-due!"

Brian and the chief were making their way to their rig, not
running, when the dispatcher called them.

"Manhattan to Battalion 5."

Brian keyed the mic on the second handie-talkie. "Battalion 5."

"Battalion 5, you get your ticket for box 1-1-2-9? Fire, first

106

floor of a multiple dwelling?"

"Ten-four, Manhattan. Responding."

"Ten-four. Manhattan to Ladder 88?"

Captain Gorm: "Ladder 88, ten-four, Truck and Engine responding."

"Ten-four, 88."

The tools were away, and the rigs started. Everyone not in full gear, which was everyone but Charles, was putting on the rest of their gear. Except Pete. As the Engine chauffeur, he'd have no reason to go inside the building, so he didn't bother with his gear. He checked to see that everyone was on the rig, turned on his flashers, pulled away from the curb around the Battalion's rig, and headed toward 150th Street. Fagan followed him, and Brian, after pulling a broken U-turn, had the Battalion rig right behind them.

They drove off toward the fire, a caravan of blaring sirens and flashing lights.

IN THE CAB OF the Engine, Bahms smiled as he put his gloves on. Kenny opened a Jolly Rancher and popped it in his mouth. Charles could feel his heartbeat in his jaw. Bahms leaned over to him and whispered.

"You alright, bud?"

"I am," Charles answered, as he tried to remember these scenarios in the academy.

-12-

JOSH WAS IN HIS car, half a mile from home, listening
to Kenny G on the radio, when the call for fire came in. Years
ago, he had installed a store-bought scanner to the dashboard
in his car. It was always on, tuned to the Manhattan fire dispatcher. The scanner didn't work as well as the department
issued ones you'd find in a firehouse or a department vehicle,
but the reception was decent, and he was able to listen to both
the scanner and his car radio simultaneously.

When he heard the dispatcher announce the call for fire
at West 150th Street, he felt a familiar thrill. Engine 80 and
Ladder 23 were closest to that address, so 99 and 88 would be
second-due, but still: fire's fire.

As he turned into his driveway, the boss in Engine 80,
Maureen O'Malley, contacted the dispatcher, sounding urgent
but not panicked.

"Engine 8-0 to Manhattan."

"Engine 8-0."

"Ten-seventy-five the box."

Josh smiled. *Ten-seventy-five*. A confirmed fire. Josh pictured the men and women jumping out of the rigs, grabbing
their tools, and rushing into the building. He put his car in
park but left the ignition on so that he wouldn't lose the scanner or the air conditioner. Unbuckling his seatbelt, he leaned
back and smiled. "Harlem's going to work," he said out loud,
and smacked the wheel.

A MINUTE EARLIER, BACK on Engine 99, Charles was looking up at a screen, reading the ticket.

There were two flat-screen monitors on the rig, one up front, on a swivel for the boss and the chauffeur, and one in the back. The monitors showed the ticket information: the address, the reason for the call, what due they were, and the other firehouses responding. It also showed a description of the building—height, size, roof access, location of standpipes, whether there were sprinklers. Charles read it all twice.

Pete made the turn on to West 150th Street and Kenny, whose seat faced backwards, turned to see out the front of the rig. Firefighters from Engine 80, the first-due Engine, were grabbing lengths of hose off the back of their rig and heading to the building. Charles didn't see any fire yet, but his pulse quickened. This seemed like the real thing.

They all heard the first-due Engine boss contact Manhattan, and before the dispatcher could respond, Charles was following Kenny off the rig and running over to Engine 80.

"We're second-due," Bahms called to Charles, a step behind him. "We don't stretch our own line—we back up the first line."

"Right," Charles said. He'd learned that in the academy.

Captain Emmett went straight into the building. Pete ran past Charles to the side of 80's rig, where their chauffeur was, and asked what he needed. Bahms did the same thing with 80's controlman at the back of the rig, and Kenny led Charles to the sidewalk where lengths of hose from the first line led into the lobby of the building.

Charles knew what to do. He had done it a hundred times in the past four months. He grabbed one part of the hose line and pulled it left of the entrance while Kenny grabbed behind him and pulled to the right. When they were finished, there was a large S shape from the rig to the building. Captain

Gorm, Paul, and Danny hurried past them carrying hooks, a water can, and forcible entry tools. Paul smiled at Charles and said, "Turn your bottle on, kid."

Charles reached behind his back and turned on the cylinder in his mask but didn't put his face piece on. The clean air in his bottle was limited, and he didn't need it just then.

The fire was on the first floor, and it didn't take long for Engine 80's guys to get to the fire apartment and ready to move in. Their boss called over the radio, "8-0 to 8-0 chauffer, start water."

The chauffeur acknowledged, and a moment later, water filled out the hose from the control panel to the street, through the S shape on the sidewalk, into the building. Their control man followed the filled line in, and Charles and Kenny went behind him. Bahms stayed outside.

The lobby was smoky, but not very. A woman in pajama pants and a sports bra stood barefoot in the hallway in a puddle of water holding a little girl with tears on her face but who was no longer crying. Charles was behind 80's control man and Kenny behind him, and all three lifted the hose line off the ground and helped move it forward.

Captain Emmett came out of the apartment with the neck of his hood pulled up over his nose and mouth. He nodded at the woman and waved at the girl, then went over to stand beside Charles and Kenny.

"Mattress fire," he said quietly. "It's already out. Nothing serious."

"Ten-four," Kenny answered, and spit out the Jolly Rancher.

"Still," Emmett said, smiling at Charles. "You're having an exciting first day."

"Ten-four," Charles said, and permitted himself a smile.

JOSH DIDN'T KNOW IT was a mattress fire, but figured it was something like that. Not too long after the ten-seventy-five was given, Brian, the chief's aide, had contacted the dispatcher. He told them that they had one hose line stretched and in operation, and that the main body of fire had been knocked down. Five minutes later, he was reporting that both primary and secondary searches were negative, which meant that everyone was accounted for, there was no extension of the fire, and operations were wrapping up. Whatever it was that had caught fire was big enough that the water can Truck firefighters carry wouldn't have been enough to put it out, but small enough that the whole scene was under control in half an hour. It had to be either a single piece of furniture or a glorified stove fire.

Josh smiled at the thought of the probie going to a fire on his first day. For everything else firefighters did, going to and putting out fires was the job, and real fires were few and far between these days. Sure, it was good for the city and the people that new construction, new laws, and new awareness initiatives by the department were making homes and buildings safer, but as far as Josh was concerned, practice was the only thing that made perfect. If the young guys didn't go to fires, how could they get good at fighting them? It was a… what did they call it? A Catch-22. Or something.

Nevertheless, this was a good omen for the probie's career. Some junior guys were white clouds: they went months before they ever saw a fire. There was no set season for fire duty, but in Josh's experience, going to a fire early in your career often meant you'd go to a lot more.

"Good for you, kid," he said to the scanner, and smiled.

Josh turned the car off and pulled the key from the ignition. He popped the door and flinched at the heat. A little after ten o'clock in the morning and the temperature was already in the nineties. It had jumped at least ten degrees since he left the firehouse. Yesterday, when he stopped working on Athena's wall unit to head in for the night tour, he had every intention of going back to the garage when he got back home, but the lack of sleep last night and the temperature this morning was killing his motivation. He only had a few hours before he had to go back to work, so he decided to nap instead.

In his bedroom, he sat on the side of his bed, his ankle on his knee, wrestling a stubborn knot out of his shoe. Mildred wasn't home. He pulled at the laces and tried not to think about the situation with her, but the more he struggled with the knot, the more the negative thoughts bubbled to the surface.

He dropped his foot to the ground and sat back, the knot solid on the bridge of his foot. He stared at his shoe, not really seeing it, and shook his head. How did he screw things up this much?

HE AND MILDRED HAD gotten married almost twenty years ago. Every night, the week before their wedding, they talked about the future and the family they'd start—two boys, one girl—and the adventures they'd take and the house they'd buy down South, and the clothing line

Mildred would start. She would name it Milagros," after her mother.

But then they'd come home from the honeymoon to a piece of mail from the fire department telling Josh that he'd passed the entry exam and would be moving on in the hiring process. That process consumed the next twenty months, and as a result, their plans were put on hold. That hold was extended another nine months, when Mildred missed her period. Athena was a blessing, but she was only a piece of the puzzle. The picture wasn't complete, but the more time passed, the more it faded.

The delay always felt temporary, though. Like things were just around the corner from getting back on track. First, they had to get through the hiring process. Obviously, they couldn't move down South at the time, but maybe they could later. Josh could maybe transfer to another fire department in a southern state. But then Athena came along, and they didn't want to make any big moves or decisions while she was young. Then, being a junior guy in the firehouse, Josh was required to spend a lot of time there. In a rare argument, once, Mildred said that it had begun to feel like dates and times important to the firehouse meant more to Josh than dates and times important to their family. By the time he had ten years on the job and Athena was turning eleven, he had only been home for three of her birthdays. He hadn't noticed that, but Mildred had.

Then when it finally seemed like, because of his seniority, things were starting to change for the better, Josh decided to take the lieutenants promotion test. When he wasn't working, he locked himself away in his den and studied. It'd paid off. He passed the test and was promoted in the first round of promotions the following year. That made him a new lieutenant, which in the officer rank made him junior all over again. He was assigned to Ladder 88 in Harlem and for Mildred, dinners and birthday celebrations at home went back to being a two-person affair. He hadn't noticed. She had.

Josh loved his family. He didn't think Mildred or Athena ever doubted that. When he was home and he wasn't studying, he was there and present and he was confident his love was obvious to them. Theirs certainly was to him. Especially Athena. She loved his job and she made him feel like a superhero. When she was young, he'd bring her to the firehouse every weekend he worked. The guys treated her like their own and their kids were like siblings to her. Matt and Meg were like unofficial godparents to her and they had probably been around for just as many birthdays as Josh had, if not more. That was no good. But he hadn't noticed.

Then, last Christmas, Josh had gotten home after working a day tour and found Mildred upset. Not mad, but distant. Athena had gone to a friend's house for dinner and Mildred was alone on the couch with an apple pie scented candle burning on the coffee table. After some coaxing, Josh had gotten her to tell him what was wrong.

"I don't want to do this anymore," she said, tears welling up in her eyes. "I can't."

"What do you mean? Do what no more?"

"This. Be your second family."

"What!" He was confused. And a little pissed. No way in hell could she possibly think he was having an affair. No way in hell. "Second family? Second to who?"

"To the firehouse," she answered, and tears fell down her face.

Josh was silent, processing the statement. He thought hearing her accusing him of cheating would be the last thing he would expect. He never even considered this. Second family? What did that mean? Of course the firehouse was a family to him. The fire service was a calling. Not just anyone could do it. The men and women you served with not only put their lives on the line *with* you, they put their lives on the line *for* you. How could they not become family? But that didn't make Mildred and Athena a *second* family. He didn't love anything in the world more than he loved them.

As if reading his mind, Mildred wiped her cheeks and said, "I know you love us. I know, Joshua. We both do. But we deserve to be loved more than your job. Not the same."

THAT CONVERSATION WAS SEVEN months ago. Over that time, Josh had tried to show Mildred that his family was second to nothing. But it seemed that a line had been crossed. She did a good job of looking like herself when Athena was around, but when it was just the two of them, she'd go cold. Then, in May, when Athena had gone overseas, Mildred stopped sleeping in their bed. She hadn't said the *D* word yet, but every time Josh came home, every time they spoke, he was afraid of hearing it.

Now, Josh stared out the window and played with a tuft of hair, thinking about how different things had gone from when he and Mildred lay in bed in St. Maarten planning their future. He looked out into the sunny day, uncertain what the future held. Uncertain, even, of the present. He had no idea where Mildred was now. He thought about his promotion next year and wondered what his life would look like then. Still no sons, obviously. Still no house down South. Mildred likely wouldn't be running a clothing line. Athena would probably be living on her own. Would he be too?

He turned from the window, caught a glimpse of himself in Mildred's vanity, then looked away quickly.

-13-

AFTER THE MATTRESS FIRE, Charles was introduced to the firefighters in Engine 80. Then he, Bahms, and Kenny helped them repack the hose line on their rig. When they were done, they went back to their own rig, where they took off their masks and coats and gloves.

On the rigs, the seatbacks had cushioned cutouts to accommodate the mask assembly which encompassed an air cylinder with forty minutes of clean air strapped to a harness and secured to the wearer with shoulder and waist straps. . Charles sat down and pushed his back in place, then freed his arms and put the shoulder straps back on their hooks.

Kenny did the same, then unsnapped his coat and pulled off his hood. He said, "How was that? Not bad, right?"

"No," Charles agreed, though his adrenaline was pretty high.

"Make sure you shut your bottle off, bud," Kenny said to Charles.

"He means your mask," Bahms said. "It could get confusing because everything has a bunch of different names for it. Mask, bottle, cylinder, tank. They're not technically interchangeable, but we all use them that way."

"Got it," Charles said, and he half turned in his seat to shut it off.

"How would you know if you left your bottle on?" Kenny

116

asked.

"The PASS alarm would go off," Charles answered confidently.

Bahms: "After how long?"

"After twenty seconds it'd go to a low alarm. Then a loud alarm twelve seconds after

that."

Bahms held out his fist and Charles bumped it with his own.

Kenny asked, "Do you know why?"

Charles wasn't sure what Kenny meant and he said so.

"The PASS alarm is basically a personal motion sensor," Kenny said. "Once the bottle is turned on, the motion sensor inside the mask is activated. If you don't move for twenty seconds, that creepy alarm sounds. The first one is low because only you need to hear it. Once you do, and you move, it goes off."

"I understand."

"The thinking is that if you heard the eerie alarm for twelve seconds, and didn't move a muscle to silence it, you're probably not able to move. You're probably in distress. The second alarm is louder so that other firefighters could hear it and come to help."

Charles nodded. "Ten-four," he said.

Kenny shrugged. "It's a humbling thought, but also kind of comforting. Someone will always come for you. You're never alone if you're in trouble. God forbid."

Pete opened the driver's door and climbed in, and a moment later Captain Emmett got in on the other side.

Emmett turned to Pete and said, "Let's go back and pick up Charlie's car."

Kenny, continuing his train of thought, said to Charles, "That's probably the biggest thing about the firehouse. Trust.

No ego, no self-doubt. At the end of the day, you should know that no matter what, I'm gonna be there for you, and I should know that no matter what, you'll be there for me." He squinted. "You know?"

Charles nodded, understanding. "I know."

From up front, Pete said, "You know nothing, Jon Snow."

THEY PICKED UP CHARLES'S car and he drove it back from the dead-end street to the firehouse at normal speed, with Pete following behind him in the rig. When they arrived, he pulled into an empty spot in the lot and Pete backed the rig in through the garage door.

Inside, Brian, came from the housewatch with a notepad and pen, and stood beside Charles.

"Charles, what's your schedule?"

"What do you mean, sir? Today?"

"No, I mean when are you scheduled? Today and tomorrow day?"

"Yes, sir."

"Okay. Do you have any plans for tonight? Joe Morrison, one of the guys from the Truck, had an emergency with his mom. He was supposed to come in tonight. If you can stay and work for him tonight, he'll work for you tomorrow day."

"Of course I can stay. But if he has an emergency, he doesn't have to come in tomorrow.

I can do both."

Brian shook his head. "No," he said. "You can't. You can't work longer than twenty-four hours at a time. It doesn't work like that, anyway. You're working his tour, so he has to pay you back. It's not about being nice or being a probie."

"Okay."

"So, you're good for tonight? You sure?"

"Yes, sir. I can do it."

"Great, thank you. And, Brian. Not sir."

AFTER THAT, BAHMS WALKED Charles through "committee work." Every bathroom was cleaned, every garbage can emptied, every floor swept then mopped. Every kitchen surface cleared of anything used or unused for breakfast that morning. All the sheets from beds laid in the night before were thrown in the washer, then dryer, then folded and put away in a locker. The stripped beds were remade with the sheets cleaned from yesterday's committee work.

Bahms had Charles clean the bathrooms alone. "It's not like a hazing thing or anything like that," he explained. "Everyone participates in cleaning, but as the most junior guy, you wanna do the dirty jobs. It's fair. Everyone before you did it as the probie too. At one point, everyone is the most junior guy."

So Charles washed and disinfected every surface, and when he cleaned the stalls, he made sure to put a pre-wipe on top of every roll. When he was done, everyone else was done with the rest of the committee work. There were still sheets in the dryer that would need to be folded and put away when the cycle was done, but everything else on the checklist Bahms had gone over had been checked.

"How long do you think it would have taken you to do everything by yourself?" Bahms asked. They were standing on the apparatus floor near the Engine. A couple of guys were sitting on a couch behind the Truck where the fans mounted near the ceiling blew the strongest. Kenny was on his phone in the lot. Everyone else was in the kitchen.

"I'm not sure," Charles answered. "A while."

"A long while," Bahms agreed. "It would have taken any one of us a long time to do all that work alone. But it took us

119

all working together no time at all. Get it?"

"I do."

"Here's a hint about being a probie. Everything we do with you and to you is for a reason. Nothing is done just for tradition's sake. Well," he held up his hands, "scratch that. A bunch of things are done for tradition's sake, but there is rhyme and reason to it. We train like we play. Nobody does anything for the benefit of the house by themselves. From cleaning or cooking to, like, repairing a broken sink, nothing. The same way nobody operates on the field alone. We work as a team the entire tour. Doing committee work together makes all our lives easier; working as a unit on the field makes all our jobs easier. And safer."

"I understand."

"I know you do."

AFTER LUNCH, GUYS WENT their own way, doing their own thing until the next call came in. Most guys went upstairs to a room with a big screen TV and several couches. A few went up to the gym to work out. As a probie, Charles wasn't allowed to go to the TV room, so Bahms suggested he use the time to study the training books on the computer in the kitchen. That way, he could sit down and relax in an airconditioned place, but still be on the first floor in case a run came in.

Charles filled a cup with water, then sat down at the desk in the kitchen. He pulled out his cellphone and started to text Libby, but hesitated, his thumbs hovering over the touchscreen keyboard. It was his first moment to himself since the supermarket, and he had time to think. He looked around the kitchen, taking in everything but not really looking at anything. Only a few hours ago he was anxious about what to bring for breakfast, now he was causally sipping water after lunch, having come back from a fire. Charles hadn't actually seen anything burning and he didn't really do much to help put it out, but how crazy was it that he was there? In the building, on the line—a fireman.

A sad smile spread across his face. He wished he felt differently about this. Happier. But complete excitement felt insincere.

He took a long drink from his cup, put it on the desk, then looked down at his phone and tapped the screen to wake it up. But then Paul Oldman came through the door, lighting a cigarette, and Charles put his phone away. Paul raised his head and blew a lung full of smoke toward the ceiling.

"How's it going so far?" he asked.

"Good, sir."

Paul flinched. "Cut the sir crap. We're all firemen."

"Sorry," Charles said, then shook his head. He hated how much he used that word. Sorry, not sir.

"It's cool. I'm just saying, this isn't the academy. We'll know you have respect by taking your job seriously. In the firehouse and out on runs. Understand?"

"Yes…yes."

Paul laughed. "You were gonna say sir again, I caught that."

"Sorry."

Paul turned away and spat in a garbage can near the coffee station. "And stop saying sorry so much. Even if you are. Owning up to a fuck-up doesn't mean apologizing a thousand times. Just recognize it and fix it." He spat again. "I'm not saying calling us sir is a fuck-up, I'm just saying."

"I understand."

"This is a good group of guys and the greatest job in the world. It really is. You're part of it now. Don't be so nervous. What do you got today, the nozzle?"

"Yes."

"Best seat in the house. It can be scary when you're new, but you don't let anybody know that, right?"

Charles nodded.

"When you get that first big fire, and you will, it could come any minute. When you do, you get behind the nozzle and know: I got this. Understand?"

Charles was upset with himself. He hadn't known his insecurities were so evident, but this was now the second person to give him a pep talk. He didn't like that. But maybe it was normal. Maybe everyone was worried about how they'd do until the time came and they were on their knees in front of a raging fire. Maybe that's when all the confidence came. Maybe that's when you realized you were ready. But he didn't like it.

Charles met Paul's eyes. "Got it," he said, and hoped he sounded convincing.

Paul nodded. "Good."

-14-

AFTER ALAN HAD STABBED the tire that morning, he'd run down the stairs to the subway, jumped over the waist-high turnstile without paying his fare, and found an empty spot on the platform to wait. Fare evasion was illegal, but that didn't matter because people did it all the time. Besides, the city always took half his check every two weeks, the least they could do was give him a free ride.

The train schedule said that the next train would be there in two minutes, and he leaned against a pillar to wait.

It took four minutes. The first car entered the station slowly, then stopped, the rest of the train still hidden in the tunnel. People on the platform looked up from their phones or books, questions on their faces. Some looked at the arrival screen for an explanation but didn't find one. The motorman was in the front, talking on a radio.

Alan looked around. Was this about him? He looked everywhere, physically doing a three-sixty on the platform. Nothing. No cops or transit workers. No supermarket jerk-off. So what was this about? Why had the train stopped?

He considered leaving the station, but that turned out to be unnecessary because the train groaned and squealed, then started to move again. It crawled along the length of the platform and stopped at the other end with all cars in the station. The conductor poked his head out of the middle car and a moment later the doors opened. Alan stepped back to let two women wearing leggings get on before him. They smiled and thanked him, and he smiled back.

Inside was comfortably cool. He found an empty twin seat in the corner of the car near the doors that led to other cars. He leaned his head against the train's wall and blew out. The doors that led to the other cars opened and a clean but unkempt man wearing a backpack and holding a cup stepped through. Alan pulled his legs out of the way and the guy nodded his thanks. He walked to the middle of the car, then spoke up.

"Please excuse the interruption, ladies and gentlemen. I'm sorry to disturb you. I'm homeless and hoping to make a few dollars to get breakfast. I want to sing something for you all, and if you enjoy it, I'd be thankful for a small donation."

Alan looked away, wishing he had headphones. He hated when beggars approached him.

He closed his eyes and tried to ignore him, but then the guy started singing and, damn! The dude was good! Alan opened his eyes, shocked. And he wasn't the only one. Everyone stared. The two chicks in the spandex had their hands on their chests. An older woman across from Alan opened her wallet by touch because she couldn't take her eyes off him. Other passengers reached into their bags and pockets.

Alan wasn't one of them. The dude was good, but Alan was almost in the same boat. He needed his money. He couldn't sleep in the check cashing place another week, or however long it took Candace to get over this. He was miserable there. If Rob didn't convince Jackie to take the stick out of her ass, Alan might have to stay in a motel for a couple nights.

The thought upset him. He leaned back and closed his eyes again. This was so stupid. He should be at home right now cleaning the dishes from breakfast with Candace. Or on his way home from walking her to work. Or in bed watching *CBS This Morning*. Not on the fucking subway going downtown for no reason.

He didn't want to wait another week. He didn't want to wait another day, he had to fix this. Now.

Flowers? That could work. Candace loved flowers. All women did. There was a florist next door to Kim's Shoes. He could get her a dozen roses. One red and eleven white: do it classy. Bring them to her school around the time she got out. She'd see them and touch her chest the way those chicks with the leggings just did. Maybe she'd cry. They'd hug and things would be okay again. He'd have his home and his wife back.

Alan opened his eyes, turned his leg, and pulled his wallet from his pocket. He pulled the cash out a little and checked to see if he had enough for a dozen roses. He hadn't noticed that the beggar had finished singing and started around with his cup. Alan looked up and saw the dude standing not quite over him, smiling expectantly.

Alan looked at the cup, then at the wallet in his own hand, and sighed.

"Got me," he muttered, shaking his head. He pulled out a one-dollar bill and stuffed it in the cup.

WHILE ALAN WAS ON the train, Candace and Hanna were walking to Candace's school. Hanna had cooked them breakfast earlier, and as they ate, Candace invited Hanna to come along for the day. She told her that the kids would love to hear from a professional writer. Hanna didn't believe that for a second, but didn't want to be inside all day, so agreed to go.

They walked in silence. They were both exhausted. Last night, after Candace had gotten off the phone with Alan, nei-

ther of the two women had gone back to sleep. Hanna stayed
in the bedroom, on the bed beside Candace, hands in her
pajama pockets, and neither spoke. Not long after that, they
heard the sirens.

When they'd heard the bell on the intercom, Candace said,
"You can't be serious."

"What an asshole," Hanna said, and when Candace looked
at her questioningly, she said,

"What? You don't think it's him? You don't think it's Alan
calling them, just to be a dick?"

That specific thought hadn't crossed Candace's mind, but
once Hanna said so, Candace was sure she was right.

They got off the bed and headed to the living room. Candace buzzed the entrance downstairs, and a minute later there
was a knock on the door. A man spoke loud enough to be
heard without exactly yelling, "Fire Department." Candace
unlocked and opened the door. Outside were three firefighters.
One lieutenant and two others. Candace didn't know anything
about the hierarchy of the fire department, but she knew the
lieutenant was a lieutenant because the leather patch on his
helmet said so. And because he had been there Saturday night
too.

When she opened the door, the lieutenant looked slightly annoyed and very tired, but determined to hide both. He
smiled and said, "We received a call for fire in this apartment.
Is everything okay?"

"Yes, everything's fine."

The lieutenant nodded and asked her to remind him of her
last name, and when she told him, he turned away, grabbed a
radio on his chest, and called someone. When that person responded, the lieutenant said, "Ten-ninety-two, apartment 6B,
last name Johnson." Then he looked up and asked Candace if
she knew who was making these calls.

"I don't know for sure, but it's probably my husband. He doesn't live here anymore. I'm really sorry you guys are wasting your time."

"No worries, ma'am. Not your fault," the lieutenant said. "But if you talk to him again, tell him he can go to bed…" he laughed and shook his head. "Bed. Hear me? See how tired I am? Jail. Tell him if he keeps this up, he can go to jail. Okay? It's against the law to make false claims to 9-1-1."

"I will. Sorry again."

The firefighters left and the two women had gone back to bed, but not fallen asleep. Now, as they walked to Candace's job, Candace wished she hadn't invited Hanna, so that Hanna could've stayed home and slept.

When they got to the school, Candace spent a few minutes in the principal's office introducing Hanna to Lucy, then the two headed to her room to get set up. While she prepared her room, they spoke about Alan and about the weekend and about last night and they apologized to each other although neither knew what the other was sorry about. Then they hugged.

ALAN GOT TO THE school about an hour before noon. Noon was when Candace's students went to lunch, and he wanted to be sure to get to her while they were still in class so they could cheer or giggle or clap or whatever it was kids did for mushy crap. He nodded at the school safety guy whose name he couldn't remember, and signed in.

He started to head inside, but the school safety guy stopped him.

"I gotta announce you, pal," the officer said. He pointed to a bench behind Alan. "Have a seat. I'll send you up in a moment."

Alan frowned. "I'm her husband. I've been here before."

"It's not that," the officer answered. "Times have changed, I guess. You know, school shootings and stuff. She just has to give the okay, then you can go on up."

"I wanted it to be a surprise."

The officer shrugged. "I really don't know what to tell you. I could tell her she has a visitor and not say your name if you want. But if she asks who it is, I gotta tell her."

Alan was disappointed but understood. He said, "Okay," then sat down. The school safety officer used a walkie-talkie to contact someone else, and Alan waited. He stared at the flowers and felt better just thinking of her reaction.

He'd gotten a dozen red roses. As it turned out, all colors weren't equal. A bouquet of eleven white and one red rose was almost twenty dollars more than a dozen red. He wasn't a cheap guy, and sure Candace was worth it, but he just didn't have a lot of cash. He wasn't worried, though. As he walked from the florist to the school, a bunch of women looked at the bouquet and smiled. A dozen red may not be classy, but it was classic, and that was just as good.

ON THE SECOND FLOOR, a different school safety officer tapped her knuckles against the window of Candace's door, and when everyone looked, she opened it.

"Sorry, Candace. You have a visitor downstairs. Want 'em escorted up?"

"Huh? Do you know who it is?"

"I do," Hanna said, and Candace looked at her. "I'll go talk to him. I'll be kind, okay?"

Candace ran the fingers of both hands through her hair and exhaled. She was standing by the board and now she leaned her butt against her desk.

"Is everything okay?" the second officer asked.

Candace looked up and forced a smile for the kids' sakes.

"Yes," she lied. "Just a silly thing." She looked over to Hanna. "Be nice about it."

"Atta girl," Hanna said. Then she disappeared into the stairwell.

ALAN WAS SMILING TO himself and looking at the bouquet in his arms. He would've preferred the white roses, but this really was a nice arrangement.

Someone came down the stairs and entered the first-floor hallway, and he looked up expecting Candace. Instead, Hanna was there, arms folded, eyeing the bouquet with a sneer.

What the hell was she doing here?

Alan stood and she let her arms fall to her sides as she walked to the waiting area. Neither person spoke for a long moment. Then Alan, uncomfortable, started toward the stair-well.

Hanna shifted her weight so she was leaning in his direction, and behind him, Alan heard the officer at the desk stand up.

"She's busy," Hanna said.

"What?"

"What's going on?" the officer asked.

"She has a real job. She doesn't have time to come down here and entertain your corner store flowers," Hanna said, then smiled brightly. "But you can give them to me. I'll be sure to take care of them."

Alan, feeling the anger rising in his gut, took a deep breath. He didn't need this. He didn't come here for a problem. He came here to *fix* the problem. Why was she even here?

He shook his head. This whole mess started the day Hanna came over. If he could just talk to Candace, maybe she would see that. Hanna was the fucking problem! He had to tell her.

Alan went to pass her again, but Hanna stepped in front of him. The officer stepped from behind the desk, and everything went downhill.

IF ONE OF THOSE three were recounting the story, it might take some time to tell it properly, but the reality of what happened was pretty quick. Alan went to his left and Hanna's right, and she stepped in front of him to block him. He was mid-stride and didn't have time to avoid the contact, but he dropped his shoulder and made it a bigger impact than it might've been.

Hanna spent a lot of time in the gym doing CrossFit and Wing Chun, and as a result had great balance. She was already stepping toward him when she saw him drop his shoulder, so she half turned and thrust her bodyweight behind her own shoulder, and they bounced off each other, more or less back to where they started.

Except that when the school safety officer saw Alan going forward, he stepped toward him and was in the spot where Alan started. Alan nearly collided with him, but the officer pushed him back and he stumbled back in Hanna's direction. Hanna planted her feet and stiff armed him, and this time he did fall back into the officer.

Alan, feeling like a tennis ball, screamed, a frustrated outburst. He grabbed the roses by the stem and threw them down, pedals scattering across the floor.

His fists were balled, and his body shook with every angry breath he took. His feet were planted a little more than shoulder width apart, and his head hung like a bull. Hanna was the opposite. She rocked calmly back and forth, one leg forward, the other back, breathing easy.

Lucy came running out of the office, probably because of the scream, and looked them over. "What's going on here?"

"Nobody move," the officer said, glaring at Alan and Hanna, then grabbed his radio and called for help.

UPSTAIRS, CANDACE HAD GIVEN the kids free-play and told them to keep it down. She was near the hallway door, trying to hear what was happening downstairs while keeping an ear toward her classroom.

Hanna came up the stairs running her fingers through her hair. Behind her was the school safety officer who had knocked on the door. Candace looked back and forth at the two.

"What happened?" she asked.

"There was an altercation," the officer said. "You two have to stay up here. Lucy will come up and talk to you."

The officer went back down the stairs and Candace grabbed Hanna's shoulder and led her out of sight of the kids.

"What happened?" She asked. "Did he hit you?"

"Not really. I think he's drunk," Hanna said, calmly. "The guards detained him and called the police. He's going to jail."

-15-

JUST BEFORE FIVE P.M. that evening, Matt walked into the firehouse to start his shift. He saw Charles crouched beside the back of the Engine with Bahms, going through an open compartment, and he went over, spoke with them quickly, then headed upstairs to the Engine office to relieve the captain. He and Emmett spoke a few minutes about the day tour, then the captain went into the bathroom in the office to shower. Matt left and went across the hall to the

Truck office. Captain Gorm was sitting in the officer's chair reading an article by Ray McCormack in *Firehouse* magazine. When Matt peeked in, he looked up.

"Matt. What's up, buhby?"

"How's it going, Capt?" They shook hands. "You working tonight?"

"Negative. Joshy Jobs is coming in."

"Ah. I thought so," Matt said. "Are you marching in the parade Thursday?"

Captain Gorm frowned and swiveled his chair to face the calendar on the wall. "Is Thursday the fourth?"

"Yes, sir."

"Crap. I didn't realize it was so soon." He faced forward again. "Umm…am I marching? Negative. I'm taking my kid to an event at West Point. We're gonna stay there 'til Saturday. You just reminded me, I gotta see if Josh will work for me

Friday night." He lifted his eyebrows. "Unless you can?"

Matt smiled apologetically. "Sorry. I'm already scheduled Friday night."

"No problem, buhby. Josh will probably do it. He loves being here."

MATT CHANGED AND WENT upstairs. He worked out for an uninterrupted hour, then went back to the Engine office and washed up. When he left the office again, he heard Sade playing from the radio in the Truck office and he smiled.

"Joshy Jobs," Matt said slowly as he entered the office. "What's up, buddy?"

"Matty Q. As I live and breathe." Josh stood and held out his hand, but Matt came around and hugged him. Josh hugged him back, and after a moment said, "I'm a fan of the lovin', brother, but that little bump poking my leg is makin' things a little awkward, know what I mean?"

Matt laughed and backed away. He stepped backward to the bed, moved a t-shirt out of the way, and sat. Josh sat back in the chair behind his desk and leaned back. Neither man spoke for a moment, then Josh said, "Uh-oh."

Matt looked a question at him. "What?"

"You tell me. You look like you got something deep on your mind. You about to fire me?

We gettin' a divorce or something? What's up?"

Matt smiled. "No, no. Nothing like that." He took off his cap, ran his fingers through his hair, then put the cap on backward.

"What, then?" Josh asked. He was smiling, relaxed. "Is this about me or you? You knock some broad up?" Matt made a face and Josh sat up, astonished. "Bullshit! No you didn't!"

"Yeah, I kinda did."

"Meg?"

Matt laughed. "What the hell? Of course, Meg. What do you think?"

Josh leaned back in his chair, hands on his chest. "Brother. I know you don't mess around, but I was scared for a second. I'd kill you if you were dirty-dicking."

Matt chuckled. "You and Meg, both."

Josh stood, beaming. "You're gonna be a poppa!" He grabbed Matt by the shoulders and pulled him up. "My boy's gonna be a pop-pop!" They hugged again. "Congratulations, Matty!"

He kissed Matt's cheeks, then leaned back. "I'm just glad your dick works."

Matt chuckled again. "You and Meg, both."

They separated, sat down again. "So tell me the story, brother," he said, pulling his chair closer to the bed. "When did you guys find out?"

"Just yesterday. Last night."

"I'm the first to know!"

"Well, Meg was the first to know…" Josh spread his hands. "…but no. I called my mom earlier, and Meg told her family." Matt took his cap off again and stared at it. "I ever tell you about Beth? Her aunt?"

"Meg's aunt?"

"Yeah."

"I don't think so. Why would you?"

"'Cause she's crazy. She's, like, spiritual but not religious, really. You know? Like, she's not into the whole power from the universe thing; she thinks there's a higher power, but it isn't the God of any organized religion."

"Okay." Josh shrugged. He was amused.

"Meg's family thinks Beth has visions or something. Not like she's psychic or anything like that, but like she knows things. She has divine intuition or something. Anyway, Meg told Beth about the baby—or told her mom and her mom told Beth—and Beth calls Meg up earlier and tells her to be careful. She asked if Meg or I were sick."

"Sick? With what?"

"I don't know. Cancer or something. She says babies mean death."

"What the fuck?" Josh sat back, a mixture of confusion and disbelief on his face. "Well, not babies. New life. New life means death. If someone you love is coming into the world, someone you love is on their way out."

Josh stared at Matt, open mouthed.

"Can you believe that?"

"No. I can't." Josh shook his head.

Matt scratched his scalp. "Who says that to a new mother? What kind of idiot tells a cancer survivor who just found out she's pregnant that a baby means someone is gonna die? Who?"

"That asshole," Josh said, angry. "What a douchebag. How's Meg? Is she okay?"

"No! She's upset. I mean, yes, she's fine. She doesn't believe in that stuff, really. But Beth has been right about a lot of things, and, you know, no survivor is ever really completely cancer free. Plus," he held out his hands. "This job. So Meg is a little paranoid." He shook his head and stared at his cap. "It was just a stupid thing to say to a pregnant woman."

Josh stared at him a moment. He sat forward in his chair and said, "Matty, listen. There's nothing more important than family. Believe me. But sometimes family is nuts."

Matt laughed, put his hat back on. "Yeah."

Josh: "I'm serious, brother. If some rando on the street came up and said that crap to you guys, you wouldn't think twice about it. But because it was Meg's family, you're gonna let it worry you? That's crazy. She's not psychic. God or the universe or whatever isn't whispering things to her. People make themselves look like fuckin' prophets all the time by takin' guesses.

Know what I'm sayin'? It's like horoscopes. People expect them to be right so they make the things that happen fit." He squinted. "You get me?"

"Yeah, yeah. I get it. You're right. It's just...you know..."

"I do know, but this is one of the best moments of your life. There are no two people on this planet who deserve to be parents more than you two. You've wanted this for forever. Don't let that psycho ruin it. Be happy, brother! This is great news."

Matt smiled. "Thanks, Joshy Jobs. I am. We both are. I'm not really worried about it. Meg is healthy, I'm healthy. We'll be fine."

"Exactly right."

"To be honest, though, we were both kinda worried about you."

"Me?"

"Yeah. Not about what Beth said. Before that. You've looked distracted lately. And Meg said Mildred hasn't been herself much either." He paused and waited for a response. When Josh didn't offer one, he continued. "You mind if I ask if everything is okay?"

Josh smiled, moved his chair back, and put his feet back on the desk, ankles crossed. A long ten seconds passed in silence, then Josh said, "You ever feel like life is a tuxedo and you're a brown pair of shoes?"

Matt gave a small laugh. "I don't even know what that means."

"Sometimes I feel like...I'm doing me, a hundred percent. But I'm doing it wrong. Know what I mean?"

"Not really. What do you think you're doing wrong?"

"Life, brother."

Matt looked surprised. "Are you crazy? You? You're like my role model."

Josh laughed. "God forbid. You don't know everything."

Matt turned up his hands. "No one knows everything. People never know all that's going on. So what? You deal with it like a champ. I see you as much as your family does, and your attitude and strength never cease to amaze me."

"Yeah." Josh looked at the ceiling. "Tell you the truth, sometimes I hate how much strength being strong takes."

Matt looked at him and didn't know what to say. The office was quiet but for the low sounds of the men talking and moving around downstairs.

Then the tones went off. The Engine had a run. Josh looked at Matt and Matt stayed where he was. Joe Kohler, the senior man in the Engine, spoke over the loudspeaker. "Engine goes, Engine only. EMS assist. 2967 Seventh Avenue, apartment 5 David. Assist EMS with a carry down. Engine only." That was followed by two bells and then it was quiet again. Matt stood and smiled and Josh returned it.

Matt said, "We'll finish this later?"

"Sounds good, brother," Josh answered. But they never spoke of it again.

THE EMS RUN WAS for a forty-nine-year-old male who, by all indications, had suffered a stroke. EMS arrived and determined that he should go to a hospital. He lived on the fifth floor of a walk-up and was more than slightly overweight and unable to walk comfortably on his own.

The two EMTs weren't able to carry him down alone, so they called the fire department for help.

The run came in at five minutes to six p.m., so it was still technically the day tour, but Pete had been relieved by Kohler,

Captain Emmett had been relieved by Matt, and Bahms had been relieved by Jimmy Harris, a red-haired man with long sideburns. When Engine 99 got to the building, only Charles and Kenny recognized the EMTs from the run that morning with the baby. And the EMTs recognized them too.

Towns, the EMT with the purple-tipped dreadlocks, looked up when the guys walked in and smiled. "Hey, guys, thanks for coming. Sorry to bother you."

"No problem at all," Kenny said, pulling on a pair of gloves. "We're bringing this gentleman down?" The patient was already in an EMS chair wrapped in a sheet and secured with straps.

"Yeah. We wouldn't be able to do it, just the two of us."

"Cool. Let's do it." Kenny smiled. "Sir," he said, leaning toward the patient. "We're gonna take you down facing forward. It's gonna feel weird having a chair that you're in being carried, but don't worry. We won't drop you. All you have to do is keep your hands and elbows in and we'll do all the work. Okay? Resist the urge to grab the railing. Trust us. We're not gonna drop you. Got it?"

The man agreed and Kenny rolled the chair through the door of the apartment and to the steps. Matt went down first, a few steps, then Jimmy and Charles went a couple steps, turned, and faced the patient. They both grabbed a small grab bar near the patient's feet. Kenny and the second EMT grabbed one handle each from the back of the chair. Towns grabbed the bags they'd brought in. Jimmy looked at Charles and asked if he was good. He was. Then he asked Kenny if they were good and they were too.

"On your count," Kenny said to Jimmy.

"On three. Two. One. Lift!" The four men lifted the chair straight up, a foot from the ground, and Charles and Jimmy started walking backward. With each step, Matt called

out how many stairs they had before they got to the landing. When they got there, the chair was put down, the men,
stretched, readjusted, made sure everyone was okay, and then
did it all again. It took just under two minutes to get to the
lobby. Once down, the other EMT leaned the chair back on its
wheels and rolled the patient out to the street, then to the back
of the ambulance, where Charles and Jimmy helped him onto
a stretcher.

"Thank you, guys, again," Towns said. "Oh, and nice job
this morning," she said to

Charles and Kenny. "The baby made it."

Charles spun around to Kenny, his face bright. Kenny held
out his fist and Charles punched it. He bit the inside of his
cheeks to keep from smiling too broadly.

"Good job," Kenny said. The men dumbed their gloves and
got on the rig. Kohler sat up front listening to the dispatcher
on the radio and alternately puffing on a cigarette and sipping
a Red Bull. EMS rolled past them and squawked their siren.
Kohler tapped his horn in response, turned off the emergency
lights, and headed back to the firehouse.

WHEN THEY GOT BACK to quarters, Kohler and Jimmy
went over the rig with Charles. They had him tell them what
was in a compartment before he opened the door. Bahms had
done a good job going over it with Charles earlier, so for the
most part he was pretty accurate. That process took longer
than it might have because they were interrupted by two runs.
One EMS and one call for smoke which turned out to be kids
playing with fireworks in the hallway of an apartment building. While they were going over the rig, Josh and Matt were
in their respective offices doing paperwork.

Around nine o'clock they had dinner. Half a chicken a
man with yellow rice, string beans, and biscuits. Kohler had

spent some time in culinary school, and he made a dry rub that made the chicken fantastic. But they weren't at the table for more than five minutes before the tones went off and they were out the door again.

After dinner, Kohler took Charles to the basement for a drill. It was mostly just talk about tactics, but nearly everyone from 99 and 88 went downstairs to watch. Kohler was big and bald and unconsciously tucked his shirt down over his belly and rubbed his head from back to front then back again whenever he paused to think of ways to explain something.

Per Bahms's advice earlier, Charles was in full gear, but he was the only one. It was warmer down there than on the apparatus floor.

In the basement, there were different stations where they could simulate real world scenarios and practice. An open space was used for new Engine probies to practice stretching a line and advancing it. A doorframe held up by steel beams that could be fitted with different types of doors was used to train on forcible entry. One wall held a board of locks where they trained on gaining entry without destroying the door for non-emergency situations. To the right of the forcible entry door, an elevator door where they trained on elevator mechanics, hung from the ceiling. Behind that was a hand-constructed maze, three feet high and three and a half feet wide. The maze had a series of obstacles made to simulate navigating a cluttered apartment with poor visibility. Kohler led Charles to the forcible entry door and leaned against the frame.

"The thing you gotta remember," he said, "is that everyone has a role to play. Things work out best when everyone does their own part. The Engine works as a team and the dick-wagon, I'm sorry, I mean the Truck company, the Ladder, works independently. But we all operate as a cohesive unit. I'm talking specifically about operating at a job right now. Okay?"

"Yes, sir."

"Okay. So let's just go through this," Kohler said, then tucked his shirt and rubbed his head. He pointed at a hose line on the floor by the stairs. "We're gonna stretch that line to this door." He nodded at the forcible entry door. "As the nozzle-man, you want to bring your entire length to the apartment door, all the way up to the coupling, right?"

Charles nodded. "Yes."

"Go ahead."

Charles went to the stairs, picked up the lead length of the practice hose. It was folded back and forth in the shape of a horseshoe. He picked it up from the center and hung it in the crook of his arm like a purse. He walked back to the door, the second length trailing behind him.

Then he dropped the line.

"Get low," Kohler said. "Heat and smoke rise. It's cooler and clearer low down."

Charles knelt and Kohler knelt beside him. The other guys in the basement repositioned themselves to see clearly. Matt stood to the right of the door, crossed his arms, and watched.

Kohler continued. *Tuck. Rub.* "Okay, so, we got the whole first length at the fire door," he said. "Your part is done for now. What does backup need to do?" "Spread it out," Charles said.

"Flake," Kohler answered. "I mean, yes, spread it out, but we don't say spread, we say flake. Right? Go ahead. You wouldn't flake your own length normally, backup would, but for the sake of the drill, show me how you would flake it. We're just bullshitting; it's okay if you fuck up."

Two members of Ladder 88, Joe McCann and Pete "the Greek" Constance, walked over to where Matt was on the other side of the door. When Charles grabbed the hose line to flake it out, Mike Puchane, the senior man in Ladder 88, who everyone called "Pooch," went and joined them. Charles flaked the same way he and Kenny had done earlier in the day for the mattress fire, making an S shape with the line. When he was done, he knelt again.

"You feel good about that?" McCann asked.

Charles looked at his work. "Yes, sir."

"Joe. Not sir."

Jimmy laughed. "He's met, like, a dozen Joes today."

"That should make it easier to remember," McCann said.

"In a fire, it gets hard to see," the Greek said, interrupting them. "If it gets bad and you need to bail, the hose line is also your way out. You just get a hand on it and follow it back out to the hallway or out of the building." He pointed at the S shape Charles had made on the floor. "The back and forth is unnecessary. Just make it a straight run if you can. If not, just one turn will do. Understand?"

"Yes, sir. I mean…"

"No, that's fine," the Greek said. "You can call me sir."

AFTER CHARLES DID IT again, Pooch discussed everyone's role in a fire and why it was important that everyone did their own job.

When he was done, Kohler said, "Everyone has different roles to play. The dick-wagon forces entry, finds the location of the fire, and isolates it if they can. They vent the smoke from the roof and the windows and search for civilians. But none of that will matter if the Engine doesn't get the hose line in position and in operation. Water puts out fire. As the nozzleman, if you don't do your part, the job doesn't get done. Got it?"

"Got it."

"Good." He wiped his forehead. "Now let's get out of here, I'm sweating my balls off."

They put things back as they were, then headed up the narrow stairwell. Charles noticed a wooden plaque above the doorframe, just below a dim fluorescent light. Everyone reached up and slapped it once they were under it. The wood was faded and grimy from years of dust and sweat. The words on it were carved by hand. Pooch did the carving and did a good job at it. It was the first time Charles had seen the plaque, but he recognized the words from a motto he'd heard at the fire academy: *Let No Man's Ghost Return To Say My Training Let Me Down.*

FOR THE REST OF the night shift, there were only a handful of calls. One came at three in the morning. A prank call. When the tones went off, the guys working were annoyed, but not very surprised.

-16-

MONDAY AFTERNOON, AFTER THEY'D left the school, Hanna told Candace she was

going to run home to get a change of clothes and maybe pack a bag so she could spend the night for a few days. She promised to bring back dinner, then hugged Candace and waved down a cab.

Candace walked home in a funk. It had only been four days since she kicked Alan out, but she felt as if the whole world had changed. It felt overwhelming. Too many problems needed to be addressed and she didn't know where to start.

By the time she'd gotten to her building, it was all too much. She grabbed the mail from her mailbox in the lobby, made her way to the sixth floor, and accidentally dropped her cellphone when she reached for her keys. Then she broke down.

She sunk to the floor, dropping her bag and the mail, and cried. She wasn't aware how loud her sobs were, but at that moment she didn't care. Behind her, a lock turned, and she looked around. Her neighbor, Mrs. Tabacco, stood just inside her apartment, frowning. She considered Candace for a second, then started to shut her door. Candace turned away, leaned her head against the railing, and closed her eyes. Didn't hear the door close.

She opened her eyes again and was startled to find her neighbor standing beside her. Mrs. Tabacco was a weathered woman, with white hair and leathery skin. She was wet from sweat and the honey-colored dress she wore clung to her body. She looked frail, but with a vitality in her eyes. Maybe not a physical strength, but strength nonetheless. Stamina.

The older woman got carefully to her knees and started gathering the mail.

"Oh. Oh, no. Thank you," Candace said, rising. "Please, it's okay. I'll get it."

Mrs. Tabacco leaned back and rested her hands on her thighs. "It's Johnson, right?"

"Yes, ma'am. Candace."

"My name is Sheryl."

Candace smiled and wiped her face. "I know."

"Is your husband home?"

Tears welled up in Candace's eyes and she wiped them away before they fell. "No, ma'am."

Sheryl nodded. "Come inside. Have some iced tea." She rached up and grabbed the railing to pull herself up and Candace stood and helped her. When Sheryl was on her feet, Candace stooped and gathered her things, then the two women went inside, and Sheryl closed the door behind them.

MRS. TABACCO—SHERYL—POINTED to a sofa behind a small, neat coffee table and invited Candace to sit. Candace headed that way and looked around. It occurred to her that this was the first time she had been in another apartment in the building. Sheryl's apartment was a mirror image of her own. The kitchen was on the left, a few feet from the entrance, whereas

Candace's was on the right. The living room was parallel to the entrance and the bathroom was through a door off the upper left corner of the living room. The bedroom was a smaller space than the living room, but a decent size, and it was along the right wall. The far wall in the bedroom separated Sheryl's apartment from Candace's. Because the only windows in the bedrooms led to a fire escape, tenants weren't allowed to put air conditioners in them, so both bedrooms were equipped with ceiling fans. Sheryl's bedroom door was open and Candace noticed a table fan facing the head of the bed and felt a flash of sorrow. Someone Sheryl's age shouldn't have to suffer this heat.

Sheryl busied herself in the kitchen getting glasses and ice and pulling a pitcher from the fridge. Candace smiled. She thought old ladies making pitchers of iced tea or lemonade only happened in shows on TV-Land or the Hallmark channel. And even if it really was a thing, Sheryl Tabacco was the last person she would expect to do it. Maybe if she were hosting guests, but even that was an odd thought. Sheryl wasn't the friendliest neighbor. In fact, she had a reputation in the building for being the mean old lady married to the sweet old man. At least until he passed away last year. It felt odd to Candace to be sitting in Sheryl's living room waiting for tea. Still, Candace thought this might be the most visitor-ready home she had ever been in.

"Kevin used to love iced tea."

Candace was in the center of the sofa, looking underneath the coffee table, astonished by how clean it was. "I'm sorry?"

"Kevin. My husband." Sheryl nodded at a photo on the TV stand. A younger version of herself and a good-looking man stood by a bridge, smiling broadly.

"Oh, my goodness! That's you?" Candace asked. She stood and walked over to the stand. "You look so beautiful. You guys looked great," she said, picking up the photo. "What occasion was this?"

Sheryl carried two glasses over to the couch and set them on the coffee table, then sat down. "That was the day before my birthday. Almost forty years ago."

"You look so happy."

"We were."

Candace put the frame back where she got it, careful to do it neatly, then sat down next to Sheryl. She took one of the glasses, sipped from it, and coughed. Very sweet. "Thank you for this," she said, clearing her throat.

Sheryl looked at her and nodded. "Are you happy?" she asked flatly. Candace looked up, surprised. "Right now," Sheryl said. "Are you happy? You know what I'm asking."

Candace looked away. She watched the cubes of ice in her glass and thought about the last few days. "No. Not right now."

"Where's your husband?"

A pause. "I'm not sure."

"Is that why you were crying?"

Candace put the glass down on the coffee table. It was a light-colored wood and there was a ring of perspiration from when Sheryl had put it down earlier. Candace put it back on the same spot. "Not exactly," she answered.

"But he's the reason?"

"Yes. I guess."

Sheryl shook her head. "That's no good." She turned to the photo on the TV stand. "Kevin and I had a routine. We lived every day the same way for over thirty years. It's why I still make a pitcher of tea for two when there's only one to drink it. I'm stuck in the past." She turned and faced Candace. "The past can be seductive. We always wanna go back to the good times. But life don't work that way. You can't start over. People nowadays don't get that. You can't start over. You can start again, but you can't start over. You gotta do right the first

147

time or you gotta learn from your mistakes and do better the next time. A marriage, a *real* marriage, has love and respect and…" She paused, searching for a word. "Reliability. You can't do that over. If it's not done right the first time, there's no need pretending it'll change."

Tears welled up in Candace's eyes again and she looked up to keep them from falling.

"We split up. I kicked him out."

"Drink some tea," Sheryl said. Candace reached over and took another sip, and the sugar shock helped. She wiped her eyes. Sheryl pushed herself up and stepped from behind the coffee table. "Come with me."

Candace put her glass down again and the two women walked into the bedroom, which was pristine. The bed looked like a showcase in a furniture store. Against the wall that separated the two apartments stood a dresser, maybe four feet tall. On top were two plants on either side and between them, an urn. Candace didn't know how to react. She folded her hands in front of her and lowered her head.

Sheryl stood in front of the urn with her back to Candace. "I don't know what he did. Your husband. But I see you two all the time and I've never seen on you what happiness should look like," she said. "I've seen plenty from him that I wouldn't put up with. A lot that I wouldn't have to 'cause Kevin would never cause me to." She put one hand on the dresser, just in front of the urn. "A woman should only shed tears *for* her husband. Not because of him," she said, quietly.

HANNA BROUGHT BACK A bucket of chicken, corn on the cob, potato wedges, and coleslaw. They worked on opposite sides of the kitchen getting the things they'd need. Candace got the plates and utensils, Hanna some bottled waters from the fridge and paper towels off the roll. They carried those things over to the table by the couch and set them down. Hanna pulled a wedge from the bag and closed her eyes when she ate it. She smiled contently, and when she opened her eyes again, Candace grinned at her. Neither woman spoke for a moment, then Candace stepped forward and they hugged.

"Thank you for being here," Candace said.

"Every time."

THEY ATE THEN STACKED the dishes and water bottles somewhat neatly on the table. Afterwards they watched episodes of *Game of Thrones* on HBO MAX until they fell asleep and had weird dreams. At a few minutes after three in the morning, the buzzer from the doorbell downstairs woke them.

Hanna had dreamt about fighting an army of swordsmen empty-handed and woke up defensive. Candace just sat forward. This was now the third night in a row that her doorbell buzzed. She wasn't expecting it, but she wasn't surprised either.

For a minute, the two women, just sat on the couch in the glow of the TV screen, wiping their eyes or rubbing their faces. When the bell buzzed again, Hanna moaned and mumbled, "I really, really hate him."

Candace leaned forward, put her hands on her thighs, and pushed herself up. She ambled to the door and buzzed the fire department in.

Hanna stood and stretched, then started grabbing the dishes and the garbage. Candace stood by the door and waited for the knock. She heard their heavy gear on the last flight of stairs and felt bad. What a waste of their time this was.

There was a knock on the door, then a familiar voice. "Fire Department!"

TWENTY MINUTES BEFORE THAT knock, Alan was on a bench across the street staring at the window. He had been there over an hour but wasn't aware of it. He'd been preoccupied with more important things.

Like earlier.

He hadn't actually been arrested. Two police officers arrived and simply grabbed his arms above the elbows and escorted him out. He was smart enough not to put up a fight.

They put him in the back of a squad car and took him a few streets down to the precinct. On the way there, one of the officers pulled up his rap sheet and saw his two priors: one for possession, the other for disorderly conduct. He was an addict and a drunk they figured, but he wasn't either of those things today. Because he hadn't resisted when they escorted him out, and because, in the school, he hadn't really attacked anyone, as far as the two officers were concerned, Alan hadn't done anything that he could be arrested for.

All the same, they took him to the precinct to impress upon him the seriousness of participating in a disturbance at a school.

When he left the precinct, he called a kid who worked the streets in Washington Heights and Harlem. He bought an eight ball of coke from him, then went to the bathroom in the park behind the soccer field on 135th Street. He'd been there for longer than he intended, and when he'd finally left, both the coke and the sun were gone.

He had gone to Ritechek, sat on his crate, and put his phone to charge. Not five minutes later, he left and sat across from his building. He lay his hands at his sides, palms up on the bench, looked up at the glow in his window, and didn't move. His mind went a lot of places that had no connection to each other and ended up back in the school. Something was wrong there.

He'd been to the school before, and they'd never stopped him from going in. What were they hiding?

His hands clenched. He was upset and uncomfortable. And gross. He'd been in the same clothes for three days, now. He was sitting outside in the middle of the night, sweating his balls off, while Hanna was probably in his living room relaxing on his couch, no care in the world.   He leaned forward and wrung his hands. Then he stood and thought about the payphone. The calls were starting to feel childish, but he had to do something. What else was there? He started to head to the payphone on 145th but changed his mind.

Imagining Candace and Hanna upset wouldn't be enough tonight.

Alan crossed the street, headed to the door of his building, and yanked the handle. It didn't budge and he didn't really expect it to, but he had to try. He looked around for someone he may know. No one at all. He shook his head and cursed. Nothing ever worked right for him. He turned back to the door and tried the handle again. No luck.

He could break one of the windowpanes in the door. That was a thought. Everyone was asleep, so no one would see him. He looked around for something to use, and as he did, a guy came out of the building looking down at his cellphone. He almost bumped into Alan, but glanced up in time to side-step him, and Alan ran forward and caught the door just as the latch touched the door frame. He pushed it open and was inside.

At the foot of the stairs, he looked up and sighed. It wasn't just the trek up that he was thinking of. This was a risk. Cellphones could be traced. But it was a chance he had to take. He needed this.

Alan wiped the screen of his phone on his shirt, then pushed the home button. After entering his code, he tapped the phone icon and the keypad came up. He stared at the screen, thinking twice.

He had to do it.

He tapped the three buttons, then pressed the phone icon again and held the phone to his ear.

"9-1-1, what's your emergency?"

CANDACE OPENED THE DOOR to a familiar face. The lieutenant looked tired again, but not like he was sleepy. Like he had a lot on his plate. His name, if she remembered correctly, was Josh. The last time he was there he had called someone and spoken in some kind of military or radio code and the person had responded, "Ten-four, Josh."

Now, he was with two guys she hadn't seen before, and the three men knew they were there for no good reason.

"Good morning, ma'am," Josh said.

Candace smiled apologetically. "Hi, guys. Josh, right?"

He laughed, eyebrows raised. "Yeah, Josh. It's crazy, right? I've seen you more in the last few days than I've seen my own wife!"

Candace laughed too, even though it wasn't funny. Hanna came beside her and smiled.

Candace said, "I'm really sorry." They were whispering— Candace because she didn't want to wake Sheryl, and Josh, she figured, out of reflex politeness. "I don't know what to do. I thought he was in jail. I don't know how to stop him from calling."

"Forgive him, that's how. Take him back," Josh joked. Candace smiled, and looked away. Josh reached in and touched her shoulder. "That was a bad joke. I'm sorry."

Candace shook her head. "No, I'm the one who's sorry. You guys have important things to do. I feel terrible you've gotta keep coming here." She looked past him at the other two men. "You guys want, I don't know, can I offer you something to drink or something? Water? I have orange juice…"

"And beer," Hanna added.

They laughed and the other two passed on the offer, then headed downstairs.

Josh leaned away from the open door toward the stairwell that led to the roof. "8-8 to Battalion 5, ten-ninety-two."

"Ten-four, Josh."

Josh turned back and shrugged. "Well. See you tomorrow night, I guess." They all laughed, and he said, "Good night, ma'am."

Candace smiled, still apologetic. "Candace."

Josh smiled back. "Have a good night, Candace."

"Good night, Josh."

He turned, glanced over at the stairs going up to the roof, smiled again, then headed down. Candace watched until he was gone from view, then closed the door.

ALAN WAS IN FRONT of the bulkhead door, at the top of the stairs that led to the roof. He'd called 911 from the lobby, then hung up and ran up there to wait. He heard the firemen come up to his apartment and he heard conversation when the door opened, but they were speaking low.

He couldn't make out what they were saying, but no one sounded very upset. His position was no good, he needed to hear better. Had to get closer. It was a risk, but if he didn't hear or see what was happening, what was the point? He tiptoed down a few steps from the landing and looked below.

There were three firemen. Two stood near the stairwell, barely paying attention, and the third, probably the boss, was right at the door, laughing.

Laughing?

Alan still couldn't hear what was being said, but he saw the fire boss laughing and he heard Candace laugh in response. What the hell was going on?

Candace said something, and the boss answered, and Alan heard nothing. They were whispering. They were *trying* not to be heard. Why, though? What was so damn important it had to be secret?

Then the boss reached in and touched her. Alan couldn't see her, so he couldn't tell exactly where, but wherever it was, he touched it for a long time. Was he caressing her face? Her hair? Who the hell was this guy!

Candace said something and the other two guys smiled and started down the stairs. They were giving the boss some privacy!

Boiling, Alan started down to confront them, but stopped when the boss turned toward him and spoke into a radio on his chest. Whoever he spoke to responded and he turned back to the apartment. Alan eased down another two steps, not completely worried about being seen. He had to know.

The boss smiled into the apartment and shrugged and said something that Alan didn't catch. Down another step. Necessary. Candace said something in response and the fire boss's smile spread.

He said, "Have a good night, Candace."

Then, in a moment that Alan would replay in his mind too many times over the next twenty-four hours, from inside the apartment, Candace said, "Good night, Josh."

The boss, *Josh*, turned to go downstairs, then looked up and looked straight at Alan.

And smiled.

The fucking asshole.

-17-

TUESDAY MORNING, CHARLES HAD two pots of coffee made, half a dozen eggs boiling, a pre-wipe set up in the bathroom on the main floor, and was scrambling eight eggs for French toast when Joe Bahms came in. They shook hands and Bahms asked him how the night tour went. Charles told him about the drill in the basement and the prank call for fire at 8989 Douglas Boulevard.

Bahms shook his head. "That dude called again? The bosses need to report him to the Marshals. It's been every night." Charles nodded but didn't say anything, and Bahms changed course. "Anyway. You completed your first night tour and your first twenty-four and you're still up bright and early getting it done in the kitchen. Nice."

Charles smiled and thought about that, surprised he wasn't more tired. In fact, the way he felt, he could've worked another shift and have been okay, he thought. He was in a good mood.

Part of it was having heard that the baby from yesterday was okay and knowing that he'd helped. But a bigger part was the drill in the basement. That everyone had come down to participate. Like they were a team. Like his success mattered to them. There was a little pressure in that, but there was also excitement. Genuine excitement.

"And now you have the day off," Bahms said. "Got any plans?"

"No. Not really. I wasn't expecting to be off."

"Well, enjoy it," Bahms said. He grabbed a paper towel from the dispenser and wiped his forehead underneath a Yankees cap. "You got a girl or something?"

"Um, no. Not yet." Charles smiled. "Maybe I'll work on that today."

"Nice touch."

ON THE DRIVE HOME, he called Libby. His phone was hooked up to his speakers via

Bluetooth and the ring sounded throughout the car. After the fourth ring, he looked at the screen on his dashboard and worried that it might be too early, but just as he went to end the call, Libby picked up.

"Hey!"

"Hey," Charles said, smiling about the excitement in her voice. "How are you?"

"Good. Just making breakfast. How was your first day! Was it amazing? Did you slide down the pole?"

Charles laughed. "No. There wasn't any pole sliding for me yesterday. But it was a pretty interesting day anyway."

"Tell me all about it. Or do I have to wait 'til the weekend when I see you?"

"I will tell you, but I was hoping I could tell you in person today. I could get you for lunch around one?"

Charles thought he heard her smile. After a small pause, she said, "Make it two."

CHARLES LIVED IN HAMILTON Heights, a fifteen-minute drive from the firehouse barring unusual traffic. Half an hour after his call with Libby, he was home and changed and drinking a blend of oat milk, peanut butter, blackberries, bananas, and ice. He sat in a cushioned office chair that once belonged to his father and leaned back far enough to get the glass at an angle that the foamy sludge at the bottom could make its way down to his mouth. At that angle he could see the time on the microwave behind him. Barely ten o'clock.

He called his mother. She worked from home, and she picked up on the first ring. She sounded sleepy, and when Charles asked her about it, she told him that she hadn't slept well. She had tossed and turned throughout the night until about three, before giving up on sleep, she said. For the rest of the pre-daylight hours, she read her Bible or listened to an all-news station on the radio.

"Are you feeling okay?" Charles asked.

"Um…yeah. I'm okay. You know I've had this cough for a couple of weeks. I had a fit

Sunday where it wouldn't stop. I think I pulled a muscle in my back or something."

"Should you go to the doctor? Do you only feel it when you cough?"

"No, I feel it when I'm laying down too. That's why I was tossing and turning. I wasn't in pain, but I was, I don't know…I couldn't get comfortable."

"Huh," Charles grunted. "It must suck being old."

She sighed. "What do you want?"

He laughed, then told her about his day. He told her about the calls and the training and the people he'd worked with. He told her how he didn't think Fagan liked him.

"Why?"

"Why doesn't he like me, or why don't I think he does?"

"Why wouldn't he like you?"

"I don't know. It just seems like that. He seemed, I don't know, angry. Or unfriendly. I don't know."

She said, "What does his being angry or unfriendly have

to do with you?"

Charles shrugged even though she couldn't see it. "I don't know. Nothing."

"Then why would you think he doesn't like you?"

Charles paused, then said, "I don't want to say 'I don't know' again. I feel silly."

"That's 'cause you're being silly. If he's angry or unfriendly—which he probably isn't— it's the way he is. He's not those things because of you. There's no reason to think he doesn't like you."

"No, I—"

"And there's no reason for you to operate like he doesn't. You need to be the best coworker and firefighter and rookie you can be. And that's it. What more could you do at that point?"

"Okay," Charles said. He leaned forward on the edge of his chair and put his empty glass on the floor beside him.

"Have more confidence," his mom said. "And faith. Confidence in yourself and faith in God. Stop worrying about failing so much. That isn't a job where you should walk around doubting yourself. You wouldn't be there if you weren't ready, right? You wouldn't have made it out of the academy."

"Right."

"So, don't worry so much."

"Okay," Charles said, and smiled sadly. He should've invited her to the graduation. "Thank you. You're my favorite old lady."

"So funny. I'm hanging up now."

TWO O'CLOCK IN THE afternoon on a July day in New York City during a heatwave was an uncomfortable time to be outside unless you were at a beach or in a pool. Or sitting at a table under the shade of an umbrella with ice cold drinks in front of you, like Charles and Libby were.

Charles had picked her up from the bakery fifteen minutes before two. She wasn't working, but her mom and another employee, Serena, were. After an introduction to Serena and some small talk, Charles and Libby got into his car and drove five minutes to a restaurant in Lincoln Center.

They had a choice of sitting outside, inside at the bar, or waiting up to half an hour for a booth. They chose to sit outside and immediately ordered iced drinks: a virgin Piña Colada for

Charles and a frozen margarita for Libby. They ordered appetizers and picked off each other's plates because Libby started it.

As they ate, Charles told her all about his first day. She sat frozen with a mozzarella stick halfway to her mouth during the story about the baby in the bedroom. She smiled broadly and stirred her drink absentmindedly while he told her how they made a training session out of helping him with his tire. She interrupted the story about the second-due fire with half a dozen questions; and when he told her about the prank caller calling in fake fires, she sat back and sighed.

"Wow. I'm exhausted just from listening."

Charles gave a half shrug and took a drink of water to hide his smile. He was glad for her reactions. He hadn't taken credit or boasted about anything, but after going through it all for someone who was happy to hear it, he felt a sense of ac-complishment. He said, "Yeah. So, you know…all in a day's work."

Libby smiled. "A day in the life of a fireman."

"Well, hopefully not every day," Charles said.

Their waiter came by and refilled their water glasses.

"Second-due fires are bad, right?" Libby asked.

"What do you mean?"

"Like, they're worse than first-due. Bigger or something. Requiring more people?"

Charles frowned, then smiled and nodded. "I think you're thinking of second alarms."

Her face brightened and she nodded. "Yeah. What does that mean, that it's bad?"

"Yeah, I guess. It means that it requires more people. More firefighters. A first alarm is the initial call. It's three Engines, two Ladders, and a chief. A second alarm is just that same thing again. So three more Engines and two more chiefs, I mean, two more Ladders. Get it?" She nodded and he nodded back. He put his glass down and leaned forward, his forearms on the table. "So. Tell me about your dog."

Libby laughed and used her straw to fish a piece of ice from her glass and popped it in her mouth to suck on. "It's not a great story," she mumbled around the cube. "It's not a story at all, really. It's not a dog either." She laughed again. "It's a cat."

Charles laughed too, but it was forced. He was confused. "Your dog is a cat?"

"No, my cat is a cat. And her name is Dog."

He laughed for real this time. "Why?"

Libby held a hand to her chest and the other hand up, a signal for him to hold on as she chewed the ice. She did, then said "Because I wanted to name her Polly, but my mom said that Polly was a bird's name." With the ice in her mouth, she sounded like a Muppet, and Charles smiled. "So then I wanted to name her Goldy because she's light brown, but my mom said that

Goldy was a fish's name. So I was annoyed and I just called her Cat and my mom said that I was being silly, so I said fine, her name is Dog. And she thought I was joking or being stubborn or something, but it's been Dog ever since."

160

Charles stared at her, half amused, half astonished. Libby shrugged as she separated another piece of ice from the rest with her straw. After a deliberate moment, she looked up and met his eyes.

"You're insane," he said.

"Better you know now, right?" she answered. Charles smiled again and Libby popped another piece of ice into her mouth. "You're welcome," she mumbled.

AFTER LUNCH, THEY WALKED from Lincoln Center to Central Park and found an empty bench in the shade. In the grass behind them, two women and two men were laying on sheets in bikinis and swimming trunks. Across the walkway, behind the benches parallel to them, three men in pork pie hates and three-piece suits with no ties played the song "On the Sunny Side of the Street" from a trumpet, an organ, and a four-piece drum set. The trumpet's carry case was open and filled with crumpled up dollar bills and coins. Charles and Libby watched them for a while, sitting side by side, and then Charles asked Libby about her father.

"If you tell me you don't wanna talk about it, I'll be cool with it and never ask again, but I figured I should try to, you know, understand what…I don't know. I couldn't figure out…I don't know. Never mind."

Libby smiled but didn't answer. She kept looking at the band, but her eyes were unfocused. The organist was singing now.

…get your hat. Leave your worries on the doorstep.
Just direct your feet, to the sunny side of the street…

Charles regretted asking. He wanted to change the subject. He said, "You know, one of the things…" Then stopped because at the same time she started to say, "My mom's husband…" But then she stopped.

161

Libby: "Sorry, what?"

Charles: "No, you go ahead. I was just trying to change the subject."

Libby looked at him kindly. Then she turned away and continued. "My mom's husband is who I call my dad, but neither of them are my real parents. I know my birth mom died when I was a baby. If you're asking about my birth father, I don't know anything about him. But my dad, my mom's husband, he's in Polinairre Medical Center." She paused, looked at her hands, then continued. "He worked in an office in lower Manhattan in 2001. He was in the North

Tower, getting breakfast when the plane hit." She turned to him and smiled sadly. "Firefighters got him out."

Charles smiled back. "That's awesome," he said. She faced forward again, toward the band.

I used to walk, in the shade, with my blues on parade…

She said, "I was a child. I only vaguely remember it. They only had me for a year at that point and I remember having been a handful of places before. There were always adults in and out of my life, so afterward, when…" She stopped and shook her head. "I'm sorry, is this a lot? Is this too, you know, deep for a second date?"

"No, please. Not at all," he answered. "Afterward when what?"

Libby took a second to remember her train of thought, then said, "I didn't really know that he wasn't around. He was in the hospital for a few days after the eleventh, but not seeing him didn't mean anything to me because that was normal, you know?"

"Yeah, I get it."

"Anyway, I didn't realize it 'til I got older, but my mom and I became really close then.

She needed me and I liked being needed. My dad's wounds

and fractures healed and eventually he went back to work. But he kept going down to the site to volunteer, like serving food and drinks at the tables people set up near Ground Zero. Every September we go to the firehouse of the guys who got him out and sit in on their memorial service. They didn't lose anybody from their house, but they lost a lot of friends from other houses, so they have a service every anniversary and we go. My mom and I bake pastries and Dad donates a collection from his job to their foundation.

"Last year, Dad was diagnosed with a form of cancer that the doctors attributed to the time he spent down there. It's in his lungs. They discovered it, like, the Monday after Thanksgiving last year, and it didn't seem terrible, but by the new year it was, like, stage four or something." She shook her head again. "My mom...if you didn't know there was something wrong, you would never figure it out by looking at her. I don't know if it's strength, I don't think it is. Not really. I think she just doesn't know how to respond to the fear of losing him. She doesn't know what to do. So she's telling herself he's gonna be fine, you know?"

"I get it," Charles said. He was thinking of his mom. "What do the doctors say? Is it possible he *will* be fine?"

Libby didn't answer. She stared at her hands, then sat up straight and looked up, trying not to blink. The sun had moved across the sky and their bench was now only half in shade. Charles reached over her lap and took her hand, and she interlocked her fingers with his.

"You can change the subject now," she said, then blinked, and tears rolled down her cheeks.

Can't you hear, a pitter-pat?
And that happy tune is your step.
Life can be so sweet, on the sunny side of the street.

-18-

THAT EVENING, ALAN FOUND himself sprawled on a bench in the subway. He hadn't been asleep, but he hadn't really been conscious either. He'd been inside his head, tangled up in a combination of genuine memories of the last few days and horrible imagined images of Candace cheating with that fire boss. Captain Asshole.

Alan pushed himself upright and got his feet beneath him. He looked around the station, perplexed. Look at what Candace had done to him. He'd spent the whole day laid out on a subway bench like a legit bum. It was pure luck that he was okay. He could've woken up robbed or in jail. Or dead.

The station felt muggy and disgusting. Alan looked himself over and shook his head, angry. He slapped his thigh with his fist. What had he ever done to deserve this? Hadn't he been a good husband? Wasn't he there for Candace years ago when she lost their baby? Hadn't he provided for her? How could she betray him like this!

He hit his thigh again. And again. When he felt the pain in his leg, he took a long, deep breath and released it slowly. And felt a little better. A little, not much. Not enough. He needed a drink and a shower. And some time to think.

ALAN RANG THE BELL for Rob's apartment, already annoyed because he knew he'd have to jump through hoops to convince him. He didn't know if Rob would even let him in the building, but he rang the bell anyway and a moment latter the buzzer sounded, and the lock released.

Surprised, Alan pushed through the door into the lobby. Rob lived on the third floor, which wasn't a great hike, but Alan called the elevator. The number on the display showed the elevator on five, and when he pushed the button, gears shifted and groaned, and after a second, the number changed to four, then three. When it got to one, it took a few seconds for the inside door to open, and during that time a delivery man pulled up on a bicycle outside and hopped off. He removed a chain from the back of his bike and locked it up before grabbing a bag hanging from the handles. Alan turned away from him, stepped into the elevator, and pushed three. He wasn't being a dick, but he didn't feel like waiting for the dude to get inside the building.

Alan stepped off the elevator on the third floor and walked left to Rob's apartment. The door opened before he got there, and Jackie poked her head out. The expressions on her face cycled through surprise, confusion, understanding, then anger all in the space of a couple of seconds. She clenched her jaw, squinted her eyes, and called, "Robert!" Then turned away and disappeared inside.

Rob came to the door a second later. He stepped halfway out, surprise on his face, and said, "What's up, man? What're you doin' here?"

"You won't believe the shit that's been going on," Alan said. He ran his hand across his head and put on his best stressed-out face. "I just need a hot shower and a clean shirt. And a cold drink."

Rob glanced over his shoulder. "I'll get you a shirt and I'll meet you at Mikey's for a drink in a couple hours. But you know you can't shower right now, dude."

Alan closed his eyes and shook his head. "Rob, I need a break. You don't know the crap I've been through," he said. "I know Jackie doesn't like me, I get it, but I don't got nowhere else to go, man. You gotta help me out."

Behind them, the delivery man who Alan saw outside came up the stairs. He looked at a paper on the bag he was carrying, then up at the labels on the door.

Rob stepped all the way out and raised his hand. "Over here, boss."

The delivery guy hurried over and nodded at both men. He checked the paper again and said, "Fourteen seventy-nine."

Rob gave him a twenty-dollar bill and told him to keep it, and the delivery man held his hand up in thanks, then turned away and headed back to the stairs.

Alan shook his head again. "Shit. You're about to eat. I didn't know. My bad, dude. I didn't know." He turned away and started toward the stairs, head bowed. Rob stopped him.

"You're killing me, man," Rob said. "You know that right?"

Alan stood up straight and smiled. "I know."

JACKIE WAS NOT HAPPY. Not at all. When Alan walked in, she stood up, grabbed the TV remote, turned off the television, then stormed into the bedroom, remote still in hand. The two men looked at each other in silence for a moment before the door opened again. Jackie walked out straight to Rob, eyes on Alan. She snatched the food from Rob's hands, then went back into the room and slammed the door.

"Damn," Alan said, staring after her.

Rob shook his head and sighed. "Killing me."

THEY WERE IN MIKEY G's a few hours later, just after ten p.m. Alan had washed the smelly parts of himself in Rob's bathroom and was given a bright blue t-shirt that said "Viva Costa Rica" on the front. Jackie had brought it back from her sister Camille's bachelorette cruise two years ago. Camille still wasn't married.

The pub wasn't very busy, with only half the booths occupied and one other customer at the bar. Rob was nursing a Moscow Mule and was subtly watching the redhead bartender. She was less subtle about watching Alan, who was on his third Manhattan, the whiskey fueling his emotion. The bouncer at the other end of the bar was also monitoring the situation.

Alan told Rob about what he saw the night before, from the top of the stairs, and about the incident in the school. He had a theory that the only reason the school security guard stopped him from going up to see Candace was because the captain was there too, and they were trying to hide it. The very thought disgusted him, and he said, twice, "What kind of a person has an affair in an elementary school?"

Rob took a sip of his vodka and dragged his attention away from the redhead. "AJ, you're not makin' sense. You're sayin' she was foolin' around at her job with kids in the room *and* her friend?"

"What?"

"You just said the guard called for Candace, but Hanna came down. Hanna was in the room while she was foolin' around with the captain? That don't make any sense."

"Why? Hanna doesn't like me. She's probably happy Candy's cheating on me with that asshole."

Rob gave up and faced forward again. "I don't know, man. It sounds crazy. Anyway, if it's true, it's your fault."

"What!" Alan was louder than he probably intended, and the bouncer sat up straight and fixed him with a stern look. He didn't notice, but Rob did.

Rob said, "Relax, dude. I'm just sayin' I don't think she's messin' around with anybody, but if she is with the captain, she only met him after you called in a fire the first time, right?"

Alan scrambled. "No, I told you. I heard her talking about it once. Around Valentine's Day. Remember? Her school had career day the day before, and when I got home, I heard her talking on the phone about him. Remember?"

Rob didn't answer. He didn't remember because it was bullshit. Alan wasn't a great liar, but he thought he was.

THEY LEFT THE PUB when Rob finished his drink. A strategic move on his part. Alan was becoming more emotional as the night went on, and Rob thought it best to leave on their own before red or the bouncer "asked" them to.

Rob sent Jackie a text as they walked along 125th Street but didn't get a response. It was nearly eleven o'clock and there was a possibility that she was sleeping, but it was more likely she was mad. Rob felt bad, but at the moment, he was more worried about Alan than he was about her.

They stopped and bought a bottle of vodka and a one-liter bottle of water, then mostly emptied the water. They ended up on a stoop only a couple of blocks down from Alan's building, and though the windows from Alan's apartment couldn't be seen from where they sat, Alan looked in that direction and spoke as if he could.

"Why should he get her? Why should Captain Asshole have her? Afterall I've done for her. I put a ring on her finger!" He cracked the knuckles of one hand with the palm of the other.

"It's not right."

Rob took a decent-sized gulp from the bottle and bit his

tongue, then passed the bottle to Alan. There was nothing for him to say. His job here was just to be an ear for Alan to do the talking. Alan took the bottle and a sizeable gulp himself and coughed.

"I love her, man. It's not right." He shook his head. "I won't lose her to that jerk. I'd kill them first."

Rob sat up and snatched the bottle away. "AJ, man!" Rob said, startled both by what he'd heard and how it made him feel. "What's wrong with you? You gotta chill with this."

Alan turned to him and laughed. "What?"

"Do you hear yourself, man? You know what would've happened if you said that at the bar?"

Alan laughed again. "Relax, dude. I'm just talking. You know I'm not serious." He wiped his mouth with the back of his hand, leaned back on his forearms, and stared at his building.

Rob watched him, worried. Alan wasn't a great liar, but he thought he was.

-19-

THE NEXT DAY WAS supposed to be a day off for
Charles, but a little after seven in the morning, the chief's aide
called him and asked if he wanted to work the day shift on
overtime. Charles said yes, got out of bed, rushed his normal
morning routine, and was out of the house in eighteen minutes. He was at the supermarket fifteen minutes after that and
in the firehouse just after eight a.m.

He went in through the side door and stopped when he
saw everyone hanging out in the seating area behind the
Truck. He felt an unreasonable flutter of anxiety but took a
breath, shook himself. and headed toward the kitchen. saying
a general "good morning" in the direction of the group.

"Whoa, whoa, whoa!"

Charles stopped again and looked over. He recognized
most of the faces but not everyone. Bahms wasn't there. Kenny was and he was smiling. Fagan was too, but there was no
smile on his face. Neither the charming nor the scary one.

"Morning?" An older man Charles hadn't seen before
checked his watch. "The day tour is damn near over, what do
you mean, morning?"

Charles felt his cheeks flush. He didn't respond.

"You're the probie, right? David or something?" The guy
was smiling broadly. He had a strong New York accent spoken

with TV Italian mannerisms. He hadn't said much but he used his hands when he said it.

"Yes, sir," Charles answered. "Charles Davids."

"Two first names? That's fucked up. That's gonna be hard to remember, kid. How 'bout I just call you probie 'til I get used to you? You cool with that?" Everyone on and around the couches were smiling and Charles realized he was too. He liked this guy.

"Yes, sir. That's fine."

The guy turned to Kenny, chuckling. "I like when they're new. They're so polite and sweet." He said. "Remember when you were that young? Remember when you used to say, 'Yes, sir,' and, 'No, sir,' to me? Huh? Now I ask you a favor and you're like, 'Fuck off, Lieu, you fat piece o' shit.'"

Everyone laughed and the lieutenant turned back to Charles. "Jack Varmitt," he said, holding out his hand. "But you gotta call me Lieutenant or Lieu, I guess, or you'll get in trouble with these guys."

"Nice to meet you, sir." Charles stepped over and shook his hand.

"Don't forget my name now, alright? I can forget your name, but don't you forget my fucking name. Alright? That's Varmitt. Two Ts."

Charles laughed. "I won't forget."

"Good. Now, what's in the bag? What'd you bring?"

"I got a pound of bacon and a bag of grapes, sir."

"No eggs!"

Charles laughed. "No, sir. Sorry."

The lieutenant shook his head dramatically, still smiling. He looked at Kenny again,

"Kenny, c'mon, man. You gotta reel this kid in. Set him straight. Where's Joey Bahms? He workin' today?" He leaned forward and looked around the apparatus floor and ended back at Charles. He chuckled, then looked back at Kenny. "At least when you were new you brought in a whole fucking meal," he said, shaking his head again. "Job's changing."

KENNY AND JIMMY WALKED Charles through the compartments on the Engine again, once he was changed and back downstairs. Jimmy did most of the talking and echoed the things that Kenny told him Monday. Kohler walked behind them, sucking a cigarette and occasionally adding a point to what was said.

They were behind the rig, going over the number of lengths of hose there were on the back, when the tones went off. Damon, a firefighter from Ladder 88 who didn't talk much, was in the housewatch, legs crossed reading a book. He took off his glasses and looked at the screen, then swiveled his chair and hit the bells twice for the Engine and three times for the Ladder.

"One and one for CO," he said calmly. "282 McCombs Place, apartment 2C for a CO detector activation. Engine and Truck goes."

Everyone stopped what they were doing, geared up, and headed out.

CHARLES WAS TOLD THAT generally, on a CO run the Engine firefighters didn't get off the rig. Most times there wasn't an actual leak, just a faulty detector. Or the detector worked fine, but the batteries were dying and the occupant misunderstood the alarm beeps. The Truck would mitigate the problem, and the Engine would stand by on the rig.

This time though, instead of sitting on the rig, Jimmy used the time to go over building construction with Charles. Their response area had everything from two-story private houses to thirty-story high-rises. They talked about the building in front of them which was a six-story tenement. What to think about and how to operate.

Kenny pointed at the front of the building. He said, "280, 282, and 284 McCombs are all attached. Tell me about the top floor apartments. What do they have in common?"

Charles looked at the three buildings. "A common cockloft," he said.

"Good. What does that mean?"

"That the roofs are attached?"

"Well, yes, but no. I meant what does it mean that they have a common cockloft? Why is that information important to us?"

Charles swallowed. The question wasn't hard, but he wasn't sure how to answer. He said, "because the fire can spread?"

Matt was the officer, and he stepped forward and said, "Let's start with this. A cockloft is the space between the ceiling of the top floor and the roof of the building, right?"

"Right."

"So if a fire spread into the cockloft…"

"It could travel from one end of the building to the other."

"So the concern here?"

"That a fire could spread from one address to the other. I mean, one building to the other."

"Excellent," Matt said, and raised his hand for a high five. They talked about fighting fires in a cockloft. Then Lt. Varmitt called Matt over the radio. "8-8 to 9-9."

"Go 'head, Jack."

"Defective detector."

"Ten-four." The men started back to the Engine, when Jimmy stopped and said, "Charles.

You know what that means?"

Everyone followed his gaze to the corner. Two identical

girls were standing near the curb, waiting for the light. Kohler laughed. Charles looked at Jimmy, confused.

"What does what mean?"

"Twins," Jimmy said.

"Uh. I don't think so."

"It means we're going to a job, that's what the hell that means," Kenny said.

Charles laughed. "Why?"

Jimmy: "We don't question the ways of the fire overseers, Davids. It's a scientific fact that if you see twins, you're going to a fire." He shrugged. "Better get your big boy pants on. You're gonna get your first nozzle job today."

Jimmy slapped Charles's back, then continued to the rig. Kenny laughed and followed. Matt came up beside Charles and put his arm around his shoulder.

"Don't worry. You'll learn the weird firehouse humor in no time."

WHEN THEY WERE ON the rig, Matt picked up the phone receiver and contacted the dispatcher to relay the message about the detector. The dispatcher asked if both rigs were ten-eight and Matt said they were.

The dispatcher said, "You and the Truck reset your MDTs and respond second-due to box 8-3-2-9, 618 West 138th for an odor of gas in the area."

Matt acknowledged the message and hit some buttons on the monitor between him and Kohler.

Kohler keyed the mic on his handie-talkie and said, "Got another ticket. Second-due gas on 138th between Lenox and Powell."

"Ten-four. On our way," Varmitt answered.

Kohler waited for the members of 88 to come out of the building and start toward their rig before he put the Engine in drive and pulled away from the curb. As they were rounding the corner, Billy Pearson of 88 said over the radio, "Look across the street! Twins!"

ON THEIR WAY BACK from the gas leak, the Engine got another ticket for an EMS run. Matt looked at the monitor and pushed a button, then said to Kohler, "EMS. 145th and Douglass. The check cashing place." Kohler reached up and turned on the emergency lights, while Matt stepped on a pedal on the officer's side that sounded the sirens, and they sped off.

In the back, Jimmy looked up at the monitor and read, "Male caller states aided male unconscious inside check cashing."

"Take off your coat," Kenny said to Charles. "It's probably an intox, but in case we have to do CPR again. It's too hot to do chest compressions with all your gear on."

Charles took off his coat and wiped his forehead with his forearm. Jimmy found a box of sterile gloves on a shelf beside his seat and handed some out to each of them. The rig pulled up behind a taxi stopped in front of a hydrant on 145th Street, and Kohler laid on his horn. The driver checked his rearview mirror, lifted his hand in apology, then sped away. Kohler moved up, then put the rig in neutral and hit the brakes.

Matt went straight inside, where a supervisor was standing over a man sprawled out on the floor, an upturned crate beside him. Jimmy opened the EMS compartment on the side of the rig and pulled out the three red duffel bags. Kenny put the strap of one over his head and across his body and led way inside.

When they entered, Matt looked up and stood—he'd been kneeling near the patient. "I think it's an overdose," he said, and they all crouched to look. The patient was probably in his thirties, wearing a bright blue shirt and matted pants. He didn't look or smell homeless, but he didn't look particularly well kempt either. Every five seconds or so his mouth would open, like a fish out of water. Charles leaned over him and spread his eyelids.

"Yeah," he said, turning to his bag. "His pupils are pinpoint." He reached in his bag and pulled out a small vile, not feeling any anxiety at all. He'd been trained on this and was very comfortable doing it.

Jimmy took out the oxygen and Kenny helped him hook it up to a face mask that would let the air flow through without a bag being squeezed.

The two employees behind the window held their cellphones high to see over Kenny's back, and when the supervisor spotted them, he warned them to cut it out.

Charles screwed a nasal spray injector onto the vile, then bent over the guy and sprayed half the vile into one nostril and half into the other. When it was empty, he sat back, and Jimmy put the mask on the guy's face and let him continue to breathe on his own.

Ten or fifteen seconds passed before the guy's eyes popped open. He looked around for a bit, before yanking the mask off his face. "What's going on? What are you doing?" he asked, trying to sit up but faltering.

Jimmy laughed. "What are *you* doing?"

The guy pulled his knees up and wrapped his arms around them. He looked around once more, squinting in the sunlight. "What's going on?" he asked again.

Kenny said, "What's your name, my friend?"

The man was rocking back and forth. He rubbed his chin on his shoulder and looked out the window. Kenny started to ask again, and the man said, "Alan! Alan Johnson." "Alan, what day is today?" "What?" He faced Kenny.

"What day of the week is it?" Kenny asked patiently.

Alan thought about it, then grabbed his head. "Fuck, man. I don't know."

Kenny nodded. "Okay. We're just gonna hang out here 'til the ambulance comes."

"I don't need an ambulance."

"You do. You were practically dead. We helped bring you back. You don't even know what day it is. We'll just let them check you out."

"No," Alan said, trying to stand. "I wanna go home." He kept trying to push himself up, but had neither the strength nor coordination.

Kenny put a firm hand on his shoulder, keeping him down. "Where do you live, buddy?"

"8989 Douglass Boulevard."

"That's three blocks away," Jimmy said. "How are you gonna get three blocks if you can't even get up?"

Alan glared at Jimmy for longer than a beat, then looked around at the others, landing on

Charles. He shrugged Kenny's hand off, turned on to his hands and knees, then took a deep breath and stood shakily. He wobbled for a moment, then reached out for the counter.

Two paramedics walked in and Jimmy gave them a report. They each grabbed an arm and Alan didn't protest as they walked him out. Before he was gone, he looked over his shoulders at the men again, and the supervisor of the check cashing place said, "Whoa! If looks could kill."

AFTERWARD, ENGINE 99 STOPPED at the supermarket and picked up ingredients for lunch and dinner. Barbecue chicken salad wraps for lunch, steak and potatoes for dinner. When they got to the house, the guys from the Truck helped them unpack the groceries, then everyone but the bosses started preparing the meal.

Kohler filled a large pot with water to boil the chicken and Fagan started frying the bacon that Charles brought in that morning but hadn't made. Everyone else grabbed cutting boards and started dicing red onions, yellow onions, celery, garlic, carrots.

Damon grabbed a handful of blueberries that Kenny picked for nosh and went back to man the housewatch. Brian O'Neil, the chief's aide, grabbed a handful of chips and started to head to the chief's office, but had a thought and went back to where everyone was working.

"Billy," he called across the table, his mouth half full. "What's with your boy Myles Peck in Rescue?"

Billy dropped his knife, threw his head back, and laughed. "Oh shit, man. I just heard that story. Who told you? O.B.?"

Brian stuffed another chip in his mouth and nodded. "Of course. Is it true?"

"What, that it really happened or that she said it did?"

"I know she said it did. I wanna know if it's true. What does he say? Did anybody ask him?"

Billy laughed again, remembering the story. "I think O.B. asked him. I think he said it was true, but of course Peck gave some bullshit reason why."

Brian laughed out loud. "Of course he did," he said. "That dude's a load."

Fagan stepped away from the stove and walked over to the table. He grabbed a chip and looked at Charles, who was using a potato peeler to skin the carrots. Charles caught his eye and nodded. Fagan looked away and asked Brian what they were talking about.

Brian: "You know that ass-wipe who transferred to Rescue last year but has been working at the academy ever since?" He looked at Charles, "Davids, you have him as an instructor? Peck?"

Charles stopped peeling and nodded. "Yes, sir. He was part of the rope-unit team."

"He was a dick, right?"

"I don't remember," Charles said.

Brian grinned. "You're full of shit."

Fagan grabbed another chip, then headed back to the stove. "You were saying," he called over his shoulder.

Brian put his back to the wall so he could be heard by everyone. "Peck is dating an EMS chick assigned to the academy…"

Fagan turned around, interested. "A probie?"

"Nah, she's already on the job. She's got, like, nine or ten years on EMS or something like that. You've seen her before, the one with all the tats. Very pretty."

Fagan was impressed. "He's dating *her*?"

"Yeah, I don't get it either. Anyway, she was hanging out with Zac's wife. You know Zac's wife used to be EMS too. They were hanging out last week and she's telling Zac's wife all kinds of things about Myles. Things no fireman would ever want the house to know."

"Like what?" Fagan asked. "Boudoir stuff?"

Apart from Charles, everyone had stopped what they were doing to listen.

"Nope! There hasn't been any bedroom stuff. That's the best part," Brian said, and Billy laughed again, thinking about it.

Kenny stood up straight and Kohler came over from the sink. Fagan turned around, shut off the flame under the pan, and came over to the table.

Brian continued. "Apparently, last month or May or something, they go with another dude to her sister's wedding upstate in Haverstraw. Separate cars, but they went up at the same time. The other guy is from his firehouse but used to be

EMS and knows both the tatted girl and her sister. Anyway, they go to the wedding and Peck meets the family and there are, like, six sisters."

Charles finished peeling the carrots and began to dice them. His knife banged rhythmically against the cutting board until Billy grabbed his arm and said, "Yo, man! Take a break. Get your priorities straight."

Brian said, "The dude from Peck's house didn't stay for the reception. He left after the wedding. At the reception, Peck is dancing with everyone. The other sisters, cousins, the mom."

Brian laughed and shook his head. "At some point, he sends a text to the guy who left. It was a picture of a bunch of the sisters dancing and it said something like, 'Bro. You left too early.

You're missing out.' Then another one that said, 'I might've picked wrong,' or something like that. Like the wrong sister."

The kitchen was silent. Everyone watched Brian expectantly, their faces in different stages of amusement.

Kohler said, "Don't tell me..."

Brian laughed. "Yep! That idiot sent the text to the wrong person. He sent it to the tatted chick."

Fagan chuckled and shook his head. He said, "What is he, in high school?"

Billy said, "She saw it when she was giving the speech!"

"What?" Everyone faced him.

"She wrote a speech about her sister and the groom. She took the mic after the maid of honor and best man spoke, and she had the speech typed, you know, in her phone." He laughed.

"Poor girl saw the text while she was standing on the platform with the mic in her hand."

Fagan laughed, shook his head. "Nice people."

WHEN THEY SAT DOWN to eat, Chief Leland was at the head of the table on one end, and Fagan at the head on the other. The chief called across and asked Fagan if he was currently working on a lot of orders. Fagan groomed tools in his spare time for firefighters and volunteer fire departments across the Northeast.

"You know me, Chief." Fagan shrugged. "I always got a few in the works."

"My buddy is a captain in Virginia," the chief said. "They were looking to get ten or twelve orders for the firehouse."

"Send it in," Fagan answered. "Give them my info. Where in…?"

The tones sounded and interrupted him. The automated voice said "Engine! Ladder!

Battalion!"

Chairs scraped away from the table, forks fell on plates, and everyone headed to the kitchen door. Then from the housewatch, Damon banged the bells four times, fast. He said,

"Second source for fire. Everybody first-due. 453 St. Nicholas Avenue. Fourth floor. Giddyup!" Then four quick bells again.

They ran. Kohler, Fagan, and Brian pushed through the others and started all three rigs so that they could hear the dispatcher. Lt. Varmitt and Lt. Quincy ran to the officer's sides and opened their doors as they dressed so that they could listen too. The guys in the Engine got their pants on, then hopped on the rig and finished dressing there; while the Truck guys ran outside to block traffic once they had their bunker pants on. They finished dressing as the rigs pulled out of the house, and a minute after the tones sounded, all three rigs were on their way.

KENNY LEANED FORWARD, GRABBED a Jolly Rancher, and popped it in his mouth.

Jimmy looked at the screen and said, "Fire in apartment 41 on the fourth floor. Seven story building. One hundred fifty by two hundred feet." He looked at Charles. "This might be a long stretch."

"Okay," Charles said, trying his best to ignore his heartbeat.

"Two stairwells," Jimmy continued. "Well-hole stairwell in the back. Wrap around stairwell in the front."

The rig made a hard left, and everyone grabbed their seats.

Kohler leaned back and called, "Jim, this is that building with the large lobby. That one with the gold columns out front. It's gonna be a long stretch."

Jimmy smiled at Charles and Charles returned it, but only as a reflex. He wasn't really paying attention. He was praying. Praying to calm down and do well and make it out safely. But if God was only granting one prayer that day, he would settle for doing well.

They made the turn onto St. Nicholas Avenue and Kohler yelled over his shoulder,

"There's fire out the window."

Kenny turned in his seat to look out the front, and when he saw the fire, he unbuckled his seatbelt and said, "Here we go!"

The Truck was behind them, and Kohler pulled past the building so that the Truck could stop directly in front. Both rigs stopped, and before anyone was out, the chief was on the radio.

"Battalion 5 to Manhattan: ten-seventy-five our box."

Jimmy sat forward, freed his mask, and grabbed his helmet. Matt and Kenny did the same. Kohler grabbed a pair of leather gloves from the dashboard, then jumped out. Everyone else followed, hopping out, looking up at the building, and reaching behind themselves to open their bottles. Charles was last. He got out, looked up, and prayed silently one more time.

Time hadn't completely stopped, but everything slowed. All the sounds of the sirens and the streets faded, and all Charles heard was his heartbeat and breathing. He closed his eyes, held his breath for a count of two, then opened his eyes again.

Time went normal again, and Harlem came back as a roar.

AT THE BACK OF the rig, Kenny told Charles to get up on the step and grab his length of hose. His length was shaped like a horseshoe, same as in the basement, and Charles tucked his elbow under it, then pulled it off.

Matt came from around the front of the rig and yelled, "Start a line!" before hurrying inside.

A dozen or more people spilled from the building, covering their heads as they ran down the stoop. Some were barefoot, others in socks or flip flops or both. Some carried their pets, some their kids. One man, who nearly bumped into Varmitt, was carrying his PlayStation.   Billy and Danny were right behind Varmitt, yelling for people to watch out as they made their way in.

 Charles climbed down, took a few steps toward the building, then looked back to see Kenny go up and grab another horseshoe. Behind the Engine, Paul Fagan was standing on the roof of the Truck using a control panel to extend the seventy-five-foot aerial ladder on top of it.

Damon was behind him, waiting to climb it to the roof.

 Kenny came down, said, "Let's go," and followed Charles into the lobby. Jimmy was behind them, carrying a third horseshoe. Pete The Greek from 88 was outside to the left of the entrance, using a 6-foot hook to release the fire escape's drop ladder.

Through the main doors, straight ahead was the elevator, and to the left of it, a set of stairs that wrapped around the shaft up to the top floor. To the right, a hallway that led to a second set of stairs.

Charles saw Billy and Danny disappear at the top of the wrap-around stairs, and that's where Kenny directed him.

Kenny said, "Make wide turns, okay? Hug the wall opposite the elevator."

"Okay."

They headed left while Jimmy dropped his horseshoe in the lobby, then ran back to the rig to pull more hose. Engine 80 was second-due and their guys entered the lobby a second after Jimmy ran out. Their nozzleman ran inside, picked up the horseshoe that Jimmy had left, and went after Charles and Kenny, hugging the far wall. The backup firefighter from 80 grabbed the hose line behind that and followed while their control man stayed outside, making sure the line Jimmy pulled off made its way, unobstructed, into the lobby. Ladder 23, the second-due Truck, ran into the building and up the stairs, squeezing past 80's guys.

At the top of the stairs on each flight, Charles looked back to make sure Kenny was behind him, and he always was. Twice they had to stop and yell for people coming down the stairs to stay close to the elevator wall. It was a slow climb, but a steady motion, and they hadn't been in the building two minutes yet.

Halfway between the third and fourth floors, Ladder 23's boss and two firefighters ran past them and yelled on the fourth floor, "23's going up!"

Charles could smell smoke now but didn't see any. When he reached the fourth floor, Matt was at the top of the stairs. "This way, buddy," he said, and headed to the right. Charles

checked on Kenny, and when he saw him there, they followed
Matt down a darkening hallway.

Now he could see smoke, and he quickly became aware of
his breathing.

A woman in one of the apartments they passed poked her
head out and asked if she should leave. Kenny said, "Yes, but
close your door behind you."

Jimmy's voice came over the radio and said, "Control to
9-9 backup, let me know when you have enough line."

Kenny's horseshoe was mostly gone, it had played out on
the stairs, but the apartment was in front of them, and Charles
still had his full length, so Kenny said, "We're good, Jim."

"Ten-four."

The door to the fire apartment was chocked open by one of
the tools that Billy had brought up. Matt dropped to one knee,
grabbed the doorknob, and said, "Get ready."

Charles held the nozzle and tossed the center of his horseshoe back toward the stairs. Heart racing, he placed his knee
on the hose line and masked up. He took off his helmet and
put his face piece on, breathing heavy now. He pulled his
hood over his ears, then put his helmet on again and tightened
the chin strap. He could hear air scrape into his facepiece with
every breath and he thought of his dad in the hospital.

He was sweating. Everywhere. The cool air in his
facepiece dried the sweat against his forehead, but it kept
coming. He couldn't wipe it away without taking his facepiece
off, and of course he wasn't going to do that. He tried to ignore it, but it was now another thing he was conscious of.

Kenny stretched out the horseshoe, flaking it down the hall,
then came back and masked up too.

Matt said, "9-9 to Chauffer, start water."

"Ten-four, here comes your water."

Charles lifted the limp hose and waited on one knee like a

nervous man waiting for an answer. The dry line hung behind his grip, and he could feel the vibration of water racing to the front. After a moment, the line filled out and hardened and he tightened his grip on it. Then he felt Kenny against his back, like a wall. The line rose to his waist and under his elbow as Kenny took the pressure off Charles's end.

Matt held on to the doorknob. Grey smoke seeped from the top and the sides and Charles waited for him to open it. Matt said something that Charles couldn't make out over the sound of his own breathing. Kenny leaned forward, his facepiece against Charles's ear, and yelled, "Bleed the line!"

Charles kicked himself mentally, then aimed the line at the floor and away from the door. He pulled back on the handle and opened the nozzle halfway, and water sputtered and spat as it pushed out the air in the line, then flowed steadily. When the stream was full, he pushed the handle forward, closing the nozzle, and the line kicked back and rocked him. He readjusted his grip while Matt leaned close and called, "Let's go! The fire is in the living room! Down the hallway on your left, ten feet from the door! Ready?"

Charles's heart rose to his throat. He turned around to check if Kenny was ready and found him smiling.

Kenny leaned close and said, "You got this. I'm right behind you. Let's do it." He hadn't yelled, but Charles heard him clearly, and breathing felt a little easier.

Charles faced forward again, and Matt opened the door. Dark grey smoke pulsed out of the apartment. Charles got a brief glimpse of the hallway inside and an orange glow before the grey blocked his view.

Matt led the way inside, following the beam from his flashlight. Charles followed, Kenny behind him, moving in stride.

They made the ten feet in a few seconds, and Charles gasped when they got to the corner of the hall. Charles couldn't identify everything burning, but there was definitely a couch in flames and sections of the floor itself seemed to be on fire. Once they cleared the hallway, he flinched from the heat, and ducked his head for relief. Matt moved from in front and crouched beside the line, side-by-side with Charles. When he was clear, Charles pulled back the handle on the nozzle and opened the line all the way. He held it at an angle toward the ceiling to cool the area. The stream was strong and full, but he had a good grip and so did Kenny, so he didn't struggle. He whipped the front of the nozzle in a wide circular motion, clockwise, hitting the ceiling at the top of the arc and the burning floor at the bottom. When the water hit the fire, visibility was reduced. The room went dark, and he could no longer see the contents, but the temperature dropped and he felt immediately better.

Charles whipped the line four full cycles, then aimed the stream at the floor and ran it back and forth. They moved forward two feet and did it all again. Four circles, smaller this time, then a sweep of the floor and forward a couple of feet.

Through his radio, Charles heard Varmitt said, "88 to command. 99 has water on the

fire."

"Ten-four, Jack."

"Chauffer to 9-9, you're on hydrant water."

Billy was to the right of the hose line, searching the area the Engine had cleared. Danny was in the kitchen breaking the windows to clear some of the smoke. Varmitt was watching from the door of a bedroom. After a minute, Matt tapped Charles's shoulder and Charles pushed the handle forward slowly, closing the line. Billy and Danny eased past them and started clearing the windows in the living room and shifting furniture around, searching for pockets of fire.

Visibility was clearing. Sunlight pierced the air and

Charles saw why the floor was on fire. There was a large area rug that the couch was centered on. It was charred now and soaked and looked like mud.

Matt leaned close to Charles and said, "Open the line halfway. Out the window. Small circles." Then he leaned back and yelled to Varmitt, "We're gonna open up to vent!"

"Ten-four." Varmitt was in the living room now and said over his radio. "8-8 to command."

"Command."

"Chief, the main body of fire is knocked down. Primary searches are negative. Be advised 99 is gonna open up out the living room window."

"Ten-four."

Charles did as he was told and aimed the stream out the window in tight circles. The smoke followed it out and the room cleared fast. Once it had, Kenny tapped his shoulder and Charles closed the line again. Billy and Danny went back to the living room and shifted piles of rubble and broke apart burnt cabinets and tables. The Greek appeared from behind them, followed by Damon. They weren't wearing their facepieces. They began using hooks like the Greek had outside to open up the walls and ceiling, checking for fire extension.

Then Fagan was there. He walked in slowly and surveyed the room. He glanced at Charles, lifted his brows, then joined the others in overhauling.

SMOLDERING EMBERS APPEARED IN random places after several minutes of the Truck working through the rubble. When they were done, they backed out of the living room and watched the Engine do another washdown. Charles and Kenny stood as they operated the hose line because there was no more smoke or heat to cause a problem for them. Standing was a lot easier than operating on one knee, and Charles was feeling his adrenaline drain.

Kenny said, "That should be good," and Charles closed the line.

Matt: "9-9 to chauffer."

"Chauffeur."

"Joe, you can shut down our line."

"Ten-four," Kohler said.

Charles waited for the pressure in the line to lessen, then he opened the nozzle again and drained it. He coughed and used the cuff of his sleeve to wipe his forehead. Matt came over and offered him a high-five and he accepted it.

"Great job," Matt said. He looked genuinely happy. "Great job."

Charles couldn't help but smile. He turned around and the members of 88 were making their way out of the apartment. Kenny was standing there, also smiling, his face and hair wet.

"Nice job, buddy," he said. Charles thanked him, the tension all but gone. Kenny and Matt quickly gave him suggestions, things he might consider doing differently next time. Jimmy was by the door separating the first length of hose from the second to make them easier to carry down. When he separated them, he stood up straight and stretched. Charles, Matt, and Kenny made their way to him, and he gave Charles a fist bump.

"Two days at the firehouse, two ten-seventy-fives?" Jimmy said. "I gotta work with you more often."

Charles laughed and shrugged. "I guess you were right about the fire overseers."

"That's right!" Jimmy gasped. "The twins!" He laughed. "The legends are true!"

OUTSIDE, CHARLES AND KENNY climbed on top of their rig to repack the hose. Everyone else stood in a line and passed the drained and reconnected lengths of hose from hand to hand up to them. Jimmy stood on the backstep to make sure the hose was packed neatly, and Kohler was at the front of the rig with the chauffeur from Engine 80, repacking the hose line he used to connect to the hydrant.

Afterward, Jimmy helped Charles and Kenny down and firefighters from the other houses came to Charles to congratulate him. He shook a bunch of hands and gave a bunch of fist bumps, and when it was over, Kenny walked him to the Recovery and Care rig. They both got a cup of Gatorade and drank it there. Then they grabbed one more for themselves and one for Jimmy, Kohler, and the boss, and went back to the Engine. Jimmy was sitting next to Kohler, talking about what Kohler had done outside. They took the drinks and Kohler congratulated Charles.

The Greek came behind Charles and slapped his back. "Nozzle job in your first week.

Welcome to the team, brother!"

A small circle formed behind the Engine, everyone discussing what they did and what they saw. Fagan appeared beside Charles. His shirt was soaked through, his face smeared here and there with soot. He had his hands tucked into the waist of his bunker pants.

"How was that?" he asked.

"Good," Charles said, forcing himself not to say "sir." He was rocking back and forth and wasn't sure why but didn't stop himself.

"What you expected?"

"Um, I don't know. I don't know what I expected," Charles answered. "Kenny made it easy. I mean, not easy, but he made my job easier. The stretch was harder than I expected, I guess.

So many people on the stairs."

Fagan shrugged. "People get scared. Better they self-evac-uate than us having to go in and get them when they're per-fectly fine."

"I get it."

"Anything else?"

Charles didn't know what he meant. "No. That was it."

Fagan nodded for a long moment. He said, "Very well," then turned and walked away.

When he did, the circle broke up and everyone headed to their rigs.

Kenny put an arm around Charles's shoulders. "I'm proud of you, bud. You got past your doubt."

Charles smiled, thinking about that. "Thanks, Kenny."

Ahead of them, Billy was saying to Danny, "But they didn't look like tourists. We could be going to fires every day!"

Danny said, "Don't be silly, Bill. Everyone knows twins only leave the house together once a month."

Billy nodded, smiling. "Yeah, you're right. I'm being crazy."

-20-

ALAN TRIED GOING BACK to work. He was doing things wrong. He needed to take control of his life. Try to get back a degree of normalcy. He'd been out of his home for nearly a week now. As much as he refused to call himself homeless, the truth of it was hard to deny. He wasn't ready to figure out a permanent living situation, but he could go back to work. That would be a start.

AROUND TWO O'CLOCK, WEDNESDAY, Alan walked from the park on 135th Street to
Kim's Shoes on Convent Avenue. It was a ten-minute walk down streets with no shade, under a cloudless sky, and by the time he arrived, he was drenched.
He pushed open the door and stepped inside. No customers inside. He stepped all the way in and let the glass door close behind him. The air conditioner felt great. He grabbed his collar, fanned his chest, and held his head up to the ceiling. Kimberly stuck her head out from behind the wall that led to the stockroom, a small bundle of fries poking from her mouth. Her eyes narrowed, and her chewing slowed, then she ducked back behind the wall.
The sales floor was a small space, rectangular, with product on shelves along three sides and the window and door on

the fourth. There were six small benches in two rows of three, facing each other. The top of the benches were cushioned platforms supported by mirrored boxes. Customers could sit on one row of the benches and see their feet in the mirrors of the other row.

Alan sat down in the middle of a bench with his back to the window and sighed. Kimberly came from behind the wall, wiping her mouth with a napkin. She stood behind the bench closest to the stock room and folded her arms. Alan watched her and thought again how she looked like Mr. Clean when she did that, and then remembered he was still kind of pissed at her.

"What?" he asked, looking away. He caught a glimpse of himself in the mirror of the bench in front of him. The shirt Rob had given him was bright and ridiculous, and he figured that was why Rob had chosen it.

"What are you doing here?" Kimberly asked.

Alan shook his head, irritated. "What do you want me to say? What do you think I'm doing here? I came to work."

"No," Kimberly said, and it sounded to Alan like a complete sentence. He looked at her again. Words raced through his thoughts, but none came out.

Kimberly said, "I'm not gonna ask why you didn't come in yesterday. I'm not gonna ask why you didn't call. I care and I'm worried about you, but I'm done with this, Al. I have a business to run. I gotta let you go."

For a moment, Alan stared at her, mouth slightly open, unable to wrap his mind around what was happening. This week was like a bad joke and there was nothing to do but laugh. So he did. He looked away from her, shaking his head again, and laughed.

"Alan. I—"

"Wow," Alan said, interrupting her. He stood and grabbed

his forehead, the heels of his hands covering his eyes. "Unbelievable."

"Be fair, Alan. What'd you expect?"

Alan dropped his hands and stepped toward her. "Loyalty," he yelled. "Respect! Fuck!

For once, respect!"

Kimberly took a step back, startled, but recovered quickly and scoffed. "Oh, spare me,

Alan," she said, matching his volume. "Just leave. Don't talk to me about respect. You gotta give respect to get it!"

Alan's nostrils flared and he nodded. "Okay," he said quietly. "Fine."

He stepped around the bench and yanked the door open with as much force as he could and stepped back out into the heat.

ALAN CALLED JAYLEE AGAIN and got another eight ball. He took a couple hits off it in the park, then started walking. He didn't know what happened after that, but the next thing he knew, he was laying on the ground in Ritechek with firemen over him. He was jumpy and wired and he had energy to burn but no strength to use it. It was an odd and uncomfortable feeling. He hated it and he blamed the firemen.

They'd asked him a bunch of questions that he answered, but he wasn't sure what they asked and what he'd said. None of them were Captain Asshole.

Then an ambulance came and took him to the emergency room. They asked him more questions and gave him some fluids and he was free to go. His whole day gone, and nothing to show for it.

That night he ended up in Ritechek for the last time, though he didn't know it would be. He sat on his crate and stared out at the corner of 145th and Douglass at nothing. Cars and people went in and out of his field of view, but he hadn't noticed any of them.

He was facing reality. This was his fault. People only got away with what you let them get away with. Kimberly treated him unfairly because he allowed it. Because he was too nice. Same reason he let Hanna disrespect him in his own home in front of his wife. Same reason he let Candace take advantage of his generosity. It was the same reason that asshole fire captain felt free to go see Alan's wife anytime he damn well pleased. All. His. Fault. But no more. No more.

-21-

"I saw you guys on YouTube!"

"Me?" Charles held his phone to his ear and smiled. It was just after nine a.m. Thursday, the Fourth of July, and he was off from work. He was smiling because Libby called him first. He had been up for an hour overthinking the pros and cons of calling her. They'd spoken after work Wednesday and he told her all about the fire. She was excited and surprised and proud at all the appropriate times. Then they spoke about a complicated customer who had come to the bakery and ordered a pair of cakes but for people with food allergies to nearly all the ingredients. The order had stressed her out. When he woke up today, he wanted to call her to see how she was, then thought that the question felt more like a text message than a call. But would a text imply that he didn't want to talk? Would she be offended? Just when he unlocked his phone to text her, her name appeared on the screen for an incoming call. She had seen an eyewitness cell phone video of yesterday's fire.

"Well, not you," Libby said in response to his question. "Or at least, I don't think so. I was looking for your name on the back of the coats and didn't see it. But I saw the trucks from your firehouse. I saw that guy going up the ladder to the roof. He flew up there!"

"Damon," Charles said. "He did an Ironman once. He and

Pete the Greek are monsters. They do, like, three hundred pushups a day."

Libby laughed. "I don't think I've done three hundred pushups in my whole life."

"I could probably do three hundred a day, for a few days," Charles said. "But sooner or later I wouldn't be able to use my arms. Doesn't seem worth it."

"No," Libby agreed. "Useable arms are more useful." Charles laughed and she said,

"Listen. I'm sorry about lunch the other day."

"For stealing my mozzarella sticks?" he asked. "Thank you. I wasn't gonna say anything, but it did bother me."

"You're so dumb," she said. "You know what I mean. I'm embarrassed. We were having such a good time and then…I don't know. I feel like it was ruined."

Charles was leaned back in his father's old chair again, staring at the ceiling. "You're talking about what you told me about your dad?"

"Yes, idiot."

"Don't be embarrassed. Especially since I'm a firefighter," he said, the phrase still sounding odd to his ear. "It didn't ruin anything. I felt—I *feel* honored that you felt comfortable enough to tell me."

There was a moment of silence, then Libby said, "Thank you," and he heard the smile in her voice.

"Yeah, what ruined everything was when you double dipped that mozzarella stick in the marinara sauce," Charles said. "I almost threw up."

"Wow. So my mouth makes you sick?"

Charles's phone beeped in his ear and he looked at the screen. "Oh, thank God," he said. "My mom's calling me back. I gotta take this."

"Wow."

CHARLES'S MOM SAID THAT she'd heard about the
fire on the radio but hadn't seen it. The radio said it was
quickly extinguished and no one was injured. She only gave it
a passing thought because she hadn't known that Charles was
working. He told her about it and she listened in silence.

"Good job," she said when he was done. "Were you
scared?"

"No. Not, like, scared of getting burned or anything. I was
just worried about doing well. I was praying before I went in."

"Good. Looks like you were ready after all. And Bahms
wasn't even there."

"No, he wasn't," Charles agreed. "But seeing Kenny smile
before we went in made me calm. Everybody was cool. Danny barely broke a sweat."

"Well, it's not new for them. They trust their training and
they trust each other," his mom said. "And now they can start
to trust you."

Charles smiled. "Yes. How's your back? Did you sleep
better last night?"

"Um, no. I took Tylenol sometime during the night and the
pain went away, but I couldn't sleep," she answered. "I was
trying to take a nap earlier before you bothered me."

"You'll get over it," Charles said. "Or I will. Hang on." His
phone vibrated in his hand and he pulled the screen back to
check the notifications. It was a message from the chief's aide.

"Should I take overtime tonight?" he asked, putting the
phone back to his ear.

"Why not? What else would you be doing?"

Charles told her quickly about Libby and how he was
thinking of seeing if she were free later to go watch the fireworks show from the Brooklyn Bridge.

She said, "Charles, take the overtime. It may not always be
available. You can hang out with her anytime."

"Are you being wise or are you being a hater?" Charles asked.

His mother sighed. "I'm hanging up now."

LIBBY WAS ON HER way to the bakery when he called her back. He told her that he told his mother about the fire yesterday, and that she was uncomfortable but tried to hide it. Libby didn't blame her.

"Just dating a firefighter is worrisome, imagine being the mother of one! Imagine being worried to get a call every time you hear about a fire in the area that they work in." When Charles didn't respond, she said, "Hello?"

"You're dating a firefighter?"

Libby chuckled. "You're so dumb."

"You said, just dating a firefighter is worrisome. That means you're dating one, right?"

"Well, if you have to ask, maybe not."

Charles smiled. "Fair enough. I'll help you figure it out the next time I see you."

"Looking forward to it. When do you work again?"

"Tonight, actually. I picked up overtime," he said. "I was gonna invite you to watch the fireworks, but I'd have been embarrassed if you said no, so I figured if I have to work, I have an excuse."

"Smart man," Libby said. "My mom and I are probably gonna be working late tonight anyway. It's gonna be so busy."

"Yeah? I wouldn't have thought the Fourth of July was a huge pastry buying holiday."

"It's not. Valentine's Day is the only holiday great for business. And graduation season.

But we have a huge order for tomorrow."

"Oh. I see."

"Yeah. July is usually pretty slow. We had an elementary

school teacher place a decent sized order of cupcakes for her summer school students to be picked up this morning, but aside from that, we may only get a handful of people today."

"Gotcha. Well, good luck with tomorrow's order," Charles said.

"Thank you. When am I seeing you again?"

Charles smiled. "Uh, I work tonight, tomorrow night, and Saturday night. I'd suggest breakfast, but if the night tour is crazy, I might be exhausted. I'd be bad company. So let's do Sunday if you're free."

"Okay, I am." She was breathing heavy from walking a distance in the heat. "Man, three nights in a row? In this heat! You're gonna be dead by Saturday."

THE FOURTH OF JULY was traditionally a busy day for the fire department. Busy because there were lots of calls for smoke or calls for fire because the caller saw smoke and assumed that where there's one, there's the other. But the number of actual fires they went to was nowhere near the number they were called for. The callers weren't outright liars, usually—they were just mistaken. What they were smelling was usually something you'd expect to smell around the Fourth. They smelled smoke from a barbecue heating up or a grill in use. What they were seeing was smoke from fireworks being used in an enclosed area when they should have been used in the open. Or not at all. And though the improper use of fireworks could possibly lead to a fire, or injury, most often it did not. These concerned calls weren't malicious false alarms, but they were false alarms, nonetheless. They happened every year on Fourth of July weekends. They were expected. And so even though the Fourth was typically a busy day for the firehouse, it was usually uneventful.

Usually.

CHARLES GOT TO THE firehouse exactly at four and was told he'd be working on the Truck for the night tour. He was given the can position. The can-man carried a water can and a six-foot hook and usually stayed with the boss.

Eddie Short, a firefighter who used to be assigned to the Engine but had transferred to the Truck, sat across from him in the cab and had the irons position. The irons and the can firefighters worked together to force entry through locked doors; so once Charles was shown the rig and the tools he might use, they took him to the basement to do a forcible entry drill.

Joe McCann and Eddie ran the drill. Eddie brought the irons down with him. They quickly discussed what Charles had learned in the academy, then they set up a door and did it for real. Gap, set, force. The irons were made up of a forcible entry tool and a flathead axe. Eddie manipulated the tool between the door and the jam, creating a gap, and Charles used the axe to hit the tool until it was set in further and one end of the tool made it past the frame to the other side. Then they both put pressure on the other end, forcing the door from the lock or the lock from the frame. The door had two locks on it and they were through it in just over a minute.

When they were done, McCann told Charles he did well enough but that he might've gotten a better swing if he shrugged off his blankie and hit like a man.

THEY HAD RIBS AND barbecue chicken with corn and coleslaw for dinner in honor of the holiday. Eventually. It was a struggle to get dinner on the table because of how often the tones sounded. Then, after a call was completed, it took them forever to get back to the firehouse because of how crowded the streets were.

When they finally sat down to eat, Eddie said to Charles,

"Make sure you pee as soon as you feel the need."

Charles swallowed a piece of chicken and wiped his mouth. "I'm sorry?"

"You see how busy we are?" Eddie asked. "There's no worse feeling than having to pee and getting a run for fire. If you gotta go, go. Don't put it off."

Charles nodded. "Okay. Thank you."

Lieutenant Varmitt pulled a rib bone from his mouth and asked, "Speaking of which, what's with the clumps of tissue on top of the roll? What's that about?"

Eddie chuckled. "What's that, Lieu?"

"Every time I go to the bathroom there's, like, a folded piece of toilet paper on top of the roll. It's like someone was gonna blow their nose, then changed their mind."

"How many times you going to the shitter, Lieu?"

"Hey, I'm very regular. Alright? Better out than in, you know?" Everyone laughed and he turned to Charles. "You know about this? The tissue? I feel like it started when you got here."

Charles saw everyone turn to him but didn't meet their eyes. He looked at Varmitt. "Yes.

They're pre-wipes. In case we get a run while you're on the toilet."

No one spoke for a moment. Then Eddie burst out laughing. "What the fuck? What's a pre-wipe?"

Charles was confused. Had he misunderstood?

McCann asked, "Did someone tell you to do this?"

Charles looked at him, then at the amusement on everyone's face, and he sighed. He looked up at the ceiling and shook his head, smiling. Everyone laughed now.

"Let me guess," Eddie said. "Either Pete Dufresne or Lieutenant Calahan told you to do it."

Charles rested his forehead on the back of his hand and

shook his head again. "I'm an idiot."

"You are," McCann agreed, smiling. "Firemen aren't ge-niuses, but we can take care of wiping our asses."

THINGS DIDN'T SLOW DOWN after dinner. There were half a dozen different calls for fire before midnight that were either barbecues or fireworks or, in one case, incense. At one o'clock in the morning, the house got a call for a lockout/food-on-the-stove. The caller claimed that she stepped out while cooking and forgot her keys. She was extra concerned because her two-year old was alone in the apartment and was still awake when last she checked on him. Charles's heart raced at the thought of the kid, remembering the child from his first day, but by the time they were back at the firehouse, he was laughing about it.

EVERYONE WAS ON OR around the couches behind the rigs as Varmitt and Eddie told them what happened.

"Eddie and Davids popped the door, and she bullies past them and runs inside to the bedroom, down the hall."

"She straight up jumped kicked the door! Like a superhe-ro."

"Wait, was there anything on the stove or no?" someone asked.

"No! The lights weren't even on in the kitchen."

"And no baby?"

"Nope. Just her boyfriend with a chic, tryna get their clothes on."

One of the guys from the Engine said, "Not for nothing, but she deserves some credit. First, she lied about leaving something on the stove, and when that didn't get us there fast enough, she made up a freakin' baby! She earned the right to beat his ass."

Varmitt said, "He deserved that beating. She was gorgeous. Why cheat on someone gorgeous?"

That question reminded Eddie of another run he went on a few years ago and the story he told about it reminded McCann of a run he had been once, and for the next hour everyone sat around and told stories of funny runs and silly people. Some of the guys ate ice cream, and some drank water. Charles had a Gatorade. He smiled as he listened. It reminded him of when he was young and lived at home. Because of their jobs, it wasn't often that his parents and all his siblings were home for dinner at the same time. The few days when they were, they would sit at the dinner table for hours after the meal was done and tell stories. And they would laugh.

He loved it.

Then the tones went off. Eddie hurried to the housewatch, looked at the ticket, and said over the PA, "Surprise, surprise. 8989 Douglas. Apartment 6B,"

And everyone sighed.

-22-

THURSDAY WAS TOUGH FOR Candace. That morning, she left for work half an hour earlier than normal to pick up a couple dozen cupcakes she preordered from a bakery in the area. She was alone. After the incident in the school, she and Hanna agreed it would be best if Hanna didn't accompany her anymore.

The cupcakes were for both her students and the staff. For the students because it was

America's birthday and birthdays should have celebrations, and for the staff because Candace was embarrassed. Intellectually, she knew what happened at the school wasn't her fault, but that didn't make her feel any better. And it wasn't just the incident that embarrassed her. Not really. What she was most ashamed of was how much she missed Alan.

Hanna staying with her for a while was a blessing. She felt the ache of the loneliness strongest when she was alone. Things may have never been great with Alan, but there was love. It was hard to justify to her friends and family and coworkers because Alan did such a good job of acting like a jerk, but at times, when they were alone, she wished people could see what she saw.

But that didn't matter anymore. It was too late now. They'd fought and taken time apart before, but this time felt final. It was unfortunate, and it was a constant struggle not to break down and cry.

AFTER SCHOOL, CANDACE BROUGHT three leftover cupcakes home and Hanna was

excited. They drank milk and ate forkfuls and talked about how they might go to Soul Cycle later to make up for it. When they were done, they sat cross-legged on the couch and Candace told Hanna that she loved her.

"I'm food drunk right now, and maybe a little happier than I would be if I hadn't just eaten that, but seriously, I love you. I can't thank you enough for being here."

"Yes, you can," Hanna smiled. "Any thanks is too much. You know you don't need to thank me."

Candace looked into her cup. "I know."

Neither woman spoke, then Hanna said, "Don't feel bad, Candace. You tolerated all you could."

"It's not that."

"What, then?"

"I know it's crazy, so don't say so, but I miss him. Not now, or…I don't want him back in the house. I miss the way things were. When we were good."

Hanna said, "Okay," then put her feet on the floor and dusted crumbs off her lap. "Honey, listen. You guys were never good." Candace laughed, and Hanna touched her leg and said,

"Seriously. He was never good for you. Or to you, even. He did the bare minimum of what a partner should do and, you know, mostly by accident."

Candace held Hanna's eyes before looking back into her cup. She sighed, then reached up and scratched her scalp, and when she was done, her hair hung like a curtain in front of her face.

Hanna turned to face her and started to say something, but then the door buzzer rang.

Candace looked out the window. It wasn't even dark out. She unfolded her legs and went to the intercom.

"Yeah?"

"I came to get my stuff."

Hanna said, "Wow. The devil really does appear when you speak of him."

ALAN DIDN'T HAVE A plan. He was there to get his things, but he didn't know how he would move them all and he didn't know where he'd take them once he did. But walking the street and sleeping in the check cashing place or the subway was already too much. At the very least, he should have a change of clothes.

He waited downstairs, impatiently. It took longer than it should have to buzz him in, but, eventually, Candace did. When the door buzzed, Alan took a deep breath, entered the lobby, and climbed the stairs. He took the stairs slowly, and once on the sixth floor, it took almost a minute for anyone to open the door. They were trying to piss him off. They were succeeding, but he refused to show it, so he waited in the hallway like an idiot until at last the door opened.

Hanna was there in a white t-shirt, shorts, and ankle socks, looking comfortable. She opened the door all the way, then let it go and turned toward the living room. Candace was sitting on the arm of the couch, holding a glass of milk.

Alan stepped inside before the door closed and swallowed his anger. He closed the door behind him, then looked around. Nothing had changed. That surprised him. He wasn't sure what he expected to be different, but he felt as if he had been gone forever. Yet everything seemed to be exactly where it was the last time he was there, almost a week ago. The same magazines were on the coffee table. The boxes of his stuff by the couch, bedroom, and the front door were still there, untouched. The same mail was on the table by the door, with his keys on top. The fan was still near the coffee table.

"All boxed up," Hanna said. "Get 'em and go."

Alan turned his gaze on her. "I'll go when I'm ready. I need to figure this out."

"Figure what out?" Hanna said, stepping forward. She was now between him and

Candace. "If it's yours, it's in a box. Grab all the boxes and go. What's to figure out? What? Do you want another day?"

Alan ignored the audacity of that question. He looked past her to Candace. She met his eyes and he could've sworn he saw something there. She wanted things back to normal as much as he did.

He said, "Candy, we need to talk."

She started to respond, but Hanna spoke over her and said, "We are talking. Say what you need to, then get your boxes—"

Alan snapped. He yelled, "Shut up!" Then marched over to Hanna and stepped into her personal space. He had no intention of hitting her or anything, he just wanted her to think he might. He wanted to scare her.

But he didn't scare her. She didn't move or back up. She lifted her chin and met his eyes, breathing slow and deep through her nose, a hint of a smile on her face. Candace had gotten up when he went over and was now beside Hanna. Standing there glowering over Hanna, with her showing no signs of fear, Alan looked needlessly foolish and knew it.

So he slapped her.

IT HAPPENED SO SUDDENLY that all three looked shocked by it, and for a moment, no one moved. Alan was probably the most surprised. One second, he was trying to figure out a way of not looking weak, the next, Hanna was staggering backward.

It wasn't planned, but after he had done it, he felt a little better. Anger seeped from him and he felt more in control, like he had the upper hand. But then the shock was over, the women reacted, and that feeling of control passed.

CANDACE REACTED FIRST, BUT Hanna was a fraction of a second behind her, and the timing made it impossible for Alan to defend himself. Candace screamed and lunged at him and he couldn't fully turn to her before she grabbed his shirt with one hand and his ear with the other. At the same time, Hanna growled, eyes red, and grabbed a hold of his collar and caught his wrist as he raised his arm to defend himself.

Hanna pushed him backward, squeezing and twisting his wrist, the knuckles of her other hand in his throat; while at the same time Candace pushed him to his left so that all three of them were moving unsteadily at an angle toward the front door. Alan collided with the table near the door, but Candace kept pushing, lost her balance, and fell on top of him. Hanna felt the shift, let go of him, and managed to stay standing.

The legs of the table gave out under the added weight, and it collapsed. Candace and Alan slid down with a thump, her back against the table, his on a bed of mail. He groaned from pain as the set of keys stabbed him below his shoulder blade, but then his pulse increased. Hanna, her face contorted with anger, clambered over Candace's legs, dropped to a knee beside Alan, who looked dazed, grabbed his neck, and punched him on the side of his head once, twice, three times before he got his arm up and pushed her back, where she landed on her butt. Candace, meanwhile, used the edge of the table to pull herself up and, once standing, kicked Alan as hard as she could between his legs. She wasn't completely balanced, so it didn't connect the way she'd hoped, but it was good enough. He bolted up to a sitting position, grabbed his crotch, and screamed in pain, and Candace screamed back.

Hanna scrambled to her feet, grabbing one of the broken table legs, and swung it at Alan's back, a feral grunt escaping with the effort. She lifted the leg up for another swing, and when Alan lifted his arms to fend her off, Candace kicked him again, same spot as before. Alan's mind couldn't figure out where his arms were needed most and he froze, screaming while Hanna brought the table leg down against his back again. The two women stood over him, kicking and swinging and screaming as Alan screamed and cried and tried to protect himself.

Candace looked tired from the effort, and after three or four kicks, Alan caught her foot, pushed her leg up and out until she fell backward. With both arms available, Alan turned to Hanna, who stepped back defensively and lifted the table leg to swing again. Having to start from farther back, her swing took longer to reach him, and he ducked it, got to his hands and knees, grabbed another table leg and threw it at her. Hanna turned away and the leg hit her high on her back. She staggered farther from him and he seized the opportunity. He moved the mail around, found the keys, then clamored to his feet a foot away from Candace, lying on the floor. He heard Hanna move behind him and he dropped his head between his shoulder blades, yanked open the door, and ran down the stairs.

HANNA RAN TO THE top of the stairs and threw the wooden leg after him but missed. She stood there breathing heavily, her shirt clinging to her chest. Turning around, she wiped her face as best she could, walked back to the apartment, and looked at Candace. She was on her feet now, as wet and upset as Hanna felt. The apartment was hot and musty like a locker room.

"Are you okay?" Hanna asked.

Candace didn't respond. She stood with her hands on her hips, her body rising and falling with each breath. Hanna went closer, leaving the door open, and wrapped her arms around her. And Candace cried.

-23-

"Hello?"

"Rob, it's me."

"AJ, what the fuck? What happened! What did you do?"

"What are you talking about?"

"The cops were here, man. They came to my place lookin'
for you. Dude, Jackie was home! She answered the door!"

"So?"

"So! She's fucked up right now! She's pissed, man."

"About what?"

"Candace! Candace and that chick…her friend, fuck's her
name?"

"Hanna?"

"Yeah, her. They're pressing charges on you."

"On me! For what?"

"They said you assaulted them."

"*I* assaulted *them*! Dude, my fucking ear is bleeding. My
ear, dude! I can barely walk right now. They attacked me! I
was just defending myself."

"AJ, but—"

"Rob, listen, I called because I need a place to stay. Just
tonight, man. One night."

"You serious right now?"

"Rob, c'mon. Don't give me that Jackie bullshit, dude. Just

one night! I really need it."

"AJ, I don't know what to tell you. You lost it, man, like…I don't know what to tell you."

"One night, Rob!"

"No, man. Sorry. Don't come here. Okay? Seriously. I don't need cops at my place again."

"Rob, I didn't do nothing! They attacked me! I just wanna stay one night! I'll leave first thing tomorrow."

"Sorry, man. No."

ALAN HELD THE PAYPHONE on the corner outside of Ritechek to his ear. He stared at his warped reflection on the rounded stainless steel of the base. Squeezing the receiver, he waited for Rob to say something else. When Rob didn't, Alan slammed the receiver back into the base. Then again. And again. He slammed the phone eight times until there was a crack between the handle and the earpiece. Then he slammed it once more and began to cry.

His whole life he had been screwed. By everyone. His father left him. His mom kicked him out. Candace, Kimberly, Rob. Even those firemen. Everyone. What had he done to deserve it? What can a child possibly do to deserve being abandoned? What more can a husband do than love and stick by his wife? What excuse can a friend give for not being loyal? None. It wasn't fair. But that was life, wasn't it? You're born, you get screwed, you die.

Well, Alan wasn't the only one living life. He wouldn't be the only one getting screwed. He ran through that list in his head again and nodded.

Fine.

-24-

WHEN MEGHAN QUINCY WOKE Friday morning, she was surprised she had slept so well. Since the day she night the pregnancy test, the nausea had become gradually worse. And not just in the mornings. In fact, if the last week was any indication of the norm, she thought it dumb that people called it morning sickness. It should be called all-day sickness. Or just sickness.

These past few days, apart from the constant nausea and the subtle but persistent headaches, she found herself awake at times she should be sleeping because her mind wouldn't quit. She thought about whether they should take the blood test for the gender or just wait. No one waited anymore. Gender reveal parties were fun, but she imagined the feeling of not knowing if the baby would be little Michael or Michelle until she heard it crying in the delivery room would be amazing. And, on that issue, baby names were a headache all their own. The responsibility was daunting. Last year she'd spent hours thinking of a name for her iPad before

Matt asked why she didn't just act normal and call it Meg's iPad.

Since the night of the test, she also thought a lot about work. She would get maternity leave. of course, but would it be enough? Would she want to go back? She never thought about being a stay-at-home mom before, but she'd never had a baby growing inside her before either.

She didn't *need* to work. Matt was paid well enough that they'd be okay if she took time off. She'd also be saving money on what she paid every month on tolls and gas. They'd save on a babysitter too, because if she did go back to work, they'd definitely hire a babysitter as opposed to family. Meghan had no problem with Matt's family, but no one lived particularly close. As for her own family...

Over the past week, the one thing she thought about more than any of those things was what her aunt had said. More than the nausea or the headaches, what kept her up the most was that thoughtless remark. She remembered it last night when Matt set his alarm for work and went to bed. She had lain beside him with his head on her shoulder and his hand on her belly, expecting to be up all night. Again. But when his alarm rang that morning, she opened her eyes, not really remembering when she had closed them.

Matt reached over and silenced the alarm, then scooted down to lay his head on her stomach.

"How did you sleep, baby?" he asked.

Meg ran her fingers through his hair. "I know you want me to answer so you can say you weren't talking to me, but I'm not gonna give you the satisfaction."

Matt laughed and kissed her stomach. "She's a clever one, your mom," he whispered. He moved to the top of the bed and kissed her. "You in any pain?"

"Meh. *You* might consider it pain, but that's why God made women to carry the kids."

"He's a good man, God."

"Or woman."

"Fair enough. You wanna share a shower?"

Meg frowned. "Absolutely not. I'm not sexy during morning sickness. Neither are you."

Matt kissed her again and said, "You're always sexy."

"Good boy."

"You still plan to ask Mildred to brunch."

"I said breakfast," Meg corrected, her eyebrows raised. "Brunch is for people who think avocado toast is a meal. But I think I'll do dinner instead."

"Good. She could use cheering up, I think. Sure you're okay?"

Meghan smiled. "I will be."

"Okay." He looked her over, kissed her cheek, then rolled off the bed and headed to the bathroom.

Meghan stretched and turned to face the window. The sun had not yet risen. The dawn had arrived but the darkness from the night remained. She lay on her side with her arm folded beneath her head. When she yawned, a tear squeezed out and rolled down her forearm. She was still tired. Despite the sleep, it hadn't been a restful night.

AT AROUND SIX O'CLOCK Friday morning, Charles sat on one of the couches behind the Truck and thought about his dad.

His father would've loved hearing about this. All of it. The drills, the fires, that woman from last night, all of it. He would've loved the feel of it. Charles's father was the head of a large family, but also came from a large family. He would have enjoyed the atmosphere in the house— tough guys, pranks and all.

At seven, Charles went into the kitchen and started the morning procedures. He ground beans and started a pot of coffee, then unloaded the dishwasher from last night's dinner. He took out butter and eggs and placed chairs around the table. When he was done, he started a second pot of coffee, and as he did, Joe Bahms walked in carrying two bags. Charles tried to take them from him, but when Bahms didn't give them up, the two walked to the table holding them together.

"You can't do everything, buddy, I think I told you that," Bahms said, smiling. "It's not everything," Charles countered. "I wasn't doing anything else. I already started the coffee."

"Nice touch."

Bahms had brought bacon and bagels. He took the bacon out of its bag and left the bagels in theirs. Charles carried the bacon over to the stove and Bahms grabbed a pan to cook it in. When Charles took the pan from him, he didn't resist.

Bahms went upstairs to change, and Charles started cooking. He got three plates and laid paper towels flat on each of them. By the time Bahms came back into the kitchen, Charles had all of one and most of a second plate covered with strips of cooked bacon lined in a row.

Bahms looked at the plates, up at Charles, back at the plates again, then chuckled.

"Did Calahan tell you to do this?"

Charles looked at the three plates laid out side by side. He closed his eyes and shook his head.

Such an idiot.

AT NINE O'CLOCK, CHARLES put his gear away, changed, and left. He was exhausted. He hadn't realized how much until he was off the clock, but once he was in his car, he couldn't stop yawning. He was scheduled to come back in that night and the next. He thought about what Libby said about him working so many nights in a row during a heat wave: *you're gonna be dead by Saturday!* "Dead" might've been dramatic, but if last night was any indication of the weekend, he would, at the very least, be spent.

Still, he had some time to rest. There were about seven

hours before he was due back. At least four would be spent sleeping. But first he wanted to call his mom. He was up most of last night thinking of his dad and he wondered if she had done the same thing. At home he made a smoothie, turned on a fan, sat in his father's chair, and called her. She picked up after the first ring.

"Hi."

"I was hoping you would sound well rested," Charles said.

"Um, I'm not. But I'm okay. What about you? Are you allowed to sleep during a night shift?"

Charles took a sip of the smoothie. The cold felt great. "I'm not really sure if anyone sleeps. It doesn't seem like it. I mean, there are beds in the firehouse, but, you know, we're still working. There could be a call at any time. I think the guys try to relax, but not so much that it would take them more than a minute to go when the bells sound."

"Okay. I see. So, what did you do all night?"

Charles told her about the calls. He told her that most of the night he just stayed on the couch, mostly thinking about his dad. "What do you do when you have trouble sleeping?" he asked her.

"I pray, mostly," she said. Charles could hear her shifting in her chair. "I read my Bible and I pray, and I listen to the news."

"Do you ever have difficulty sleeping because you're thinking about dad?"

His mom paused. "Not really. I guess it's different for spouses than it is for children. At least, you know, grown children who are no longer at home. Not greater or worse, just different. For you, you think about things that happen in your life that you would have liked him there for, and it's a reminder that he's no longer around. For me, everything in my life he would have been there for. So everything—every moment—is a reminder that he isn't here. Not just sleepless nights."

"I understand."

"I don't have difficulty sleeping because I miss him. I have difficulty being awake because I do."

They were quiet for a minute. Then his mom sighed and shifted in her seat again and said, "But that's why I pray. My life didn't end when his did. Neither did the world. And when the world doesn't end, you gotta keep going."

"Okay."

"Okay."

Charles's family never said the words "I love you" to each other. He never knew why, but he didn't wonder much about it either. That's just not what they did. They all knew they were loved by each other, so there wasn't really a need to say it. But as he sat there in his father's chair, smoothie forgotten on his lap, he wanted to tell his mom how much he loved her.

He didn't, though. Because that's not what they did.

LIBBY AND FELICIA WERE in the living room of their third-floor apartment eating breakfast a little after nine o'clock, Friday morning. Dog was on the couch, giving herself a bath. The bakery was already open, but it was slow enough in the morning hours that Serena could manage things alone.

The news played on the television but neither of them were watching it. Felicia was reading an email from her soror-ity about an event they were hosting next month, and Libby was shopping online. She hadn't remembered what she want-ed to buy, but Amazon was showing her a bunch of things she just realized she needed.

When Felicia was done, she took her plate to the sink. The television said it would hit ninety-five degrees later and she shook her head at that. She hated the heat. She hated the whole summer. What was there to like? No particular holidays that were great for business fell during the summer. She didn't sell ice cream, or beverages, so people weren't coming in for that. She didn't swim, so the open pools weren't a draw. And she had no desire to tan, so she didn't go to beaches.

She rinsed her plate and dumped it in the dishwasher. "You coming to the shop today or no?" she called over her shoulder.

Libby looked up from her phone and glanced at the television. The five-day forecast was on the screen and Libby saw that the heat wave would continue into Sunday. "Um, if you need me to, I will. But I hadn't planned on it."

Felicia shrugged. "Nope. I don't need you to. You going on a date with Charles?"

Libby smiled. "No. I do know other people, you know."

"You're dating other people?"

"No. I *know*…I'm not…who said I was dating Charles?"

Felicia rolled her eyes and sat down again. "Are you guys hanging out or no?"

"No! I'm meeting up with Diana."

"Why not with Charles?"

"Because I know other people."

Felicia stared at her but didn't say anything.

"And because he's working."

Felicia gave a small laugh. "I see. You guys are getting to know each other, though?"

"Yeah." Libby smiled. "He's a nice guy."

"I think so. Just be careful."

"Careful?"

"Yeah. Firefighters and police officers are hard to love. They may be the most confident people in the world, but the danger in confidence is that you never expect things to go wrong.

Sometimes they do, though. Sometimes bad things happen."

"Well, you're cheerful this morning," Libby said. She
stood and headed to the kitchen.

"I'm not being negative. I just want you to know what
you're getting into."

"What am I getting into? We've been on two dates and
you're already talking about love." Libby's plate clattered in
the sink. She was annoyed but didn't really know why. "You
act like we're getting married."

"Calm down, Libeth."

Libby closed her eyes and exhaled. She may have been
overreacting, she didn't know.

The conversation just seemed unnecessary. *Sometimes bad
things happen*? Why say that?

Felicia waited for her to open her eyes again. When Libby did, Felicia said, "There's no reason to be upset, so calm
down. What I'm saying is, the closer you two get, the more
his job may make you worry. That's natural. Just expect it,
that's all."

Libby turned to the couch. She regretted her reaction. "I
understand, Mom. Sorry. I just...we're not there yet. We have
been on two dates. It's been a week! Yes, things *could* happen. But that doesn't mean they will. I don't wanna worry. I'll
cross that bridge when we get to it. *If* we get to it."

"Good," Felicia said.

"Okay. Sorry again."

Felicia smiled. Libby turned back to the sink, rinsed off
her plate, and put it in the dishwasher, then changed her mind,
took it out, and hand washed it. She took out her mom's plate
and three other dishes that were in there and washed them too.
She didn't want to sit back down because she was still upset.
But not with her mom. The conversation made her think of

her dad. As much as she didn't want to think of it, her mom was right. *Sometimes bad things happen.* And it changes everything.

-25-

BEFORE HE WENT TO the firehouse Friday evening, Charles went to Libby's bakery and ordered two dozen cannoli. Libby wasn't there, but her mother and the other woman, Serena, were. He and Felicia exchanged small talk about the firehouse and the week he'd had and the Fourth of July. When the order was wrapped, he paid, said goodbye, and left, thinking that he really liked Libby's mom. Felicia watched him leave and smiled. She liked him too.

THE CANNOLI WERE A hit. Charles got to the firehouse ten minutes to four, dropped the cannoli on the kitchen table, set up his gear, and started a pot of coffee. He went to change, and by the time he came downstairs, most of the guys were sitting on the couches behind the rigs with a cannoli in one hand and a mug in the other.

Kohler was standing near the seating area holding a large glass that had once been a pickle jar, it was filled with ice and Red Bull. He smiled when he saw Charles.

"What's up, Charlie?"

"Hi, Joe. Are you going home?"

"Yeah, but I'm driving. You can't relieve me. Relieve Jimmy and Jimmy will get me."

Charles looked over to Jimmy, who was sitting on a couch

eating a cannoli and blowing into his cup. He took a second to swallow, then said, "You got the nozzle."

"Okay."

Charles went and set his gear up near the rig. When he was done, Kohler asked, "What's the occasion? Why the pastries?"

Charles shrugged. "No reason."

"Well, thank you," he said, and there was a murmur of agreement from everyone else.

"Next time, though, put a sign that says, 'Engine only,' so the dick-wagon doesn't bust open the box like a bunch of savages the second you drop it off."

McCann was on the couch beside Jimmy, a half-eaten cannoli on his knee.

"Really, Joe?" he said to Kohler. "You really wanna talk about savagery? Who's the only one of us who finished eating before he even left the kitchen?"

Kohler shrugged. "I'm a growing boy."

McCann shook his head. "No," he said to himself. "Too easy."

AFTER THE CHANGE OF tours, Charles, Bahms, and Kenny went over the rig. Kenny gave Bahms the backup position for the tour and he took control. When they were done going through the compartments, they brought a length of hose line and two plastic orange cones outside. They hooked the hose up to the rig and the rig to a hydrant across the street, then had Charles practice advancing the line. Bahms backed him up and Pete acted as the officer and told them where the fire was in that scenario. Matt and Josh stood back and watched, offering advice here and there. In the street, the guys from the Truck directed cars around the cones and curious kids to stay on the sidewalk.

Afterward, Charles said to Kenny, "This is random, but,

can I ask, why do you put candy in your mouth for every run?"

"Not every run," Kenny smiled. "Just fire runs."

"Why, though?"

"Sucking on a hard candy forces me to breathe through my nose instead of my mouth.

My heart is already racing because it's a fire. The candy kind of reminds me to calm down.

Know what I mean?"

Charles nodded and smiled. He was happy to hear that even someone with Kenny's time felt nervous when going to a fire.

WHEN THEY WERE DONE drilling, they started dinner: deep fried porkchops with egg noodles and broccoli. Paul Oldman sliced two pork loins into twenty-eight chops and Charles took them from him and started to bread them. Bahms stopped him and said, "We gotta pound those first. They fry easier if they're thin." He went away and came back with two meat mallets and handed one to Charles.

McCann, who was cracking eggs in a bowl for a wash, said, "Speaking of pounding,

Davids, you got a girl?"

MEGHAN WENT OVER TO Josh and Mildred's home around the same time McCann was

interrogating Charles about his sex life. The sun hung above their house like a spotlight. There were only two more hours of daylight, but the heat was as oppressive as it had been all along.

Meghan parked in the driveway, and in the seconds it took to make her way from the car to the porch steps, her face was wet from perspiration. Twenty seconds of walking. Imagine

giving birth in this heat. She stopped on the top step and tried
to figure it out. What month was this? July? She did quick
math and figured that her due date was probably in April. A
spring baby. Not terrible. Spring weather was pretty nice. She
placed a hand on her stomach and smiled.

"Good job, honey," she whispered.

Mildred was obviously happy to see her. She opened the
door and hugged Meghan tight around the neck, smashing
their bodies together. Meghan laughed and hugged her back.

"Careful," Meghan said. "We're not alone."

Mildred pulled away, dropped to her knees, and kissed
Meghan's stomach above the shirt. "This baby will be fine.
Nothing will ever hurt it. Not as long as I'm around." "Well,
that was easy," Meghan said, rubbing Mildred's head.

"What was?"

"The godparent talk."

Mildred looked up, beaming. "My little munchkin!"
she said, and hugged Meghan tightly around the waist, and
Meghan laughed again.

THEY SAT AT THE dining table, ate pasta, and talked
about pregnancy. The morning sickness lasting all day, the increased bowel movements, the cravings not being as specific
as portrayed on sitcoms, but more like a general desire to eat
junk. The pain in places other than the back and ankles. The
desire for sex while alone and the disgust for anything sexual
in male company.

Mildred told Meghan about a children's store she'd gone
to earlier in the week with her friend Marey who just adopted,
and how being there made her miss the baby phase of life.

"You're gonna be tired of me by the time this baby is a
year old," she said, looking at
Meghan's stomach.

"Never. That's what godparents are for. I want my baby to be as close to Josh and you as we are to Athena," Meghan said. It was the first opportunity in the conversation for her to say

Josh's name without being obvious. She watched Mildred's face when she did and caught the shift.

Mildred smiled, leaned over the island, and refilled her glass with water from a filtered pitcher.

"Have you guys started thinking of names yet?" she asked.

"No. I mean, yes, of course, but no, we're not gonna glaze over this," Meghan said.

"What's going on with you two?"

Mildred shook her head. "Can we not talk about it?"

"Of course," Meghan answered. "Let's go to the couch. My ass hurts."

The two stood and put their dishes in the sink, except their cups, and made their way to the living room. Meghan sat in the center of the couch and Mildred moved a pillow to sit beside her. She placed her cup on the table beside the couch and Meghan put hers on the floor. Meghan half turned to Mildred and smiled. Mildred smiled back.

"So," Meghan said. "What's going on with you two?"

JOSH WAS IN A better mood than he anticipated, all things considered. He was working with a good crew on the Truck and Matt was working on the Engine and everyone was having fun with the probie, who himself was having fun. The drill earlier had gone well, the meal was good, the conversation was flowing; it was what he loved about the job—a kind of family you couldn't replicate anywhere else.

Most of the conversation during dinner was relationship advice to Charles. After some ball-breaking, he admitted that he had been on a couple of dates with a girl who worked at the bakery where he got the cannoli's. Pooch had demanded a confession that the trip to the bakery wasn't a generous act for the firehouse so much as an attempt at a quickie. He, Charles, didn't admit to that, but he had hoped to see her.

Pete asked her name, and when Charles naively gave it, both first and last, a bunch of guys took out their phones and searched social media and the internet for her. Paul found her on Facebook and his phone was passed around for everyone to see. The probie looked uncomfortable, and though Josh knew the guys meant no harm, he thought of Athena.

"Probie!" Josh called across the table. "Let me ask you a question. How old are you?"

"Twenty-four, sir."

"Twenty-four. Let me tell you something. My good friend Michael Davidson told me this when I was a probie. He was a good dude, Mikey. Great fireman, great father and husband—a real gentleman. He took me under his wing immediately before I was any of those things and he told me, he said, Josh, for the first five years of your career, don't get fat and don't get married."

Charles laughed, but Josh shook his head seriously.

"No bullshit. I'm being serious. After five years on this job, especially in this house, you're a totally different person than when you came. A better person. You'll learn things you didn't even know you didn't know. You'll be a better man for this one," he waived his hand. "Libby or whoever you end up with. You'll be in great shape, you'll know how to work with your hands like a man, and you'll know how to problem solve."

Danny: "And you'll know how to cook."

Pooch: "And you'll be the best damn toilet cleaner you can be!"

"And bedmaker!" McCann added.

"Yeah. What woman can resist a man who can fold fitted sheets?" Paul said.

Josh sighed. "Fellas, come on. I'm tryna do my sage thing here."

AFTER DINNER, MATT WENT upstairs to work out. He was interrupted by two runs but eventually got his full hour in. Afterward, he went to his office to clean up, then sat in the recliner beside the bed and called Meg.

"Hey," she answered.

"Hi, beautiful baby momma. How's it going?"

"Uh…"

"You're trying to decide how you feel about me calling you baby momma, aren't you?"

"Already decided."

"Won't happen again."

"Thanks."

Matt laughed, pulled the lever on the side of the chair, and leaned back. "So, how'd it go today?"

"Still going," Meg said. "We're here binge watching *The Blacklist* on Netflix."

"Oh, nice. I know you can't speak freely, but is she okay? Did you guys get to talk about

Josh and her?" He was whispering even though his office door was closed, and Josh was downstairs with the others.

"Yes and yes," Meg said. Then, "She agreed that they'd be the godparents." Matt heard Mildred say something in the background but couldn't make it out. "The best ever godparents, excuse me," Meg said, laughter in her voice.

"Junior will be so lucky," Matt said.

"How's work going?" Meg asked. He knew she noticed the reference to a son and decided to ignore it.

"Not crazy," he answered. "Honestly, it's been a pretty

good night."

Just then, the tones sounded, loud in the quiet of the office.

Meg said, "Great. You just jinxed it."

THE RUN WAS FOR an odor of gas in the second-floor hallway of a tenement four blocks away. It turned out to be a faulty stove in an older woman's apartment, which the Truck shut down. As they were leaving the building, Matt, Kenny, and Bahms took the opportunity to take Charles inside and show him how narrow the stairwell was for stretching a line. On the rigs, the Manhattan dispatcher called the Chief.

"Manhattan calling Battalion 5."

Chief Leland pressed the button on the receiver. "Battalion 5."

"Battalion 5, are units still operating at your box?"

"Negative. We're ten-eight."

Brian O'Neil was driving the chief and pushed the mic on his radio. "Guys, we're about to get another run." Kenny stopped speaking and the Engine came down off the stairwell and headed out. They were almost to the rig, when Brian's voice came through their radios again, louder and more urgent.

"Second-due for a store on fire. Amsterdam Avenue between West 1-3-0 and West 1-3-1.

Multiple calls!"

Everyone got on the rig and Pete peeled off after the Truck before the doors were fully closed. Charles was the only one on the Engine wearing all his gear for the gas run, so while Kenny and Bahms got dressed, he read the ticket out. There wasn't much to read because there wasn't a building number. Just the cross streets and that the caller stated, "Store on fire."

The screen refreshed and showed that Engine 80 was ten-eighty-four. Charles said, "80's there." It refreshed again and Ladder 23 showed up as on scene too.

Ladder 23's boss came over the speakers in the rig. "Ladder 2-3 to Manhattan…"

"Ladder 2-3, K."

"Manhattan, transmit our box. Ten-seventy-five."

Engine 99 followed Ladder 88 around a corner onto Amsterdam Avenue and a fire that looked too big to be real engulfed a store front in the middle of the block. Talk that Charles could barely register spilled from the radio. He took a deep breath and let it out slowly.

Kenny said, "Well damn!"

Bahms, who had been turned in his seat to see through the windshield, turned back around and pulled his gloves on.

Kenny reached into the bucket beside him and grabbed a Jolly Rancher. When Charles did the same, Kenny smiled.

Pete pulled to a stop in front of a hydrant across the street and hopped out along with everyone else. The store was only one-story high, and the flames seemed to be covering the entire front from the ground to the roof. Engine 80 had already stretched a line along the sidewalk and was preparing to operate. Ladder 23 had saws running, cutting padlocks and roll down gates. Charles and Bahms got behind 80's nozzle team and grabbed the line to help them advance it.

The chauffeur from 80 said over the radio, "Here comes your water," and Charles, who was closer to the back of the line than the front, felt the hose began to vibrate.

A crowd of people on the corner of West 131st aimed cell-phone cameras at the blaze.

Police officers stood between them and the rigs but didn't make them leave. Charles couldn't blame them for their fascination, he'd never seen so much fire in real life before.

Engine 83, the third-due Engine, stretched a second line

on the sidewalk in anticipation of the fire spreading to the stores on either side of it. A good move, Charles thought. He couldn't tell what kind of store the one burning was, but things could get really bad if either of the stores next to it caught fire. They both had pretty combustible product, he figured. To the left of the fire building was a florist and to the right was a hair salon.

-26-

ALAN WAS IN THE crowd on the corner. He watched as the fire engulfed Kim's and he covered his face so no one would see him smile. That wasn't really a danger, though. No one paid him any attention. Why would they? They were in awe of the show.

Alan watched the fire burn away that stupid awning and he smiled.

HE'D SPENT THE DAY riding the train. Once the sun had set, he'd gone to the park looking for his dealer but Jaylee wasn't there. Which was annoying. Friday early evening: there would be dozens of customers looking to score. It was dumb of Jaylee to miss the opportunity.

But Alan wasn't there five minutes before he realized why Jaylee wasn't. Cops. They were everywhere. He couldn't stay there and wait. The cops may not have been in that park specifically for him, but they would be happy to get their hands on him. He couldn't allow that.

He left the park but he had nowhere to go. He couldn't go home for the obvious reason. He couldn't go back to Ritechek because if the cops knew to go to Rob's place, they probably knew he spent his nights at the check cashing spot. Even if he could get over the filth of a motel room, he was worried about them because the cops sometimes raided those places. The more he walked around, the more he exposed himself, but he couldn't just walk into a random building and hangout in the lobby. So, what to do?

The keys! He stopped, pulled out his key ring, saw the store keys for Kim's shoe store, and smiled. He got his bearings, then turned and walked to Convent Avenue.

ALAN PASSED BY KIM'S on the other side of the street first. The store was closed, but that didn't mean she wasn't there. She often stayed after hours.

The lights on the sales floor were off and he didn't see a light in the corner that led to the stockroom and office. He crossed the street to the store side at the corner and walked back slowly. On the alarm panel inside, he saw the flashing red light that indicated the system was armed and he smiled again.

Perfect. The alarm code was 7777 because Kimberly was superstitious. The lock was at the bottom of the door. He pulled out his keys, found the right one, and crouched down.

The key didn't fit.

Alan massaged his eyes with his thumb and middle finger, then opened them wider. He just wasn't aligning it right. He tried again, but still it wouldn't go. Frustrated, he knelt to one knee and lowered his head to the lock, opened his eyes even wider, and tried again. No.   "What the fuck?" Alan checked the key in his hand. It was the right one. Why the hell wasn't it working? He tried again, and when it didn't work, he tried flipping it upside down. Nothing.

"Fuck!" He knelt on both knees now, sitting on his calves, staring at the keys, confused. What was going on? How could the keys not work? Alan looked through the glass door at the flashing red light and the reason hit him like a slap in the face.

"She changed the fucking lock."

ALAN STARED AT THE lock for almost three minutes, on his knees. With each passing minute he felt his rage increase, and for a time, he considered just bashing the windows and doors. But then he had the idea to torch the place and it felt like poetry.

He walked to a gas station a few streets away, passing a bodega on the way, and went to the convenience store at the station. At the register, he bought a pack of tissue and a five-gallon jug. It was red like on TV and he told the guy behind the glass that his car had broken down some streets down. He paid for the items and five gallons of regular, filled the jug, dropped the nozzle back in the holster, turned around, and headed back. He stopped in the bodega and paid a dollar for a book of matches.

When he was back on Convent Avenue, he stood in front of Kim's holding the jug in his left hand, his right hand curled in a fist. His face was a blank stare. He was thinking. If he broke the glass, it would probably trigger the alarm, and that would bring the police. He may not have time to get in, dump the gas, and set the fire before they arrived. He could do a kind of Molotov cocktail thing and throw the whole jug through and just let it spread where it may, but he wasn't entirely sure how to do that, and he might end up blowing himself up.

He was overthinking. It didn't really matter. He didn't care about burning the place to the ground. He was making a statement. Checking a name off the list. He wasn't going to be the only one getting screwed.

Alan pulled the cork from the jug and the smell of gasoline surrounded him. He looked around. People were on the streets, but not many on Convent Avenue, and all the stores were closed. He stepped up to the door, knelt in front of it, and opened the pack of tissue. He tried stuffing them halfway inside, but the seal between the bottom of the door and the metal frame was too tight. Frustrated, he dumped the tissue on the ground, stood up, and poured the gasoline along the length of the store, from corner to corner. When the ground was wet, he stood back and started swinging the jug toward the door and window. He aimed as high as he could, and when there was only a little left, he turned the jug over and drained it.

His heart raced now. He didn't dare look around—it'd be a shock if no one was watching—he didn't need to let them see his face. He had to be fast. He took the book of matches and tore one off. When he swiped it across the back, nothing happened. He laughed incredulously. Nothing worked for him. He tried again, and again nothing happened. The third time, he pinned the head of the match between his thumb and the pad, yanked it free, and finally a flame ignited.

Excited, he held the match to the rest of the book. A small fire appeared in his fingertips. He stared at the dancing flames, then realized he had been there too long, and threw it at the store.

-27-

THE FIRE DEPARTMENT HAD no difficulty putting
the fire out. The ground to roof blaze was a sight to see, but it
was all show and no go. The reality was, there wasn't much
to keep the fire going. Aside from a cloth awning, Kim's store
front was all glass and brick, neither of which burned. The
glass melted in places and the brick was charred, but the fire
never got inside or spread to the surrounding stores, so even
though it grew big, it went out easily.

THE FIREFIGHTERS ENJOYED DOING it. They spent
a good amount of their tours mitigating gas or CO leaks,
helping people out of stuck elevators, shutting down faulty
faucets, and assisting with medical emergencies, but fighting
fires was the job. A situation like this, where there was a good
amount of fire to fight, no one injured or trapped, and no one's
home ruined, was ideal. It didn't happen often, so when it did,
they all enjoyed it.

CHARLES NEVER PUT HIS facepiece on. There wasn't
a need. Once Engine 80 had water on the fire, there was some
smoke, but because it was outdoors, it mostly traveled up.
Once the fire was out, and the Trucks were breaking the store
front window and opening up the walls to see if the fire had

spread inside, Charles shut down his tank and spit out the Jolly Rancher.

A crowd had formed behind the police and caution tape. When 80 first opened the line, those people applauded. Now as they watched the fire department wrap things up, someone would occasionally shout out something like, "Thank you guys!" or, "You're the best!" and there'd be more sporadic applause.

Charles was smiling. He didn't take the applause personally because he hadn't really done anything, but he enjoyed seeing the people go from shocked and concerned to appreciative and relieved. He looked over to the crowd and their phone cameras and wondered if he were clearly visible. Maybe Libby was watching again.

THEY GOT BACK TO the fire house just before midnight. Everyone took a few minutes to wash up, change their shirts, and clean their equipment, before going their separate ways to relax and try to rest. The attempt was unsuccessful. About a quarter after midnight, the Engine got an EMS run for a seventy-four-year-old male with difficulty breathing. On their way there, the Ladder was assigned to a call for a water leak in the projects.

When the Engine was a minute away, the Manhattan dispatcher called them over the radio. Matt answered through the phone on the console and the dispatcher said, "99, ten-ninety-one. You're ten-eight."

Bahms looked over to Charles. "What did he say?"

"Who?"

"The dispatcher."

"He said, 'Ten-ninety-one. We're ten-eight.'"

Bahms smiled. "I heard him. What does that mean?"

Charles smiled back, not embarrassed. "It means EMS is

on scene, so we don't need to go. And we're now in service and available for another call."

"My man."

While they were talking, the screen had cleared of the EMS ticket and the numbers 10-8 replaced it. Then a ring sounded, and the screen refreshed again with another EMS ticket. Above the information, the words "assign specific units." The Engine had been assigned to the same water leak that the Ladder was on.

Kenny frowned when he looked at the screen. "EMS for a water leak? That's weird." Pete did a U-turn and they went lights and siren to the address.

As it happened, it wasn't so much a medical emergency as it was a frustrated neighbor. The "patient" was in apartment 11D. The occupant in the apartment above, 12D, had a faulty washing machine that overflowed. The water had made its way down into 11D through heat pipe chases, and aside from wetting the walls and the floor, had also wet an outlet where 11D's fan was plugged in. 11D had done the safe thing and shut off the breaker to the outlet, but was now suffering from the heat and claimed to feel faint.

Charles wasn't sure he believed she felt faint so much as angry, and, in fact, when an EMS ambulance arrived later, the "patient" refused medical attention.

THEY WERE ALL BACK to the firehouse for only a minute before the tones went off again.

The Engine was assigned to a brush fire on West 140th and Douglass Boulevard that turned out

to be teenagers playing with the remainder of their fireworks. They had directed their cherry bombs into a large pile of garbage outside a café on the corner, and the garbage had gone up in flames. There was no danger of the fire spreading.

If left alone, it would likely have burned itself out, but Matt didn't want to risk being called back, so Charles and Bahms stretched a line from the front of the rig and put it out while Kenny picked through it with a hook to make sure the water reached all the embers.

AT THE SAME TIME, Ladder 88 was back on their rig, on their way to a call for an occupied stuck elevator. The elevator was reportedly stuck on the ninth floor of a fifteen-story building. There were two elevator cars, but one had been shut down earlier in the day for a similar malfunction. That meant that Josh, along with Fagan, who had the irons, and McCann, who had the can, had to walk up to nine; but Danny, who had the roof position, had to walk all the way up to the roof where the elevator machine room was located. Paul took the hike up with him.

Fagan keyed his radio and told Pooch, who was driving, that they would be walking—a message that it would take a little longer than usual. Especially if there was an occupant who needed to be helped down. Which there was.

Pooch acknowledged him, then leaned back to wait and listened to the Manhattan frequency to see what else was going on in the city.

IN THE ENGINE, PETE was also listening to the Manhattan frequency. The guys had put out the trash fire and now Kenny was showing Charles how to refill the tank. They'd hooked up a suction line to the hydrant and Bahms and Kenny were quizzing Charles on hydrant pressures when Manhattan called them over the radio.

"Manhattan calling Engine 9-9."

Pete picked up the phone pushed the button and said, "Engine 99." He reached out his window and slapped his door two times. Kenny looked up and Pete made two circles with his finger, a signal to wrap things up. Matt walked around the front of the rig, opened his door, and looked up inquisitively.

The dispatcher said, "9-9, are you available?"

"Ten-four," Pete answered, and Matt climbed in.

"9-9, respond first-due, phone alarm box 6-9-2-8 address 8989 Douglass Boulevard and

148th Street for a fire, sixth floor. 9-9, receive?"

Matt rolled his eyes. "This idiot, again?"

Pete shook his head and scratched his scalp beneath his cap. "At least we're already out and he isn't waking us up." The monitor between them rang and the ticket appeared. Ladder 30 was assigned first-due Truck because Ladder 88 was still at the stuck elevator.

Matt said, "The Truck isn't on this one," meaning 88. "They must be on another box.

We're gonna beat Ladder 30 in."

"By a lot probably," Pete said. "They know it's bullshit."

"Yeah," Matt agreed. "I'll run up and talk to the wife. If the chief isn't in by the time I'm done, just give the ten-ninety-two."

"As you wish," Pete said. He looked back to make sure everyone was on the rig. They were, and he pulled away.

Kenny looked at the monitor in the back as he sat down and shook his head. "At least we're already out," he said.

Matt started putting on his coat. He knew it was nothing, but he didn't want the occupant to think he was unprofessional. It was usually the Truck boss who went to the door first, so this would be Matt's first time meeting the woman. He leaned forward to get his arm through his sleeve and saw a glow up ahead. On his left, Pete just passed West 143rd, and in the corner of his eye, Matt saw the chief's rig pulling away from the firehouse on their way to respond. But he wasn't thinking about that. He was looking ahead, not believing what he was seeing. The dispatcher came over the radio and said, "Manhattan calling Battalion 5."

Now Pete leaned forward. The rig slowed briefly, and he said, "Oh shit!"

POOCH HEARD WHEN MANHATTAN assigned 99 to the chronic false alarm box, and he laughed. For that guy to call every night was just childish, but Pooch kind of respected his diligence. He keyed his radio and said, "The Engine and the chief are going to 8989 Douglas right now."

Josh: "Wow."

McCann: "Aw. We missed that?"

Pooch was looking through the gallery on his phone at pictures he had taken with his sons at the beach earlier, trying to decide which he was going to make his Facebook profile picture, when Manhattan called the chief.

"Manhattan calling Battalion 5."

"Battalion 5."

"Battalion 5, we're filling out your box. We're getting multiple calls and reports of people on the fire escapes. Rescue has been assigned."

Pooch sat up straight and tossed his phone to the side. He keyed the mic on his handie-talkie, started to speak, but paused when he heard Lt. Quincy's voice call Manhattan, excited and out of breath.

"Engine 99 to Manhattan."

"Engine 9-9, K."

"Ten-seventy-five our box. Fire out the windows on the top floor."

Pooch, his brows raised and finger still keying his mic, said, "Oh shit."

JOSH PUSHED THROUGH THE stairwell door into the lobby at a sprint and followed McCann and Fagan out of the building and to the rig. Pooch had already given a signal for the elevator and gotten them assigned to box 6-9-2-8. They replaced Ladder 30 as the first-due Truck but were farther away than 30 was. So, as soon as the last guy was on the rig, Pooch leaned on the horn, stepped on the gas, and sped off.

KEITH NICHOLS OF LADDER 30 was a thirty-six-year veteran of the department. He pushed
30's rig fifty miles an hour down 145th Street, laying on his horn every time he approached an intersection. Engine 59 was two seconds behind him. He loved this. As Keith got closer to Douglass Boulevard, in his side mirror, he saw the lights from 88's rig coming up behind 59. He didn't hear their sirens over his own, but he knew 88 was in a rush to get there. More of a rush than he was because it was their first-due box, and they were the last ones assigned to it. Keith checked his mirror, then moved to his right and eased off the gas. The rig slowed a little but not much, and 59 did the same. Ladder 88 caught up, then sped past them, sirens blaring, and Keith leaned out his window and yelled, "Yeah!"

Without slowing, 88 made the turn onto Douglass Boulevard. Keith cut his wheel to the left and followed, then stepped on the gas again, Engine 59 still two seconds behind.

Mike Puchane from 88 Truck came over the handie-talkie and said, "Thank you, brothers."

Keith said, "You got it," and fell in behind, the three rigs racing to the scene.

-28-

MATT'S DOOR WAS OPEN before Pete came to a
stop. He jumped from the rig with his tools and was off to the
building. Fire pulsed from the side windows on the top floor.
The B apartment. He thought of the wife. God forbid she was
in there.

He pushed through a small group of people coming from
the building; some worried or scared, others confused and
barely awake, nearly all in pajamas. Or less. He went through
the main door, chocking it open as he passed.

He smelled smoke as soon as he entered the lobby. Only a
light haze hung on the first floor, but people coming down the
stairs were coughing, their teary eyes the only parts of their
faces uncovered by their shirts. Matt ran up the first flight
to the half landing and looked up toward the second floor.
The haze was darker there—not blinding, but heavy enough
to make him think the door to the fire apartment was open.
Which wasn't good. That much fire was definitely looking to
spread, and an open door would give it all the room it needed.

Two young women came from the third floor, holding
hands, pinning their collars over their mouths and noses. One
pointed up and said, "Fifth floor. 5B, I think."

"Got it," he replied, and, "Thank you. Stay to your right
going down."

The women released each other's hands and went past him,

one behind the other, holding on to the railing.

Matt continued up, a familiar rush of adrenaline starting through him. On the fourth floor it was harder to see and harder to breath. He dropped to a knee and masked up. He wasn't out of breath, and despite the adrenaline, he was calm. He ran up to the fifth floor. It was hotter there than on the floors below. He went over to the foot of the next flight and looked up, but the beam from his light barely pierced the heavy smoke. At the half landing, he took a step up and looked toward the fire apartment. It looked like the entrance to hell.

Red eerily silhouetted the doorframe, tongues of flame lapping out at the hallway walls and ceiling. He crouched, wincing from the heat on his head, and duck walked up the stairs, then turned around and went back to the half landing. It was no good. The whole apartment was on fire. He couldn't get to the door to close it if there even was a door. It could've been burned through. He'd have to wait for the line.

CHARLES AND BAHMS ENTERED the building just as the two young women were leaving, and the one who'd spoken before repeated that the fire was on the fifth floor.

Charles, sucking on a Jolly Rancher, carried the nozzle horseshoe. He started up the stairs on legs that felt numb.

"Fifth floor?" he asked, confused. A stupid question because he'd seen the fire on the top floor when they pulled up, but the woman at the door sounded so confident.

"Six," Bahms said behind him. "She probably lives on five. The smoke's not lifting."

They made their way up to the second floor, then the third, sticking close to the wall, trying to keep the hose line from hugging the railing. At each landing, Charles waited for Bahms, who occasionally had to pull the line up the stairs for more slack. On the third-floor landing, Charles noticed how hard he was sucking on the Jolly Rancher and tried to calm himself.

It was slow going. Ideally, at least five people would help stretch the first line, but the second-due Engine hadn't arrived when they'd entered, and Kenny was busy outside pulling the amount of lengths they would need off the back of the rig. When they made it to the fourth floor, they were breathing heavy. They stopped and masked up there. Charles pushed the Jolly Rancher to his cheek with his tongue and took a deep breath. When they were done, Bello tapped his back and they kept going.

It was a lot hotter on the fifth floor. No wonder that woman thought the fire was there. Charles was breathing through his nose but he could still feel the heat in his lungs. He stopped at the foot of the stairs going to the sixth floor and waited for Bahms to catch up. The candy wasn't working. He wished he could spit it out, but he couldn't; his mouth was covered by the facepiece. He felt trapped and tried not to panic. Bahms came up behind him, his face close to Charles's ear.

"Don't sweat it, bro," he said loudly. "A little fire or a lot, it always goes away with water. Okay?"

"Okay," Charles said loud enough to be heard. Then to himself he said again, "Okay." Bahms slapped his back, and they climbed the stairs to the half landing.

THEY COULDN'T SEE UP there. Charles didn't even see the light from Matt's flashlight until he was nearly standing beside him. The boss placed a firm hand on his shoulder, and Charles stopped.

Matt yelled, "Flake the line from here! We don't have control of the door!"

Charles nodded. He laid his horseshoe down and Bahms took the center of it and ran back down to the fifth floor to flake the line away from the fire. Charles knelt on the line behind the nozzle and looked up to the fire apartment. It was strangely clear up there. The stairway, just half a landing down, was dark, but it was bright on the sixth floor, like the fire burned up all the smoke. *It always goes away with water.* He wasn't so sure.

Bahms had finished and was back behind Charles. Then Josh appeared at the foot of the stairs, followed by Fagan and McCann. They were all masked up. They stepped over the hose and around the men to the sixth floor, standing, but the heat brought them to their knees. Josh yelled for the other two to take the door for 6A and Fagan and McCann crawled up the last few stairs into the oven.

Meanwhile, Matt said, "9-9 to Chauffer. Start water."

"Here comes your water."

At the door to 6A, Fagan stood to a crouching position, separated his tools, dropped the axe, and stepped on it. He tried the knob, but it was locked. McCann grabbed the axe from under his foot and Fagan quickly gapped the door. They both grimaced from the heat next door but kept working.

The hose filled behind them, and Charles opened the nozzle to let the air out, but the line was kinked in a few places where it folded on the floor below. Charles knelt on it so the pressure wouldn't pull it down the stairs and Bahms hurried down to relieve the kinks. By the time he was back behind Charles, Fagan had the door to 6A forced.

But not open. There was something on the floor behind the door. Fagan leaned on the door and felt it move slightly. He dropped to one knee, snaked his arm in, and felt behind the door. Smoke seeped into the hallway over his arm. Whatever was keeping the door closed was out of reach. Fagan pushed the door harder, sliding the object back enough to get in. The smoke spilling out was heavier now, but they could see a glow coming from a backroom.

Fagan crawled inside over a towel, checked behind the door, and found an old woman in a night gown, sprawled out on the floor, not moving.

-29-

EARLIER, SHERYL TABACCO HAD gone to bed
after spending what felt like hours on the toilet. She'd been
backed up and the effort used to relieve herself combined with
the stifling summer heat made her dizzy and weak. The sun
had long gone but the heat and humidity were unaffected by
its absence. The air felt sticky and uncomfortable. Her bedroom's ceiling fan hadn't worked for years and the portable
fan beside her radio on the nightstand only pushed hot air. The
digital readout on the radio showed 1:58 a.m. It was tomorrow
already. Her birthday.

Sheryl spent the first two hours of the sixty-eighth year of
her life struggling to take a crap.

She lay in bed, frowning at the ceiling. Outside the bedroom window, she could hear the sounds of a typical summer
Friday night in Harlem. She couldn't speak for the rest of
New York, but that old saying was definitely true of this part
of the city: it never slept. And lately it felt like Sheryl didn't
either. That night, like most nights, she lay in bed staring at
the ceiling, angry.

Sheryl was angry for a bunch or reasons. She was angry
that she had to set hours aside just to use the toilet. She was
angry that setting time aside to crap was, on most days, really
the only thing she needed to set time aside to do. She was

angry that it was the middle of the night and it felt hotter than
it did in the middle of the day. Or *as* hot, or whatever. Mostly,
Sheryl was angry at Kevin, her husband. She was angry that
he'd passed away and left her alone. All alone in this sleepless
city on this backward planet that for some reason got hotter
when the sun went down.

Then she heard the Johnsons fooling around in the apartment next door and she was upset about that too.

Or maybe it sounded more like rough play. "Horsing
around," Kevin used to call it. There were grunts and heavy
breathing and things being bumped into or knocked over. And
there was laughter. They were either horsing around or fooling
around, but whatever it was, pissed her off.

She felt like a fool. She'd gone against her better judge-
ment and invited Mrs. Johnson into her home. She'd felt bad
for Candace when she saw her on the stairs, but deep inside
Sheryl knew. She knew the Johnsons would likely end up
back together. She never liked that man, and she should've
just stayed out of it. Now they were next door horsing around
in the middle of the night when people were trying to sleep,
for crying out loud.

So Sheryl was angry. She rolled out of bed and slammed
her window shut. It hadn't provided any cool air anyway. She
went to the bathroom, grabbed a towel from the rack, and
used it to cover the small gap at the bottom of her apartment
door. It may not have done much to help block the sounds
from her neighbors, but she had to try some damn thing. She
stomped back to her bed, climbed in, stuffed a pillow under
her head and squeezed the sides against her ears.

"For crying out loud," she complained.

BUT IT WAS TOO much. The heat, the inconsider-
ate neighbors, the loneliness, the pain—all too much. She

couldn't do it. Why fight it? At Kevin's funeral last October, Mirna, his brother's wife had sat beside her and held her hand. When Sheryl would start to cry, Mirna would squeeze it and tell her to be strong.

One time, she said, "Be strong, Sheryl. You gotta be strong for Kevin. He would want you to be happy."

Such a ridiculous statement. Pure nonsense. A stupid person's idea of a smart thing to say. Kevin didn't want her to be happy; he was dead. He didn't want anything anymore. And truth be told, neither did she. So why fight it?

No reason to. So Sheryl didn't. She couldn't be strong, so she stopped trying. She let it all go. Her strength. Her hope that the pain would pass, even her anger. And she squeezed her eyes shut and cried.

THEN THE SKY FELL. It landed just below her chest and knocked the wind out of her. Her eyes popped open and her head shot up, but the rest of her body stayed pinned where it was. It took more than a second to catch her breath and the panic of suffocation gripped her. She grabbed her neck with both hands, screaming silently. The world was quiet, dim, and she felt no pain or discomfort other than the fear that she would choke to death. Then finally her throat opened, she took a breath, and felt the pain.

Sheryl gasped and cried out, staring into a cloud of fire. Her mind struggled to make sense of what was happening. She looked down at her body and saw the ceiling fan balanced half on her and half off the side of the bed. She looked up again at the flames in the air and knew they would come down and take her.

But they didn't. They moved along over her head and spit out small burning chips. Tears rolled down her face. She tried a deep breath and screamed out from the pain it caused. She cried harder now, tried to scream intentionally, but couldn't. She coughed and felt fluid in her throat. An ember from the rolling fire on the ceiling landed on the sheets at the foot of her bed and glowed there. It sunk deeper as it burned through, and as it fell, it grew. Sheryl watched it and the panic increased. She pushed the wooden blade of the fan and gravity took it to the ground beside her bed. She went to climb off and cried out again from the pain in her leg. Something was broken above her knee. She didn't know what, but she felt it.

The fire was spreading. Smoke came up from the sheets and down from the ceiling. Fear moved her. She grabbed the side of her bed with both hands and pulled. Her body rolled off, away from the fire, and she landed on the floor, her back arched by one of the fan's blades. She screamed again. It came out as a cough and left blood in her mouth.

Her feet were still on the bed, and the spreading fire met her heels and singed her, but this time she didn't scream. Her mind didn't register the pain; it had too much else going through it. She rolled again and felt tied up. Her gown was clinging to her and restricting her movement. But she did move. She dragged herself by her forearms half a foot at a time out of the bedroom, toward her front door.

Moving was hard. Breathing was hard. Sheryl cried as she crawled, and crying was hard. A shadow moved over her along the ceiling, following her. It would beat her to the door, she thought. It wouldn't let her leave. But Sheryl kept crawling. She thought of Kevin. He died at home. It was a dreadful sight, but it was the best thing for him. He would have hated to be in a hospital with people taking care of him. He was strong, and he died that way. He wouldn't have given up. He wouldn't have let the shadow win. So she kept crawling.

She hit the front door with her wrist. Gasping for air, she tried to lift her head but couldn't. The shadow grew. The

252

doorknob was three feet above her. If she could just reach it and get to the hall, she'd be safe from the shadow. But she couldn't stand and she couldn't lift her arms. *Be strong, Sheryl. You gotta be strong for Kevin.*

Kevin. He was still in the bedroom, on the dresser. Alone, under a river of fire. Tears mixed with ash and soot on her face. She shouldn't leave him, even though he left her. She had to go back for him. She had to be strong.

But she couldn't. So she stopped trying. She let it all go. And the shadow took her.

-30-

WHEN JOSH REPORTED THAT the fire had extended to apartment 6A, the chief made it a second alarm. By that point eight different live videos of the fire were streaming online, and many news outlets were paying attention. When a body was carried out by two firefighters and put onto a stretcher, all those media outlets had a reporter or photographer headed to the scene.

KENNY FOLLOWED THE CHARGED hose line into the building. Engine 59 was behind him, and when their members got on the line, Charles and Bahms were able to move more easily, but not much faster.

They started by hosing down the doorway of 6B. Once there was water on the fire, the visibility decreased drastically. Matt crouched behind them and shone his light into the apartment, but it didn't help. The light reflected off the heavy smoke. Charles couldn't make out his surroundings, but he could see the glow, so he moved slowly and alternated between whipping the line and sweeping the ground.

He sensed more than he could see when they made it inside. The space grew and the temperature rose. The air in his facepiece turned hot. The floor felt fluid, and he couldn't tell if it was tile or hardwood or carpet. The glow was all around him and even the air felt like it was on fire.

Danny had taken the aerial ladder on the rig to the roof and now he opened the bulkhead. Despite the humidity, the open bulkhead door made a big difference. The sixth floor began to clear, and when Danny smashed the skylight, the smoke and heat lifted faster.

Charles didn't notice the change in the hallway, but the visibility near the front of the apartment got better. Enough that he could see the outline of objects. Everything was on fire.

Everything he could see and much that he didn't.

His heart pounded in his chest and he nearly choked on the Jolly Rancher. The line was heavy, and though they just started, he was starting to feel the strain. But stopping wasn't an option. There was fire all around and Bahms was behind him, moving him forward.

Matt grabbed his shoulder and yelled something to him that he didn't get. He cracked the nozzle down halfway so he could hear better, but Matt yelled at him to keep it open. Matt got in his view and pointed to the ceiling. Charles looked up and a shallow river of fire rolled above his head. Charles untucked the line from under his arm, pinned it beneath his knee, bent it, and aimed the nozzle straight up. The water hit the ceiling and mushroomed, scattering the flames like roaches in the light. Then Matt was pulling his shoulder again and leading him to the right.

Charles was feeling fatigue. His grip was slipping, and he felt like he was losing control of the line. He stopped and Bahms stopped behind him, then pushed the line up further between

Charles's arms and held it there. Charles reset his grip, regained control, took a deep breath, and continued, grateful for Bahms's help.

A SECOND LINE WAS on its way up to apartment 6A. It was being stretched by Engine 80. Their stretch was harder because of the first fully charged hose line and half a dozen men on the stairs.

While they stretched, Paul, who had followed Danny up the aerial ladder with a power saw, started cutting a hole in the roof. After Danny opened the bulkhead, most of the smoke in the hallways and on the stairs cleared. Engine 80 didn't have to mask up on the fourth floor like the others had, but because the sixth floor would be crowded, they got to their knees and masked up on the fifth floor. The captain of 80 knelt beside 5B and noticed movement out of the corner of his eye. He turned to face the door and saw light smoke spilling from the door frame. He wiped the outside of his facepiece and looked again. Smoke. He removed his glove and felt the door and it was warm.

The captain grabbed the mic on his handie-talkie to tell the chief but was cut off by Paul with an urgent message: heavy fire in the cockloft.

CHARLES HADN'T HEARD THE report of fire in the cockloft, but Matt did. They were making progress, but slowly. They'd knocked down the fire in the kitchen, headed to the bathroom, then doubled back to the kitchen for a pocket of fire they missed. Moving was difficult. Piles of clutter strewn every few feet had burned through and made unstable obstacles to crawl over. They'd extinguished all visible fire to the right of the front door and were heading through the living room when Paul gave the urgent message about the fire in the cockloft. Matt wasn't surprised.

LADDER 30 WAS ON the sixth floor as well, searching the other apartments on that floor.

They'd searched 6A after the old woman had been pulled out and hadn't found anyone else, but they couldn't give the bedroom a thorough search. Their can-man closed the bedroom door, watched it, and waited for the second line. The other members of Ladder 30 checked the C and D apartments.

Kenny was inside the Johnsons' apartment, on the line five feet behind Bahms. They were making their way across the living room toward the bedroom. Fagan was to their right, breaking the windows in the living room while McCann cleared out the kitchen.

Josh had searched in and around the piles of clutter to make sure no one was there and now he was to the left of the line, closer to the apartment door, following the nozzle into the bedroom. It was the most likely place to find someone, if there was someone to be found. He thought of the woman who lived there. Candace. He bent down and moved a burnt piece of furniture. It was heavy and his heart was racing, but not from the effort.

THEN THREE THINGS HAPPENED all at once. The captain of 80 Engine gave a report of fire in the apartment below them. His message wasn't clear because, at the same time, Danny reported that the roof had become untenable, and everyone was getting off.

Then the ceiling collapsed.

LIBBY WAS HOME IN bed but still awake. The evening with Diana had been exactly what she needed. They'd planned to go for drinks but opted for gourmet ice cream instead. It was too hot to walk around, so they sat in Diana's car and ate while they talked. Diana had just started working at the airport, and she tried to convince Libby to apply. The schedule, she said, was flexible enough that Libby could still help her mom out at the bakery a couple of days a week.

Not to mention the flight and travel benefits.

The conversation segued to Charles. Diana was slightly annoyed she was only just hearing about this guy but was willing to forgive Libby if she promised to ask Charles about any single coworkers. Libby promised.

When she got home, Libby saw a video of the shoe store fire, and smiled broadly when she spotted Charles's name on the back of his coat. She took a screenshot of the video when his coat was clearly visible and sent it to him in a text message with a smiley face emoji just before one in the morning.

Now, nearly two hours later, she was sitting in bed, her pillow between her back and the wall, watching a live video of the incident on 148th and Douglass. She wasn't smiling.

The entire top floor seemed to be on fire. Beneath the video, a scrolling thread of updates said the fire had spread to an apartment on the floor below and, subsequently, the department had ordered an evacuation of all civilians and personnel. The fire was now a third alarm.

-31-

MEGHAN WOKE UP NAUSEOUS. She'd only slept an hour or so before the "morning" sickness invaded her dreams and forced her awake. She swung her feet off the bed and bent over, hands on her knees, trying to figure out if she needed to puke or not.

She was in Athena's room. It was after midnight when she and Mildred finished talking and Mildred refused to let her drive home. Meghan had driven to and from that house more times than she could count. She knew Mildred wasn't worried about her safety; she just didn't want to be alone, and Meghan was okay with that.

She wasn't very tired when she got to the room, so she texted Matt to see if he was awake, but he hadn't responded. She lay back and thought about the talk earlier. It was sad that two people as good as Mildred and Josh, two people who loved each other as much as they did, might end up unhappy.

Meghan hadn't had any advice for her. They'd talked for over an hour and Mildred seemed happy to be able to vent, but there was no real resolution. Just a quiet understanding before they hugged.

Now, as Meghan sat on the edge of the bed fighting back morning sickness in the middle of the night, she thought about

Matt. He was on the same career path as Josh, really. He'd just been traveling without baggage. But things were different now.

Her phone was on the bed beside the pillow. She turned around, reached for it, and checked to see if Matt had responded. He hadn't. But she had a missed call and voicemail from Pete Dufresne. Pete? Why?

Meghan's heart raced. Her aunt's voice invaded her thoughts. She looked at the missed call, looked at the time it came in, and threw up.

THE MEN ON THE roof were likely the cause of the collapse. By the time the first rig had gotten to the scene, the fire had already made it to the cockloft. It had burned through the roof beams in the Johnsons' apartment and traveled along the beams in the neighboring apartment. By the time a hole had been cut by the fire department, fire had already made its way across the hall to the roof beams in the C apartment but hadn't burned all the way through.

When the men got off the aerial ladder onto the roof, the roof felt solid enough. When Pooch got to the roof, Paul and Danny and the roof-man from Ladder 30 were already walking around and working up there. Pooch was the first to feel the roof move, like standing on wet sand by the shore. The others felt it too and they all hurried to safety just as the collapse occurred. The roof-man from Ladder 30 went to the fire escape. Fire pulsed from the windows, and he stood on the ladder near the roof, unable to go down or get back up. Paul and Danny went in the opposite direction toward the bulkhead door and made it safely to the landing inside at the top of the stairs. Pooch went back the way he came, toward the aerial ladder. The structure held there, and he stepped on the roof's parapet and climbed back on to the aerial ladder. As he made his way down, a dust cloud came through the windows of the sixth floor toward him and he stopped moving. Then he heard the chief order everyone out of the building.

ENGINE 80 HADN'T YET charged their line, so their captain had them grab the dry hose and bring it back out. He watched them head down, then looked up toward the sixth floor. He wanted to go check on the guys up there, but that wasn't his job. His job was to get his men out safely. He stood there a second longer, trying to make sense of the noise up there. Then he slapped the railing, frustrated, and followed his men down.

THE CEILING HADN'T FALLEN in 6C, but Ladder 30's boss saw flames escape the base of the fan in the bedroom and heard the commotion from the collapse across the hall, so he was moving his team out before the chief even gave the order.

The hallway was chaos. Engine 59 crowded the entrance to 6B, yelling and pulling pieces of rubble away from the door. Their shouts were undistinguishable over the radio transmissions and the rumble of the debris being thrown. Embers of fire sprouted from pockets in the collapsed roof and spread over the wreckage and the men beat them down with their gloved hands and sleeves or whatever they could, because their source of water was pinned somewhere inside. A cloud of smoke and dust hung over them and they worked low to better see what they were doing. Danny and Paul crawled down the stairs of the bulkhead, coughing. They hadn't been wearing their facepieces on the roof. The can-man from 30 Truck had come out of 6A and now he used his can to spray the pile of debris at the door of 6B while the others made their way through it. Ladder 30's boss turned away from the hallway, back into 6C, and gave a mayday for the firefighters trapped inside the fire apartment.

EVENTUALLY THEY CLEARED A path. The distant eerie sounds of PASS alarms chimed in the darkness. The men moved a large piece of roof that had fallen near the door and kept moving forward. They found Kenny just inside the living room. He was on his knees, hands on his thighs. The boss from 59 Engine crawled up in front of him, avoiding small pieces of burning tar, and grabbed his shoulders. Kenny was shaken but coming out of it, and when the boss shouted, "Okay?" he nodded. The boss told one of his men to get Kenny out, but Kenny refused. He reached down, found the hose line, and followed it deeper into the apartment.

DANNY AND PAUL WENT inside behind 59 and 30 and went to the right. They were masked up now. Engine 99 would likely be with the hose line, so 59 and 30 would find them. Danny and

Paul were worried about 88's guys, who could be anywhere.

They got to the kitchen and found McCann. He was lying on his side, covering a hole in his facepiece, coughing. Danny silenced McCann's alarm and Paul got him to his feet. He had difficulty standing on one leg, so Paul grabbed him around the waist, and they followed Danny back the way they'd come.

WHEN THE CEILING FELL, a section clipped the back brim of Charles's helmet, yanked his head back, tweaked his neck and pulled him off balance. The section that hit him was the tip of a larger piece that had collapsed behind him and pinned Bahms. Charles dropped the line, tried to balance himself, and ended up on his hands and knees. He sat back, readjusted his helmet, and cried out from the pain in his neck. The apartment was darker, but there was more fire. The front of the line whipped back and forth beside him like the tail of a snake. He tackled it, tucked it beneath his arm, and tried for more slack, but the line didn't move.

Then he heard the yells from the door. He looked over in that direction, saw the ceiling on the floor, and realized what happened. A PASS alarm started behind him and he turned around, panicking. It was coming from either Bahms or Kenny. Or the boss. Charles looked toward the door again, toward the yells. They were coming to help, but he couldn't see them. Again, he felt claustrophobic. Above him was nothing but jagged pieces of wood beneath the dark sky, and he felt trapped. Fire engulfed the rubble behind him. He flinched away from it and his heart raced. He looked around for anyone from 88 but could barely see anything through the dust cloud. He was alone.

More PASS alarms sounded. Charles started to close the nozzle to help clear the debris off the others but stopped. *Things only work out well when everyone does their own job.* He took a deep breath, heart in his throat, then moved forward and bent the hose line back, aiming at the fire between himself and the front door.

MATT HEARD A SOUND like thunder and automatically looked up. The collapse wasn't one synchronized event. The roof landed on the ceiling and a crack splintered across like lightning. The ceiling held for a second before giving in. When Matt saw the crack spreading, he stood to a crouching position and pushed Josh away from where he thought the ceiling would fall. Josh, caught off guard, stumbled forward and landed face down. Matt turned toward Charles and Bahms, but the thunder roared again, and fear gripped him as a thought of Meg flashed across his mind and the ceiling fell.

FAGAN WAS OKAY. HE was at the window when the roof caved in and most of the ceiling held where it met the walls. He cleared some wood and plaster off himself and waited for the dust to settle to get his bearings. When he had, he heard the guys from 59 and 30 moving wreckage in the living room, searching. Beside the small eruptions caused from the collapse, the fire in the bedroom was still burning. Fagan crawled that way to see if he could close the door and contain the fire to that room. As he got closer to the door, he saw the probie operating alone. Charles was on his knees with the line bent back to the front door, clearing out the new weeds of fire sprouting between 99 and the exit.

Fagan turned away and continued to the bedroom. Piles of ash and pieces of ceiling and chunks of tar from the roof were hot beneath his hands and knees, but he kept moving. People yelled over the handie-talkies and in the apartment from panic, or urgency, or just to be heard through their masks. PASS alarms blared and echoed off the walls like surround sound. But he kept crawling to the bedroom, and when he got there, he found Josh.

He hadn't realized an alarm was so close to him until his knee was on Josh's cylinder.

Josh was laid out on his stomach, pieces of ceiling covering his head and shoulder. Fagan didn't call out for help; he didn't think he'd be heard. He flipped Josh over and checked if he was breathing but couldn't tell. He got off his knees and turned Josh so that his head was facing the door. Crouching, he grabbed Josh's beneath the shoulders, stopped, let them go, went into the bedroom, and pulled what was left of the door shut. Then he got back in front of Josh, grabbed under his arms again, and duckwalked to the front door, his path cleared of fire by the probie.

CHARLES KNOCKED DOWN THE new fire in the living room. He was breathing heavily and couldn't hear anything over the air sucking into his facepiece. When a path was cleared, he aimed the stream out the window to clear the smoke, then shut down the line.

They found Bahms first. Two guys carried him out. Charles sat back on his knees, still holding the nozzle. He watched them, unmoving, and he pictured Bahms back in the firehouse kitchen, smiling. *Nice touch.*

Because Charles wasn't moving, his PASS alarm started. Kenny crawled to him, silenced the alarm and put an arm around him.

It felt to Charles like forever before they found Matt. They grabbed him under his arms and hurried to the door. As they dragged him out, they yelled his name and shook him, but he didn't respond.

Kenny waited for them to get the boss out, then with his arm around him, he led Charles to the door. Charles pulled the nozzle behind them and when Kenny noticed, he said, "You don't need that anymore, bud. Your job's done."

FIVE AMBULANCES WERE OUTSIDE, and more were on the way. One had already taken Sheryl Tabacco to Harlem Hospital. Josh was put on a stretcher in the next one, Fagan sitting beside him in the back. Danny had gotten on another with McCann, who was sitting upright on his stretcher despite his paramedic's instruction for him to lie back. Bahms and Matt were on stretchers in another two with BVMs on their faces, their coats open and their shirts cut. Kenny rode with Charles in the last ambulance. They were both on oxygen, having their vitals taken by Towns, the purple-haired EMT. Pooch and Paul hopped in the back with Bahms. Pete climbed in with Matt. He watched as the EMTs worked and he listened to the beeps on the monitors.

ABOUT AN HOUR LATER, Mildred and Meghan were in a cab, holding hands. Earlier, Mildred had just gotten off the phone with Paul when she heard Meghan vomit in the next room.

She hadn't had time to fully process the call. She had time now, though, and she spent it trying to keep her lip from trembling and her mind from racing and assuming the worse.

They weren't dead. At least they weren't when Paul called. "Bad shape," he said. They were all being seen by doctors, and they were alive, but they were in *bad shape*. What else would he say? Plenty of times in the past, Josh was at a fire that made the news and she feared getting a phone call. She supposed that was normal. Every major fire or major event, she feared that call. But she never thought about how it would go. If he died, would they call her to tell her? Probably not, right? It wouldn't be a phone call from some bigwig in the department she'd never heard of or spoke to before, it would be one of the guys, face to face. They wouldn't want her to have a breakdown all alone. They cared about her too much. The firehouse was like family. They would be there for her when she found out and probably be there for her forever afterward. Even as she and Meghan were getting dressed to go, several of the guys who weren't working called them and offered to pick them up. They took a cab because none of those guys lived very close and neither of them felt like driving themselves, but Mildred knew that whatever happened when they got there, they wouldn't have to deal with it alone. The firehouse family wouldn't let them.

LIBBY ACTUALLY WATCHED CHARLES walk from the building and into an ambulance. At that point, she'd already woken her mother up and they were sitting beside each other in the dining room, watching on her phone.

A civilian had been pulled from the building first. The person recording hadn't had a great view of it. Libby panicked until she read the thread of updates below the video and found out that it was an occupant from one of the apartments. Sometime later, a rumble sounded, followed by a cloud of smoke, and the firefighters started streaming out of the building. Charles was the last one out and it felt like a long time before she saw him. He was supported by another guy but he was walking, and Libby leaned back and smiled. Her mom rubbed her leg and took the phone from her. Libby closed her eyes, too late. Tears pushed through and rolled down her face, slowly at first but faster once she felt them.

"He's okay, sweetie," her mom said. "He's fine."

Libby nodded but didn't respond. It wasn't only Charles she was thinking of.

-32-

CHARLES HAD ELEVATED LEVELS of CO, slight burns on his knees, and some literal bumps and bruises. His burns were treated, and he was given an ice pack for his neck but told that there was no real damage done, a miracle by most standards. "It'll hurt to turn your head for a while," the nurse had said. "But you're a fireman. You can handle it." When the evaluation was finished, he was given an IV, vitamin water, and oxygen and told he'd be able to leave later in the day if he felt up to it.

He was on a bed in the emergency room of Harlem hospital. A half-drawn curtain separated him from the hallway, and in it were dozens of EMTs and fire chiefs, nurses and police officers standing around discussing the fire. Kenny came from behind the curtain. He was wearing his bunker pants and boots and a damp t-shirt. His eyes were red and he looked spent, but he smiled, offering a high-five, which Charles accepted.

"How you feeling, buddy?"

"Okay, I think. My neck hurts a little, but she said I'll be fine."

"Yeah. But you'll still take a leave. We'll get you settled with the medical office in headquarters tomorrow, or, you know, later today. Stay out for as long as you need to feel a hundred percent."

"Okay, thank you."

"I'm serious. We'll talk about it later, but don't come back until you're ready. Don't worry about the fact that you're a probie."

"Okay. Are you okay?" Charles asked.

"Yeah, I'm good. I'm just worried about Quincy."

"He's not awake?"

"No. Not yet. Calahan woke up a few minutes ago. Bahms was either always awake or woke up on the bus. He and McCann had breaks, but they're gonna be fine."

"Breaks? Like bones?"

"Yeah. Joey's arm and McCann's leg. Calahan might have a concussion. I didn't hear clearly, but they're still with him too."

Charles asked, "Did we get everyone out?"

Kenny smiled again. "Yeah. Everyone's accounted for. You were the last one out, buddy.

Good job tonight."

"Thanks, Kenny." Charles thought of lunch with Libby earlier in the week. She had smiled at him, admiration on her face, and said, "A day in the life of a fireman." It was silly, but he hadn't really felt deserving of the title then. Or the admiration. If she knew the level of anxiety he'd felt that first day... He felt like a phony.

But now, as he sat on the bed, covered in soot and bruises, getting praise from Kenny, he remembered her words and her tone, and he smiled.

GUYS WERE ARRIVING AT the hospital. Everyone who was off had been notified by Pete and they all got out of bed and headed there, some with their wives. Kenny stood to go meet them, and to borrow a phone to call Jennifer, his wife.

"You have anyone you should call?" he asked Charles.

Charles stood too but shook his head. "No. I live alone."

"The news doesn't only play at *your* home, bud. I'm sure people who know you have heard about this or will when they wake up. Plus, that app that everyone has on their phone now.

The whole thing was live."

Charles thought of his mother. *I read my Bible and I pray and I listen to the news.* He nodded and stepped out into the hallway. Joe Kohler walked up to him and hugged him.

"You alright?"

"Yes, sir. Thank you."

Kohler introduced Charles to his wife Kathleen, and she hugged him too.

Charles said, "Joe, could I borrow your phone, please. I wanna let my mom know I'm good."

"Here, sweetie," Kathleen said, and handed him her phone. "His phone has been blowing up all morning. Go call your mom and whoever else you need to. Find me when you're done."

"Thank you, ma'am." Charles went back to the bed and dialed his mother's house phone.

He didn't know her cell number by heart and wasn't sure she even kept it on at night.

By the third ring, he'd had second thoughts. He shouldn't have called. It would suck if she was finally getting a good night's sleep and he woke her up just to tell her that there was no need to worry.

The phone rang a fourth time before the receiver lifted and his mom answered.

"Hello?" She hadn't been asleep. She didn't know who was calling and she sounded scared. It broke his heart.

He said, "Hi, Mom," and a moan escaped her throat, something dropped, and she began to cry.

Charles closed his eyes and waited. He put the knuckle

of his thumb to the corner of his eye, and it came back wet. After a moment, he started to say something, didn't manage it, cleared his throat, and tried again. He said, "I'm fine, Mom. Don't cry. I'm really okay."

"Okay. I know."

"I'm in the hospital, but they said there's no real damage."

"Okay." She was speaking slowly, trying not to choke on her words. "Is everyone else okay?"

Charles thought about how to answer that. "We don't know yet. Everyone is alive, though."

She was silent for a moment and Charles knew she was still crying. Sometimes relief was worse than fear. She cleared her throat. "The news said that two were in critical condition." Charles shook his head. He didn't know that. He figured Lt. Quincy and Lt. Calahan were the two, he wasn't sure. But how long ago had his mom heard that report? How long had she been wondering if he was one of them?

"I didn't know that. But I'm okay." He thought of Lt. Quincy and hoped he was too.

JOSH WOKE UP IN bed and might've been convinced that it was all a dream if not for the throbbing pain in his head. It took him a second to realize he wasn't up in his office at the firehouse or at home in his bedroom. The fluorescent lights above him were harsh and unnerving. Machines beeped and hummed close by and a low rumble of voices came from somewhere beyond them. When he tried to turn his head, his vision blurred and the pain in his head pulsed, so he stopped. He closed his eyes again. He thought about Mildred. He thought about dinner at the firehouse and everyone breaking the probie's balls because of his girlfriend. He thought about the laughs.

Then he thought about the fire. He thought about the

woman in 6B. He thought of the old lady Fagan had found in 6A. About the probie, whipping the nozzle back and forth and making a push into the fire like a veteran. He thought about sensing something was about to go wrong before it did. And he thought about Matt pushing him from behind.

He opened his eyes and tried to sit up, but his vision blurred, and his head throbbed and he was gone again.

THE NEXT TIME HE awoke, Mildred was there. He came to quietly, without movement, and looked up at the fluorescent lights. He blinked a few times until his mind had caught up, then, remembering the pain from his last attempts to move, he only moved his eyes and he saw her.

She was standing beside his bed. Kathleen Kohler was standing next to her, holding her hands. They were listening to a doctor who stopped talking when she noticed Josh was awake.

She came around to the opposite side of the bed as Mildred leaned over him.

"Hey, Josh. How are you feeling?" the doctor asked.

He thought about it and realized the throbbing had quit. He turned cautiously toward the doctor, and his vision didn't blur. He reversed course and turned toward Mildred, and when he met her eyes, they smiled.

MILDRED HELD HIS HAND as they listened to the doctor. All things considered, it wasn't terrible news. He would hurt for a while, but he'd live. And, if he wanted, he could go back to work. When the doctor left, Josh asked the women how everyone else was. When they told him that Matt hadn't woken up, he looked back and forth between the two, searching for words he'd never find. He gave up and turned away. Kathleen squeezed Mildred's hand and left.

Mildred found a chair and pulled it to the bed, sat down, and took his hand again. Josh turned back to face her, and his face was red. His eyes were filled with tears that hadn't fallen. His lips were tight and his cheeks shook.

"Josh…"

"I won't be able to take it," he said.

Mildred didn't respond.

"I'm telling you, Milly, I…I don't think I'll be able to take it. How…?" He looked away from her and tears fell from the corner of his eyes down to his ears. She held his hand in hers and wiped her own eyes on her shoulder. He eventually turned back to meet her eyes and she squeezed his hand.

He said, "I love you. You know that. I know you know. I don't love nothing or no one in this world as much as I love you and 'Thena. You know that."

Mildred said, "I do," and it derailed him. He stared at her, relieved, and she smiled sadly.

"I know you do, Josh. We both do."

Tears fell freely down his face, and he used the back of his hand to wipe them. Mildred didn't bother wiping her face again. They were silent a while, then Josh pointed to the door and said, "But I love them too. They're family. *Our* family. I'll never choose anything over you guys. You understand? Ever! But please don't ask me not to love these guys. They…" He stopped and bit his lip to keep it from trembling. "They literally saved my life."

Mildred moved to the edge of her chair, leaned over, and hugged him. He wrapped his arms around her, and for a happy moment, his relief was stronger than his fear.

-33-

CANDACE AND HANNA WERE at Lucy's home when they found out about the fire. After the fight the day before, they'd called the police and made a report. The same two officers who had escorted Alan from the school took their statements, and when they were done, asked if Candace and Hanna had any other place to stay for the night. Neither of them were very sure if Alan knew where Hanna lived, so they rented a hotel room. When Candace called Lucy to explain why she wouldn't be at work Friday morning, Lucy insisted they stay with her, at least for the weekend, until Candace figured out a long-term plan.

They waited until Lucy was off of work, so it was a little before seven in the evening,

Friday, when they got there. Lucy's kids, Olivia and Gavin, were still awake and happy to have guests. The kids knew Candace from school and hugged her around the waist when she came in, then ran inside and signaled for the women to follow. They gave Candace and Hanna a tour of the bedroom they shared, and a tour of the living room and bathroom, careful to point out which toothbrush belonged to whom. They showed their monogramed juice cups and drawing boards, and pillows and cereal bowls. When Gavin pulled out his toy chest to show them his collection of Spider-Man action figures,

Lucy put an end to it. She gave them control of the remote and the freedom to put on any DVD they wanted, a gift that any other time would have made them ecstatic, but this night, only made them pout. They knew they were being manipulated. With the kids out of earshot, Candace and Hanna told Lucy the story of the day before, with detail. Lucy was mostly angry but a little scared. She didn't have a huge place, but she told Candace she was welcome to stay as long as it took the police to find Alan. Candace thanked her but insisted, despite the events of the day, there was no reason to worry. First thing tomorrow, she would have a locksmith, or the super of her building change the locks on her door. Whether or not the cops picked him up, Alan wouldn't step foot in that apartment again. After tonight, things would be fine.

THE KIDS HAD FALLEN asleep on the couch, and Lucy and Candace carried them off to bed. Then the three women opened a bottle of wine, sat in the living room, and talked. Hanna talked about *Thursday Knight*, her latest book, and what inspired it. As she spoke, Lucy went on

Bookshop.org and ordered a copy. Then Lucy spoke about how she hadn't read much fiction since she became principal. All the recent books in her library were books on education or business or leadership. She was looking forward to reading something just for fun. Candace didn't do much talking. She was happy for the conversation, but she wasn't really paying attention to it. She was preoccupied with how dramatically her life had changed in just one week. Things might end up better because of it, but they weren't good now, and it was all she could do to keep from screaming.

THEY TALKED AND DRANK themselves tired. Lucy didn't have a spare room or bed, but neither Candace nor Hanna minded the couch or recliner. Lucy had just gotten up to get them sheets and pillows when Candace's phone rang. Everyone stopped and looked at the time and they all thought the same thing. Candace sat forward on the couch and looked at her phone on the coffee table. She didn't recognize the number.

"It's him," Hanna said. "Calling from a payphone or something. It has to be."

"Did the cops you spoke to earlier give you a number to call?" Lucy asked.

"Yeah, but to the precinct. Not a direct number or anything," Hanna answered.

"So, let's call. Maybe they can find the payphone based on the number or something."

Candace didn't say anything. It probably was Alan. And maybe they should call the cops and let them know he was calling, but at that moment, she didn't want to. Not for love or pity toward Alan, but because she was tired. It had been a long week, and she'd been dealing with these things for longer. She wanted a rest. She needed a break.

The ringing stopped, and the number disappeared, and a message of a missed call flashed across the screen before it went black. Candace looked up and caught them watching her, not judging, but concerned. No one spoke. Then Hanna's phone rang. She leaned back, stretched her leg out, and pulled her phone from her pocket.

She looked at the screen and frowned.

"Is it the same number?" Lucy had come back to the couches and Hanna turned her phone so the other two could see it.

Candace nodded, also frowning. It was the same number.

Lucy: "Alan has your number?"

"Definitely not."

Candace said, "Pick up. On speaker."

Hanna did. "Hello?"

"Hi, Hanna?" A woman's voice.

"Who's this?"

"Officer Sanchez. We were together yesterday."

"Oh! I'm sorry, yes. Is everything okay? It's very late. Or very early."

"I know, I'm sorry. Um, are you guys together? You and Mrs. Johnson. Is she with you?" The officer sounded confused.

"Yes. Right here. You're on speaker."

"Is...is my call the first you guys are getting tonight?"

"Yes. Why? What happened?"

The three women were all seated now. Leaning toward the phone.

"Um. I'm sorry, I...I just assumed. Mrs. Johnson?"

"Yeah?"

"Candace, there was a... your husband set your apartment on fire."

"What!"

Candace and Hanna stood; Lucy sat up straight.

"I'm sorry to be the one to tell you. The fire started hours ago; I assumed you already knew. I thought you'd be there. We—"

"Hours ago? Was it bad? Is it out?"

"I don't—well, the fire department is still there. The building has been evacuated."

"What!"

"The roof collapsed. The top floor is pretty much gone. I'm sorry to be telling you this way, I thought you knew. No one was found in your apartment, so we assumed you were in the crowd."

Candace sat down. Her head was spinning. Lucy got up and sat beside her, wrapping an arm around her shoulders.

Hanna stared at the phone, stone-faced, her arms folded. She sat down and rested her phone hand on her knee.

Candace looked up. "Was anyone hurt?"

"Well, like I said, the fire is still ongoing. But a number of people were taken to the hospital, yes. Mostly firefighters, but also your next-door neighbor."

Candace stood and Lucy's arm dropped. Candace said, "I'm on my way."

-34-

EARLIER WHEN SHERYL WAS in bed glaring at the
ceiling, she was upset with Candace for having been crying about
Alan one day, then horsing around with him in the middle of the
night the next. If Sheryl wasn't upset, she might have considered
that the sounds of grunting and heavy breathing and bumps and
thumps could just as easily be a fight as horse play. If she had considered that it could be a fight, she might've considered that it was
probably a man fighting a woman and she might have called the
police. If the police had been called at that point, Alan might have
been caught earlier and the fire may have never had the opportunity to start. But on top of hearing the grunting and breathing and
bumping and thumping, she also heard the laughter. So, to Sheryl,
it didn't sound like a fight.

AS IT HAPPENED, WHAT Sheryl was hearing was none of
those things. The Johnsons weren't horsing around or fighting.
What she heard weren't the sounds of two people bumping into
things or each other; what she heard was the sound of Alan Johnson emptying shelves and drawers into piles with one hand, then
dousing them with gasoline from a five-gallon jug with the other.
What Sheryl heard wasn't arguing or conversation, what she heard
was Alan Johnson talking to himself.
And laughing.
He wasn't gonna be the only one getting screwed.

When he had emptied the jug, Alan stood with his back to the kitchen and looked around.

The apartment was dark. He hadn't turned on any lights, but the curtains were open and there was enough light from the streets to see by. And what he saw was a mess.

His heart was racing. He wasn't really at a point of no return. Not yet. On the floor were piles of everything from books to electronics. In the bedroom, more piles of clothes and sheets and linen. But five gallons didn't go as far as he thought it would. The smell was powerful, and the living room floor shimmered like pavement on a hot day, but the apartment was more dry than it was wet. This didn't have to happen.

But she deserved it. Her, Hanna, the captain…they all deserved to come back to this place burned to the ground. If he couldn't stay there, why the hell should they?

Alan threw the jug at a wall, turned, and went to the fridge for a beer. This was dumb. He shouldn't be here right now. Not "here" like in the apartment, "here" in this situation. In life. Candace should have never kicked him out. Big deal, he cheated. She was doing the same thing!

He only did it once. Or twice, maybe. Candace was acting like he'd been sleeping around their entire marriage. She was acting like his damn mother. He was back to living on the streets with nowhere to sleep because, again, someone who should be in his corner claimed he had a problem.

He held up his bottle in a toast and said, "Now nobody sleeps here." And laughed.

When he finished his beer he tossed his bottle into the sink. In the drawer beneath the counter, he looked for matches, but all he found were ketchup packets and duck sauce. He opened the refrigerator again to check there, then realized how silly that was and laughed again. And kept laughing, uncontrollably. He stood there in the glow of the fridge light, tears streaming down his face, laughing. When finally he stopped, he shook his head and picked up a roll of paper towels from the floor, then carried them over to the stove. They were soaked in gasoline and heavy because of it. At the stove, he used the back of his hand to wipe his forehead and it came back wet. It was a hot night. *About to get hotter*, he thought, and started to laugh once more, but controlled it. He turned a knob on the stove, and after a series of ticks, a flame appeared. He wiped sweat from his eyes with the palm of his hands and felt a sting from the gasoline.

"Fuck!" he spat and used the sleeve on his bicep to wipe his eyes again. He blinked away new tears and took a deep breath.

Alan stared at the flame and sighed. Candace had really screwed things up. He could've forgiven her if not for yesterday. But some things had to be punished. Some consequences couldn't be avoided.

Alan closed his eyes and sighed again, and for a moment he felt nothing at all. Then he opened his eyes, reached out with the roll of towels, and touched it to the flame.

A ball of fire erupted in his hands, and he screamed in pain. He dropped the roll, shook his hands, then checked himself for burns. The fire was at his feet now and growing. Angry, he kicked the roll away and it landed in the living room on a pile of books and magazines and exploded.

Darkness disappeared in a flash. The pile of books became a bonfire. Flames shot from it and followed a trail of gasoline to another pile behind it. That pile exploded silently and spread to another. Alan watched slack-jawed as the place lit up, pile after pile. He watched the fire spread around the living room and remembered that the curtains were open.

Avoiding the windows as best he could, he ran from the kitchen, coughing, beads of sweat appearing on his forehead. He reached the apartment door and tried to open it, but it didn't budge. Panic rose in his chest and he yanked the handle toward him. Nothing.

Behind him, crackling and pops and small explosions made the hairs on his neck stand.

Sweat poured into his eyes now and he blinked furiously to see through them.

Afraid now, Alan held his breath and stopped. Be calm. What's the problem? He looked at the door and realized it was locked. Quickly, he disengaged the top lock and the one above the knob, then yanked the door open, and when he did, felt a tremendous heat on his back. He stumbled out of the apartment, coughing harder now, and ran down the half flight of stairs to his right. Turning back, he saw black smoke coming from his apartment, riding the ceiling toward the stairway that led to the roof.

"What the hell," he marveled, and backed away. He shouldn't be here. He hurried down the stairs, holding on to the railing, and rushed out of the building.

WHEN HE RAN FROM the building, he was out of breath and dizzy. He didn't know if it was the gasoline, the beer, or anxiety, but as soon as he was outside, he was on his knees vomiting. When he was able to stand again, a crowd had formed at the building, gawking and recording it with their phones. He looked up at his window, then back at the crowd, and their expressions made him smile. He watched the fire in the window until the trucks arrived, then he pulled himself away from the moment and ran.

Two blocks away he leaned up against the wall of a closed grocery store, out of the lights of the emergency vehicles and watched. After some time had passed, an ambulance sped past him in the direction of the hospital, only one person in the front. He watched it go buy, hoping, praying that somehow it was Captain Asshole inside. What were the odds? He didn't know, but they weren't zero. So he laughed.

HE FOUND HIMSELF AT Rob's building, after that. The door was locked and he pushed the bell for Rob's apartment. A second later, he pushed it again. Then a third time and held it down.

Finally, Rob answered.

"Who is it!"

"It's me, buzz me in!" Alan leaned on the door and waited for the lock to disengage, but it never did. After ten or twelve seconds, he pressed the bell again. Longer this time.

"I'm coming down!" Rob yelled through the intercom.

Honest to God, Alan was surrounded by idiots. What was so confusing? "Don't come down, buzz me up!" There was no response, and this time he laid on the button without releasing it. Lights flicked on in some of the neighbors' windows, but Alan didn't care. He was pissed.

Rob came down the stairs in green plaid pajama pants and a wife beater, his beer belly leading the way. Alan rolled his eyes. This was so dumb. Why the hell did he have a buzzer if he was gonna come down?

Rob came through the inner door, then opened the outside door, and when Alan tried to walk in, Alan pushed him back. Alan, still slightly dizzy, stumbled and fell, landing hard on his back.

He looked up, angry.

Rob glared at him. "What did you do?"

JACKIE AND ROB WERE already up before Alan got there. They were in bed watching TV, when they heard the urgent horns and sirens of firetrucks. The trucks weren't coming to their building, so at first they ignored it. But trucks kept coming. Something big was happening, and Jackie muted the television, opened the Citizen app on her phone, and saw the fire. Rob said it was Alan's building and the floor his apartment was on, and Jackie saw something in his face. Fear, not concern. She asked him why and saw that he'd considered lying. Or, at least, not telling the whole truth. She warned him that lying to her about Alan just then wasn't the best idea, and he told her the truth.

"Do you think she was still inside?" she asked him, terrified by the thought.

Before he could answer, the door buzzer sounded.

They got out of bed together. When he got to the door and asked who it was, she'd heard Alan's voice and said, "Absolutely not! If he comes up here, I'm leaving! And I'm calling the police. I swear!"

Rob asked if they should ignore him, but then the asshole leaned on the bell. Rob, angry in a way Jackie had rarely seen, slipped on some flip flops and headed downstairs. Before he pulled the door closed, he said, "Lock this behind me," and, after a thought, "Call the police." Then he left and closed the door.

"YOU'RE AN ASSHOLE," ROB said through clenched teeth. Alan didn't answer.

"Is she dead, man? Did you kill her?" Rob was standing over him, shaking. His fists were balled, and Alan felt sure that if he tried to get up, Rob would hit him back down.

Alan took a deep breath. "What are you talking about? Is who dead?"

"You know what I'm talking about, Alan!" Rob yelled. "Did you kill her?!"

Curtains were moving and faces were appearing at the windows where the lights had come on.

Alan was disgusted. He would expect this kind of a reaction from a woman. But not from

Rob. What had happened to him? Was it Jackie's fault? Rob used to be so solid. But this... Alan shook his head and started to get up, but Rob stepped over his legs.

"Stay down, man. I'm warning you."

Alan tried again. "Dude, calm down. I don't know what you're talking about. Nobody's dead."

"But you set that fire, right? I know it was you, dude. What the fuck?"

Alan tucked his leg underneath him so that he was on his knees instead of on his butt. Rob was still standing over him, shaking. Behind Rob, on the third floor, someone was at their window, aiming their cellphone at them. Alan looked at Rob, then back at the window and yelled, "Go away!" When Rob turned in that direction, Alan launched at him. He caught Rob around the waist and tried to knock him down, but only succeeded in knocking him back.

Alan hadn't gotten his feet beneath him, and as Rob stumbled backward, Alan slid down his legs and ended up on all fours. Rob was yelling something, but Aland didn't know what. He tried to stand and Rob pushed on his shoulders to keep him down, and Alan grabbed Rob around the waist again. This time he had a better grip, and he lifted Rob in the air. But he was still dizzy, and Rob was heavy and fighting back and they collapsed to the floor, Rob on top.

Other people were shouting now. Alan figured it was from the windows but wasn't sure.

He was trying to free himself, but Rob moved up and was sitting on his stomach, his crotch in

Alan's face and his knees pinning Alan's arms. Alan struggled and bucked, but Rob stayed on top.

Then from somewhere far away, but not too far, Alan heard police sirens. He tried harder to free himself, but he didn't have the strength, and after a minute he screamed. Tears fell down his cheeks and he gasped for breath beneath Rob's weight. He stared at Rob through watery eyes and couldn't get them to focus.

The sirens were closer, and Alan stopped struggling. He cried freely now. Rob moved back a little, straddling Alan's waist, and it was easier for Alan to breath. Lights from a police car turned the area a flashing red. Shouting and footsteps and then Rob slid off of him.

Alan turned to his side and coughed and spat. When he could breathe normally, he said,

"I just wanted to come home. I just wanted to go home."

Then hands grabbed him and pulled him up.

-35-

THE SUN ROSE AT a quarter to seven on Saturday. By the
time it was light outside, every local news station had reporters at
the fire building or the hospital. Or both. They all had Alan and
Candace and Sheryl's names. And Matt's.

By the change of tours, every television in every New York
City firehouse kitchen and housewatch was tuned in to the news
for updates.

After they'd left the fire building, a few members from 59 and
30 had been looked over by medics for minor injuries or smoke
inhalation and had been released. After 80 and 23 and 59 and 30
had cleaned up and changed out their tools and personnel for the
start of Saturday's day tour, all four rigs made their way back to
the hospital to join the growing vigil of off duty members, civilians, and reporters hoping for a change in Matt's condition.

Engine 99 and Ladder 88 were put out of service and another
Engine and Ladder from a slower part of the city were sent to
cover their response area. All the active members had washed or
changed before heading back to be with Meg. Josh was still being
monitored but was allowed to sit in a wheelchair in Matt's room.
Mildred sat beside him, her hand in his, watching the numbers on
Matt's monitor.

AT NOON, CANDACE AND Hanna were escorted into the hospital through an employee entrance. Candace was wearing a baseball cap and carrying a large tote bag. They'd met Officer Sanchez at the scene of the fire and were astonished at the destruction. The entire sixth floor had been damaged. Candace had asked the marshals to take her up, and after a warning that it could be a futile trip, they did. Her apartment was a pile of rubble beneath the morning sky. Nothing to salvage. But that wasn't why she had gone up. When they were done, she asked to be taken to the hospital.

Neither Candace nor Hanna had ever met Matt, and although they hoped he would be okay, he wasn't who they were there for. The crowd of people outside were there to support the first responders who had risked their lives to save the lives of others, but no one was there for the one life they definitely *did* save.

WHEN FAGAN PULLED SHERYL from her apartment, he hadn't felt a pulse, but one was there. She was passed from person to person down the stairs to the fourth floor. Then two members of Engine 80 carried her the rest of the way out.

A lot of damage was done to her body when the fan fell on her, and she was rushed into the OR. Several times, while the doctors operated, complications caused her blood pressure to drop or her heart to slow, along with touch-and-go moments when they feared they would lose her. When they were done, however, she was closed up, and breathing on her own. She would be in the hospital for a good while, which the doctors figured was fortunate because her home was destroyed, and it seemed she had no family.

When Officer Sanchez brought Candace and Hanna to her room, the nurse asked their relation. Candace told her they were friends and the nurse responded, "She has a long, painful road ahead of her, but I think she'll be okay. Your friend is a strong woman."

Candace smiled, relieved, and stepped over to a table near the bed. She placed the tote bag on top, opened it, pushed the sides down, and pulled out Kevin's urn.

CHARLES WAS IN LINE at the hospital cafeteria, waiting to purchase a fruit bowl and a bottle of coconut water. All around him were guys from his house, both current and former, and their families. Men and women from the upper echelons of the department, along with chiefs and officers from the division. Eddie's brother who ran the departments press desk was with his boss talking to Eddie. Fagan shook hands with the Fire Commissioner, and she told him that she'd be in touch with the house to check up on everyone, She walked away with some people following her, and Fagan came up beside Charles and nodded. He'd changed into his work duty uniform.

"How ya feeling?"

"Good, sir," Charles said, but truth was he was exhausted. He was nervous and worried about Matt, but at times it was hard for him to focus on that because of how tired he felt.

"Have you been in to see Bahms or Calahan yet?" Fagan asked.

"Yes, sir. I saw them both. I haven't gone in to see Lt. Quincy. I don't know if his family would rather be alone."

Fagan raised his eyebrows and sighed. "I haven't gone in either. But we'll be here when the dust settles and we know the outcome."

The person in front of Charles paid for their items and Charles stepped forward. He put the fruit and water on the counter and reached in his pocket for his wallet, but Fagan already had his out and handed his card to the cashier.

"I saw what you did up there," Fagan said. "After the collapse.

I saw you get up and finish the job." The woman put the fruit and water in a bag, which she handed to Fagan. He held on to it and said, "You getting up and knocking down that fire made it possible for the guys to pull out everyone who was hurt. If Quincy lives, you helped saved his life. Remember that. I certainly will."

Charles didn't answer. He stood silent, a knot in his throat, and waited. Then Fagan held out his hand and Charles shook it. Fagan handed him his bag and Charles tried to thank him, but nothing came out.

Fagan said, "Keep up the good work." Then turned and walked away.

THE HOSPITAL MADE ACCOMMODATIONS for the members and their wives to wait.

Meghan, Josh, and Mildred were in Matt's room, and everyone else was close by. Folding chairs were brought in and crowded into the waiting room and everyone ate food from the cafeteria or from vending machines while they talked on their phones or responded to texts or halfheartedly watched the television screen.

At five, when the news came on, the fire was the top story. Everyone watched the first civilian cellphone video, and no one ate or talked. The story covered everything from Alan Johnson, who was being held on multiple charges with the possibility of more, to the woman in the apartment next door, who doctors said was in serious but stable condition thanks to the efforts of the first firefighters on the scene, to Matt, who was still in serious condition. When the next story started, everyone looked away and many of the wives squeezed their husband's hands.

MEGHAN HADN'T SEEN THE news story. There wasn't a television in Matt's room. About an hour ago, Meghan had moved her chair closer to Matt's bed and laid her head on her arm and her arm on his leg. She hadn't cried. When she and Mildred arrived at the hospital, Brian O'Neil had met them in the lobby and led them through the crowd. Mildred was taken to Josh and Meg to Matt's room. When she walked in and saw him on the bed with a tube in his mouth and a half dozen people working on him, she remembered what her aunt had said. But she refused to panic.

She didn't believe in supernatural predictions or psychic abilities or any of that. She believed in cause and effect. And strength. And faith. Matt was a runner. He ate well and worked out every day. And he was good. His job was dangerous, and some hazards couldn't be avoided, but if anyone was able to beat this, he was. They were. Together. So she wasn't going to worry. She would wait, and he would be fine.

She had laid her head on his leg and watched his chest rise when he breathed. His breaths were slow but full. A monitor he was hooked up to beeped once every few seconds, and when she laid on his leg, she had the impression it beeped in sync with his heartbeat. She didn't know how many beats per minute was normal, but the beeping from the monitor was steady and consistent. So she wasn't going to worry.

The rhythm of his breathing and the sounds of the monitor were hypnotic, and worrying was exhausting, without realizing it, Meghan dozed off.

SHE STOOD IN HER kitchen on her phone, laughing. She dried her hands on a hand towel, then picked up a warm baby bottle. She squeezed some of the milk out on to the back of her hand, then licked it off and laughed again at the person on the phone. She wiped the back of her hand on her thigh, then left the kitchen and went into the living room. Beside the couch, a wooden crib, with the initials M and M on the panel. She walked over to it and looked down at her son. A hand was on the back of her head massaging her scalp. Matt. He was standing behind her and she smiled. He said something she didn't understand, and she groaned.

MEGHAN WOKE UP IN Matt's hospital room, her head on her arm and her arm on his lap. And his hand on her head.

When she realized, she sat up and Matt looked at her, a faint smile on his face. Josh was sitting up straight in his chair, and Mildred was on her feet.

Meghan stared at him, her eyes welling with tears. She thought of the dream: the crib, her son, his hand in her hair. She took his hand in hers. "What did you say?"

Matt said, "How's it going, beautiful baby momma?"

And Meghan cried.

-36-

THE HOSPITAL STAFF RELAXED the rules on visitors, and over the next ten minutes everyone from the house made their way into Matt's room. There were handshakes and half hugs and kissed cheeks. Charles, unsure of what was appropriate, stood near the bed and smiled until Matt called him over. He was intro-duced to Meghan and she hugged him.

"Thank you for my family," she said, and Charles smiled.

AFTER THAT, CHARLES MOVED back to make room for others. Most everyone was paired up. All the wives were there, and if they weren't paired with their husbands, they were paired with each other, so Charles slipped out of the room. He made his way back to the waiting area and was surprised to find Libby and her mom seated there, talking to Paul Oldman.

Libby stood when she saw him, and he felt his pulse quicken. He walked over to where they were, slowly, fighting the urge to move faster.

Paul stood. He said to Libby, "Nice meeting you guys. Hope to see you again." He smiled at Charles, then left, patting Charles' butt as he passed.

Charles stood in front of Libby, silent. Her eyes were filled with tears, but she smiled.

"We brought you guys some snacks," she said, turning briefly to her mother. "Hospital food is okay, but their pastry selection sucks."

"You guys are awesome. Thank you," Charles said, staring at her. He wanted to kiss her.

"The hospital just let you guys in?"

"Well, they have a cart or something where people are dropping off flowers and stuff, so we were gonna leave the snacks there, but he…" she pointed in the direction Paul had gone, "…he was outside smoking a cigarette and then he came up to me and said, 'Are you Libby?' He knew we were here for you."

Charles thought back to dinner when they passed the phone around. It felt like so long ago. He smiled and shrugged.

She met his eyes and said, "When he brought us in, he said, 'All the other wives and girlfriends are inside,' so we didn't have to wait outside."

An irrational moment of panic flashed through Charles, but he recovered quickly and stood up straight. Libby smiled broadly now, unconsciously wringing her hands.

"So," Charles said. "You're dating a firefighter?"

Libby laughed, full of nerves. Her tears fell freely, and she wiped them away with both hands.

"Well, if you have to ask…"

ACKNOWLEDGEMENTS

This book would be about twice as big if I added enough pages to properly thank everyone who has supported me on my long route to publication. So, to save ink and possibly a small forest, I'll do those thank you's in person.

Nevertheless, I do want to thank my mom and my sisters Christina and Crystal for helping me get No Man's Ghost to a place where I can submit it to an Agent. Miranda@Mirandareads.com finished that job for me by shredding the book apart and helping me put it back together in a readable form. For the same reason I want to thank Amanda, Kat, Mirna (Smoochie), Rachel and Marissa. Thank you for Beta reading and helping me clean it up.

USA Today best-selling author Mara White was with me and this book from the very first chapter, helping me transition to a novelist. Without her help I'd have never finished, and Charles and Alan would still be running around on my laptop. Thank you, Mara.

This book is dedicated to the members of the FDNY Harlem Hilton firehouse past and present, as well as their families; but I still want to say thank you. You all have taught me much about life and love, respect and pride. And cooking. I am so much better for it. Well… maybe a little less healthy because of the cooking. Still, thank you guys.

I also want to thank the "Bums on Da Hill," for hosting me for six months while I polished this book and searched for an agent and took a ten-hour nap after getting my second vaccine shot. I loved my time with you guys and will always appreciate your kindness and support.

Jack and Mike Rochester of Fictionalcafe.com, and Donald Webb and Edward Ahern of BewilderingStories.com gave me my start by publishing my first short stories; but they continued to support me and my career after that. Without you gentlemen, I wouldn't have had a resume with which to attract an Agent and Publisher. Thank you guys for my career.

Of course, big thank you's to Jason Pinter at Agora/Polis and Chantelle Aimee for bringing this book to life and putting it out in the world. I can't thank you enough for the opportunity.

Finally, I want to thank Abby. Thank you for being the best Agent. Thank you for making so many of my career dreams come true, and for walking me through the web of doubt and discouragement. I'm very happy we found each other. I pray that I'm very successful in my career so that your faith in me is rewarded.